# Hello, I Must Be Going

Also by Christie Hodgen

*A Jeweler's Eye for Flaw*

# Hello, I Must Be Going

a novel

Christie Hodgen

 W. W. Norton & Company • New York London

For information about permission to reproduce selections from this book,
write to Permissions, W. W. Norton & Company, Inc.,
500 Fifth Avenue, New York, NY 10110

Manufacturing by Courier Westford
Book design by Chris Welch
Production manager: Anna Oler

Library of Congress Cataloging-in-Publication Data

Hodgen, Christie, date.
Hello, I must be going : a novel / Christie Hodgen.—1st ed.
p. cm.
ISBN-13: 978-0-393-06139-0 (hardcover)
ISBN-10: 0-393-06139-6 (hardcover)
1. Teenage girls—Massachusetts—Fiction. 2. Bereavement—Fiction.
3. Domestic fiction. I. Title.
PS3608.O47H45   2006
813'.6—dc22                                            2006000248

ISBN 978-0-393-33018-2 pbk.

W. W. Norton & Company, Inc.
500 Fifth Avenue, New York, N.Y. 10110
www.wwnorton.com

W. W. Norton & Company Ltd.
Castle House, 75/76 Wells Street, London W1T 3QT

1 2 3 4 5 6 7 8 9 0

B.C.P.

G.T.P.

LOVE ALWAYS

The author gratefully acknowledges a grant from the National Endowment for the Arts. Also, for their steady friendship and guidance: Grace and Bart Patenaude, the Hodgens—especially John, Doreen, and Janice—the St. Onge family, Marly Swick, Aisha Ginwalla, Kim Palmer, Amy Kellert, Christine Sneed, J. C. Levenson, John Hildebidle, Tony Ardizzone, T. R. Hummer, Kit Ward, and the impeccable Carol Houck Smith.

Hello, I Must Be Going

part one

# 1

When someone arrives suddenly, standing straight-backed on your front lawn in full military dress, not even bothering to ring the doorbell—just standing there squinting in the sun, waiting to be noticed—when someone arrives unannounced like this you can be sure he's come to change your life. You can be sure that from then on you will think of time in two ways, in the Before and Since. And you can be sure that when this person steps into the house—carrying a duffel bag so long and heavy it could well be concealing a corpse—after he settles in, taking full custody of the foldout couch, eating the entire contents of the freezer, refrigerator, and pantry, watching his favorite game shows at full volume, clogging the sink with his whiskers, filling the house with the smell of wet wool and whiskey—after all of this you can be sure he will leave as suddenly as he appeared.

This was 1980. This was Uncle Harpo.

We had spent the summer as usual—my father, Teddy, and me—lingering in an endless series of waiting rooms at the VA hospital, where my father hid behind newspapers and left me and Teddy to defend ourselves against the requests of older veterans (*Come here*, they shouted, in their smoker's croaks. *Come help me out of this chair, come scratch my back, come tie this shoe, come read me this fine print*), and where my father occasionally set down his newspaper to bully the receptionists in their crisp white dresses and peaked hats about the nature of making appointments and the generally reasonable expectation of being seen by a doctor *some goddamn time today*. We had spent our days in McDonald's restaurants watching our father write long letters on unlined paper to government officials, complaining about the quality of physical and psychiatric care he received at the VA. To keep us quiet he indulged us in pancake breakfasts, and we speared our sausage links with our plastic forks so zealously that we took up bits of the Styrofoam trays on the tines, and chewed these with a strange satisfaction. We had spent our days at the pool hall watching our father lose what he considered an acceptable portion of his monthly disability check. As always he had leaned low over the tables with a fierce concentration, and struck the balls so hard that they wouldn't drop, only circled the rims of their intended pockets and sped back out onto the smug green tables. We had spent our days at the dog track sitting in the bleachers eating peanuts and swinging our legs despondently between races until the dogs sprang from the gates and our father came alive, his program rolled tight in his fist, and he'd beat it against his thigh, hollering at his skinny no-good bastard of a dog. And we had spent our days at the Howard Johnson's lunch counter, Teddy and I swiveling on the vinyl stools on either side of our father, spinning ourselves sick while he talked to the grandmotherly waitresses, reminiscing, talking always of Jack and Bobby, Jack and Bobby, their fallen, golden-haired heroes.

All summer long the Howard Johnson's waitresses had brought us food. Hot dogs, french fries, grilled cheese sand-wiches. We ate giant scoops of ice cream out of silver cups. We ate for hours and hours while our father stared meaningfully out the window at the cloudless sky, lost in reverie, making elaborate rituals of stroking his beard, of wiping the circular lenses of his glasses with his army jacket, of drawing cartoons on napkins. He drew nothing but cartoons of himself. He'd managed to capture the awkwardness of his physique—the way he slouched, as though his great height were a burden, and the way his limbs, so long and thin, seemed brittle. He'd drawn himself in various humors: amused, fiendish, rueful, bored. He'd drawn himself with two whole legs.

That summer we'd spent our evenings watching reruns. Our father fried burgers and heated cans of green beans and we ate our suppers before the antiquated glow of our black-and-white television. The Three Stooges chased each other around with hammers, clonked each other on the head. Jackie Gleason blew his top, shook his terrible fist. Dick Van Dyke swung his briefcase and tripped affably over ottomans. We went to bed while there were still traces of light on the horizon. Our mother came home soon after, and we heard her laugh at something my father had said. It was a sound made in spite of itself—the sound of someone too tired to laugh but also too tired to resist.

These were our summers. If they were strange, we didn't know it. They might have carried on for many more years with a satisfying sameness, like a Broadway show, like reruns. "I've seen this one before," we might have said. "This is the funny part, where the car breaks down and there's a misunderstanding. Afterwards they all share a laugh and go out for ice cream." We might have gone on like this forever, if Uncle Harpo hadn't shown up the summer I was ten and Teddy was seven.

We had never seen Uncle Harpo in person, but we'd become acquainted with him through a series of goofy Christmas cards and a single thirty-minute stretch of prime time when he was a contestant on *Jeopardy!* We watched as he stood shyly behind his podium while Art Fleming introduced him as Sergeant James Hawthorne. "James?" said Teddy. "Why'd they call him James?"

"Harpo's a *nickname*," my father said, and he looked at me and Teddy with a mixture of surprise and disgust. Clearly he wasn't doing a good job with us. We knew where *his* nickname—Groucho—came from. For years he'd been cracking vicious jokes while shielded behind those trademark eyeglasses, with the rubber nose and the furry black mustache. But we didn't know a thing about Harpo Marx, Groucho's little brother, that silent clown.

"You're stationed in the Philippines?" asked Art Fleming.

"That's true," Harpo said.

"And what do you do in your spare time?"

"Oh, nothing much," said Harpo. His voice was so soft we could barely hear it.

"Nothing at all?" said Art, looking smugly into the camera.

"Well, I like to read, I guess."

"Yes," said Art. "Very good." He moved on to the next contestant.

Uncle Harpo wore his army uniform, and all through the game its brassy decorations played in the light. He shifted his weight from leg to leg, declining to answer a single question in the first round. Our father stood up from his chair, outraged whenever Harpo let a question go by. "He *knows* that, for Christ's sake!" my father said. "He's a *human vault of trivia!*" During commercials our father felt compelled to explain to us the unimaginable breadth of Harpo's knowledge on every conceivable subject. "He's a real know-it-all, if you want to know the truth," he said. "He's got one of those photographic memories, and he spends his whole life reading. When he was a kid he practically *married* his encyclopedia set. He *slept* with it, for Christ's sake."

During the second round Uncle Harpo worked himself into a negative balance by missing several questions, including, "In this state tourists can enjoy fine dining and shopping at Quincy Market."

"What is Minnesota?" Harpo said.

"Minnesota!" said my father, and slapped his forehead. He and his brother had been raised near Boston, not far from Quincy Marketplace.

Soon enough Teddy was asking if Uncle Harpo would be required to pay Art Fleming the eighteen-hundred-dollar debt he had racked up. "God, let's hope so," our father said. We watched as Harpo shrugged through the rest of the game. He seemed like someone who needed a friend.

"Maybe we should write him a letter," I said. "We should tell him not to be embarrassed. That we know he's still smart and everything."

"Yes, yes, Frankie, by all means," said my father. "Send it to him in Minnesota." And so began our family's reference to the state of Minnesota as a place where all of life's mysteries and frustrations lived in harmony. "I can't find the scissors," my father would call out. "They must be in Minnesota."

Six months later, Uncle Harpo appeared in the flesh. It was mid-August, with the dark shadow of the school year settled on us, and Teddy and I had been out on a long bicycle tour of the neighborhood. We returned home to find him on our front lawn. He was dressed in his army uniform, and he stood facing the house with impeccable posture. We came up behind him, but he seemed not to notice. He was engaged in an intense staring contest with a fat garden snake that had curled up on our front steps, like a welcome mat. Teddy looked frantically between Uncle Harpo and the snake, then screamed and ran down the lawn. I would have done the same, but I was too old to get away with it.

"Well hello there, young Hawthornes," Uncle Harpo said. "You're Frankie, are you not?" He took off his cap and bowed to me. There was an unmistakable resemblance between Harpo and my father that hadn't been obvious on television. They didn't look physically alike—Harpo was shorter, and clean-shaven, and his skin was strangely pink, and all of his features were plump and round. He looked like a clown out of makeup. But there was still something similar between them—a flash in the eye, a crease in the brow. Harpo spoke in the same overblown language my father often used. Sometimes our father went for days speaking to us like our butler.

"And young Teddy," he said, bowing. "Frankie and Teddy. The New Deal and the Big Stick."

We stared at him.

"Or perhaps I'm mistaken," he said. "Perhaps the presents I've got in my bag here are for two young children a bit further down the road."

"Uncle Harpo!" Teddy cried, and came running. He leapt into Harpo's arms, and they spun around together, laughing. Once again I was too old for this, too old for the coloring books and crayons Harpo had brought for us, and too old to ignore the strange manner in which my father took the news of Harpo's arrival. When we ran in the house to retrieve him (ignoring for once the rule that we never, ever disturb him in the dark sanctity of his den, not if we had won the lottery, not if one of us was trapped under a fallen tree, not even if the house was on fire), he didn't react the way we expected. He sat in his chair for a moment, wiping the lenses of his glasses. On the wall behind him, in a framed photograph, W. C. Fields leered overtop an unfortunate poker hand. He seemed on the verge of cheating his way out of a bad deal, and my father wore the same expression. We had to pull him out of his chair and lead him down the hall by the shirtsleeves, and it was hard not to feel the resistance in him, the slight tug backwards toward the quiet loneliness of his den.

"How do you do, Groucho?" Harpo said, extending his hand.

"Well, that's a fine how do you do," said our father, out the side of his mouth. They shook hands and a shock sounded, and

Uncle Harpo bent over in a fit of giggling. Our father's eyes bulged. He had been stung with a handheld buzzer.

"The old shock treatment," our father said, in a voice too loud and quick to be his own. "You could use a few rounds yourself. I hear it does wonders."

"They tried it on me several times," Harpo announced, and crossed his eyes. "A waste of perfectly good electricity."

"What a waist!" our father said, and poked Harpo in the gut. "Let's have a drink."

After a few beers they were clowning around, singing old songs and falling into spasms of laughter. At first you could hear them straining to remember the words—they stretched out phrases, and mumbled through a few bars. But soon enough they recovered in full the bounty of lyrics stored in their memories. *"Oh, the moonlight's fair tonight along the Wabash,"* they sang, swaying their beer mugs. They hadn't seen each other since my father had left for the war. It had been twelve years.

For supper, our father went so far as to pour charcoal into the ashy belly of the old grill, which he hadn't bothered with for years. He tied on one of our mother's aprons and cooked burgers and hot dogs in the backyard. He stabbed his spatula under the burgers and then flipped them in the commanding style of a cowboy performing gun tricks. Teddy and I ate ourselves sick. We had three burgers apiece and stretched out in the grass on our backs like fallen soldiers, and only recovered when offered sips of beer. We sat next to each other at the picnic table, facing our father and Uncle Harpo, taking cold and bitter and marvelous gulps from their frosted mugs. There was no limit. We drank and drank, expecting at any moment to be discouraged.

But things had changed. Our father and Uncle Harpo were paying extravagant attention to us, reenacting their childhood in a series of long, improbable stories. Among their youthful indiscretions was the discovery of Nazi paraphernalia in a neighbor's apartment, which, out of sheer boredom, they had broken into. "And then," Uncle Harpo said, "just when we found his jacket, with the red band on the sleeve and the swastika, and we were holding it up before our terrified eyes— at that very moment, my dears, we heard the worst sound in the world." He paused. "We heard the Nazi's key scraping in the lock of the front door!" Teddy screamed. He was still a little boy in a striped shirt, and he had drunk a full can of beer. He couldn't help it.

"Teddy takes after you," said my father, and elbowed Harpo.

"I was scared," Harpo said, nodding. "I'll admit it."

"Fortunately, I kept my cool," our father said, and waggled an imaginary cigar. "I suggested the brilliant plan of hiding in the closet. As luck would have it, the Nazi was in the mood for a bath, and while he splashed around in the tub with his rubber ducky we snuck back out onto the fire escape, by the hairs of our chinny-chin-chins."

They smiled silently for a bit, pleased with themselves. That evening they had relived their former lives as escape artists, dodging the wrath of movie-house ushers, of five-and-dime proprietors, of fathers enraged by the broken curfews of their innocent daughters, and of their own father, who sometimes chased after them with a baseball bat. They had escaped the wrath of hundreds of Vietnamese soldiers, of drill sergeants, and of one fugitive Nazi.

"What's a Nazi?" Teddy asked, and lapsed into a fit of giggling. My father picked him up and began carrying him toward the house.

I was left alone with Harpo for a moment. "That's an interesting haircut, Frances," he said.

"I know," I said. I had done it myself just a week before, cutting my hair as close to my head as possible with a pair of child's scissors (the real scissors having gone missing, off to Minnesota). The result was unfortunate. My hair was thick and wouldn't quite lie flat against my skull, as I'd hoped. It sprang up in patches. To make matters worse I had a pea-sized scar behind my left ear—though no one could remember the injury—where no hair grew. I'd done this after my father had looked at me with surprise one morning. "You look so old all of a sudden," he'd said. "You look like a young lady. You hardly look like a kid anymore."

"Most people can't carry that off as well as you do," Harpo said. "You have to be small-boned. You have to be birdlike. You have to be a squirt."

"Oh," I said.

"Did you ever see Twiggy?"

"No."

"That skinny little model? Short blonde hair?"

I shrugged.

"You remind me of her."

"Oh."

"Except younger, of course. And without the psychedelic clothes."

"Uh-huh."

"And you have more freckles."

I nodded.

"And come to think of it your eyes are different. Hers weren't as dark as yours. Your hair's darker, too, of course. Actually you don't really look like her at all."

"Wow," I said, having long ago perfected the art of saying things in a tone that could be interpreted as genuine.

Inside, Teddy started screaming. "I was having fun!" he cried. "I was having fun! I was having fun!" His voice soared and fell, soared and fell.

My father returned and ordered me to bed. "Let's go, champ," my father said to me. "Hup." I was old enough to know when I wasn't wanted. It was dark by now, and fireflies blinked as I walked across the tall grass. The world was magical.

# 2

The next day was a rare day off for our mother. She emerged from her bedroom in the late morning with streaks of black makeup smeared under her eyes, with her hair in fabulous disarray. Nothing could go wrong with my mother's hair, which was long and thick and spectacularly blonde. Her hair was, she always claimed, the reason my father had married her. At first we had taken this for a joke, or at least an exaggeration, but over the years we saw what she meant. My parents had very little in common. Only a man with a fatal weakness for blondes could have married a woman so thoroughly unsuited to him.

Our mother toured the kitchen with the same somber expression I had seen the President use while visiting a town devastated by a tornado. She winced at the dirty dishes that were piled on the counter, the empty beer cans stacked in the trash can and scattered on the floor. She looked stoically at the inside of the refrigerator, which contained three pickles floating in a jar of brilliant green juice, two bottles of Tab, and a fancy, unopened box of peanut-encrusted cheese logs we had received at Christmas from Uncle Harpo. A warm half-gallon of milk sat at the kitchen table, next to an empty box of my mother's favorite cereal, which no one was supposed to touch. She picked up the box in disbelief, and a few shreds of wheat rattled spitefully in the bottom. "I just bought this yesterday," she said, stunned. There were a few precious rules in the house which weren't to be broken, and this was one of them. "What kind of a man is this?" she said, and looked at me as though expecting an answer. "Who eats a *whole fucking box of cereal*?"

In the living room, she frowned at the sleeper couch that was pulled open, with a pile of blankets tangled on top of its thin mattress. Uncle Harpo's duffel bag was stretched across the floor like a scar. His clothes were scattered, and an assortment of arms and legs reached desperately toward us. The curtains were drawn, and the room had already taken on the dankness of barracks. "Where's your father?" she asked. We shrugged. At seven in the morning, by the time we got up, our father and Uncle Harpo had already left the house, with no trace but the scandalous evidence of their early breakfast. Our mother gave us the once-over, the eagle eye. "What a fucking nightmare," she said.

When Harpo and our father returned that evening (reporting that they had gone to the zoo, a movie, and a baseball game— though from the smell of them, and the way their eyes roamed, it seemed safe to assume they had spent most of the day at our father's favorite bar, Old Blue's), our mother asked us to retire quietly to our room. This gave her the illusion of privacy, though the house was small and the rooms crowded together, and we could hear every word that passed between the three of them. "James," our mother began. She refused to call him Harpo. "If you'll be staying here for a few days, I think we should get some things straight."

"By all means, Geraldine," Harpo said. He was so polite.

"I don't want any drinking or recklessness," our mother said. She seemed to have rehearsed this line. "I'd like for all of us to behave like sensible adults."

"Sensible adults!" our father said. "That's great, Gerry. That's a good one."

"Nobody's talking to you," our mother said. "This is between James and I."

"James and me," our father said. "James and *me*."

Our father wasn't particular about much, but he was always a stickler for grammar. Usually people who hadn't finished college—people who had gone off to war and returned to spend the rest of their lives in bars and pool halls and Howard Johnson's restaurants—didn't care about the difference between *who* and *whom*, between *I* and *me*. But our father's name was Randall Hawthorne, and somewhere in our ancestry, he claimed, was greatness.

In another century, in another world, a great writer sat at his desk in the Old Concord Manse, looking out the back window on the landscape of the Revolutionary War, wallowing in the guilt he felt over his own puritanical ancestors, who had helped to persecute the witches of Salem. There he sat, writing and wallowing, wallowing and writing, lost in the past, never knowing the sad, small fate that awaited his distant progeny. Our father kept his books—paperbacks, all of them, moldy and swollen with water damage—in his den.

As the story went, our branch of the family had broken away and moved west to this booming mill city (textiles and wire and cable), but a city doomed to fail, landlocked as it was, with no river or bay to ship and receive, with everything trotted to and fro by horse. Eventually the cost of all this transport was too high, and the city folded to its competitors. The factories were shut down, their windows boarded, their smokestacks left to crumble. It was into this landscape our Hawthorne ancestors were born. We were a poor and unfortunate branch, without standing in the community. We went to church only occasionally, sitting through Christmas and Easter services wondering when they would end, thinking about the food that awaited us at home, trying to ignore the sermon—the mention of our immortal souls burning in hellfire for all eternity.

But what was the difference? Our lives were already hellish. We worked jobs as plumbers and gravediggers, as garbagemen and butchers. Toward middle age we tended to lose our minds. (Our father's strange childhood featured two occasional guest stars, uncles named Franklin and Arthur—uncles who grew long, tangled beards, who heard voices, who burst into indecipherable sermons and acts of violence against inanimate objects, uncles who wandered around town letting themselves into the houses of complete strangers and asking to be fed, uncles who died mysterious deaths, Franklin drowning in a pond, though he had always been a good swimmer, and Arthur disappearing, utterly vanishing for such a long time that he would now almost certainly be dead.) We were an endangered branch, many of us having spent our lives alone, failing to be fruitful and multiply. My father was the only member of his generation to have children.

In his own small way my father seemed to be intent on turning things around for us Hawthornes, on restoring us to our former glory. For as long as I could remember, and perhaps longer, he'd been working on something he referred to only as "the book," an epic manuscript I had glimpsed a few times, when my father had been so careless as to leave it sitting on his desk. It was a foot-high stack of white paper, tied together with twine. And though my father sometimes claimed to be close to finishing it, the book only seemed to get longer. Every night after he put us to bed our father retired to his den and devoted himself to writing. In the moments before sleep we heard the clacking of his old Smith Corona, sometimes furious, sometimes plodding and sad. And sometimes, on the days when dark moods had settled upon him, we heard the sound of our father sitting idle in front of the typewriter, the moments passing by, the quiet strain of all that he wanted to say but couldn't.

We had never read a word of the book, and knew nothing about it, except that it was a collection of our father's war stories. Nonetheless it lived in our minds as a great masterpiece, on a par with *The Scarlet Letter*. Our father had created in us a sense of awe for the Hawthorne name. We believed that somehow, through all those generations, a rare intelligence had survived and was coursing even then through our father's blood, through our blood. Under our father's care we would make something exceptional of ourselves. Already we saw our names in print.

We were, at that point, entirely our father's children. Sometimes it seemed that we hardly knew our mother, who was always at work, or sleeping after a double shift. How this came about—how our father became the caretaker and our mother the breadwinner—was something of a sad story. Just five months after shipping over to Vietnam, having been drafted during his junior year of college, our father was shot, and he returned home with the lower half of his left leg sawed off. After his discharge he'd refused to return to college and finish his degree in American history, as had been his plan. Instead he'd taken a stab at several low-paying jobs (fast-food employee, bank teller, grocery bagger, etc.), but he usually walked off in the middle of shifts, annoyed at something his boss had said or done, bothered by his coworkers, who complained about the smallest inconveniences. Then I came along, screaming and crying, crying all the time (as the story went), crying incessantly and inconsolably, crying until my mother couldn't take it anymore and gave me over to him, shoving me at him, actually, when he returned one morning from his graveyard shift at the gas station, my mother saying, "Take it! Take it away!" and running out of the house and not returning for four days, during which time my father never set me down, allowed me to sleep on his chest, held me as he cooked and ate and watched television, as he went to the bathroom, as he warmed bottles, as he walked to the gas station to quit his job, held me so long that I stopped screaming for good.

After those four days we weren't to be separated. My father

sent my mother back to her old job at Friendly's, and she was happy to go (even happier still that they were chronically short-staffed, and offered her overtime). We lived off her waitressing tips and my father's disability. He took me everywhere with him, laying me down next to him on the bench seat of his Buick, stopping occasionally to tickle me or play peekaboo, driving me all over town to his usual haunts, taking me places where babies never went, the dark stacks of university libraries, the basement of city hall (where he rifled through federal documents, looking for something, we never knew what), and all of the city's Irish saloons, where he settled me down on the bar, between bowls of pretzels and peanuts, and allowed me occasional sips of stout.

Then Teddy came along, six weeks premature, cranky and runty and prone to violent outbursts. Our mother worried that it would be too much for our father, handling two kids at once, but he assured her there was nothing to it. A third-rate vaudevil-lian could manage. All it took was a little planning. While occu-pied with a task (cooking, for instance) it was possible to amuse the children with a bit of well-timed slapstick. In the mornings, while cooking our breakfast, he made a point of dropping heavy objects on his prosthetic foot (saltshakers, gallon jugs of milk, ser-rated bread knives), then hopping around as though in pain, cry-ing, *Ha! Hee! Ho!* He faked the slamming of his fingers in cabinet doors, the singeing of flesh on the gas burner. While delivering our breakfast he walked confidently into walls. "Godfrey Daniel!" he cried, putting on an impressive display of surprise, of suffering. We sat at the table and clapped with delight.

To kill time while driving us to school, or while grocery shopping, there were always jokes. Puns, riddles, knock-knocks.

There were jokes about doctors and priests, about Irishmen, about blondes and bums. There were numerous jokes featuring talking animals, ducks in particular. (*Put it on my bill*, the duck said, when asked to pay for a tube of Chap Stick.) It didn't take much to get us going. An impression or two: the swagger of John Wayne and the scurry of Charlie Chaplin, the cocked head and furrowed brow of Ronald Reagan, who—unbelievably—was campaigning that summer for president. There was the slobbering, deep-throated Donald Duck, the stuttering (*badeeb-badeeb*) Porky Pig. There were tap dance numbers stolen from Fred Astaire and Mr. Bojangles. These he performed with a certain amount of irony, smiling, pretending not to notice the drag and clunk of his wooden leg. On his best days he was Groucho Marx. He'd come bounding into the kitchen in the morning. "This morning I woke up and shot an elephant in my pajamas," he'd announce, wiggling his mustache, waggling an imaginary cigar. "How he got in my pajamas, I don't know."

Harpo had arrived at a time when our parents' marriage was particularly strained. All summer our mother had been hounding our father to register for classes at the community college. Teddy and I were both in school, now, and it was time for my father to get back in the swing of things, to make something of himself. My father would be eating dinner, minding his own business, and suddenly my mother would swat him on the head with a glossy college brochure, something that pictured students sitting happily at their desks, hoping to be called on, their hands raised high in the air. She'd point out a class listing on the history of the Vietnam War, saying that he'd make an easy A, having seen it already firsthand. Our father would reply in his Groucho voice, which meant that he was stifling his true opinion. *Marvelous, Gerry*, he'd say. *You know me so well. You're a visionary.* Sometimes these spats would blow up into real arguments, with my mother crying and slamming doors, vowing to divorce him if he didn't make something of himself, shouting the worst cruelties she could think of—I never would have married you if I'd known you'd turn into such a goddamn waste! You could have *been* something!—and my father shouting in return—*I could have been something! You're a *waitress*, for Christ's sake!*—then disappearing into his den, going silent for days at a time.

No one was more surprised than my mother to find that Harpo's presence actually improved the state of affairs in our household. With Harpo around, my parents spoke to each other politely, like strangers in an elevator. For a few nights our mother even switched shifts at the restaurant and made it home in time for dinner. We all sat at the table together, wondering what to say, staring into the living room at the television, which had always occupied us as we ate, saving us from having to make conversation. We ate in silence, stealing glances at Harpo, who sat perfectly straight in his chair, and who made such scrupulous use of a napkin, dabbing it daintily at the corners of the mouth. When dinner was finished he stood and cleared the table, instead of letting the plates fester overnight, as was our custom. "How polite," our mother said. She seemed to be entertaining the possibility that Harpo would turn out to be a good influence, that things would work out in the end.

One night my father broke the silence at the dinner table and announced that he had registered for classes, as if the idea had come to him on its own. He was to start in a week. Our mother actually dropped her fork. "That's *wonderful*," she said, and a smile broke across her face. This was the husband she had known before the war, the husband she had worked so hard to refashion. "Tell us what you'll be studying."

"Well, I've got a class in twentieth-century British literature, a course on the Vietnam War. And a biology class. I'm told we'll be required to dissect house cats."

"That's just wonderful, Randall," our mother said. "Isn't that wonderful, kids?" There was a gleam in her eye. Perhaps she already saw herself, seated in a white folding chair, watching him graduate from Harvard, where he had transferred after his first year of community college, and where, even before graduating, he had been offered a handful of high-paying jobs.

Things seemed to be changing in a more permanent way than we'd expected. At first we thought that Harpo would stay just a day or two, a week at the most. But now he seemed to have settled in. He wasn't showering or shaving or brushing his teeth or getting dressed each morning like he had done at first, like he had done in the army. He was wearing the same thing day and night—a green T-shirt and a pair of Levi's, a pair of flip-flops. How long could he go like this? At first we kept track—*Hey! It's been ten days!*—but time is strange when you're young. By the second week the oddness of him was gone, and we couldn't remember life without him. We couldn't remember fighting over the front seat as we had always done previously, because now Harpo was there, sitting beside our father keeping him company. Teddy and I watched them from the back, trying to crack their code. They spoke almost entirely in quotations from old W. C. Fields and Marx Brothers movies. They'd drive by a store with a funny name, like Flowerbell's, and simultaneously they'd burst out with "Flowerbell! What a euphonious appellation!" Teddy and I would look at each other, roll our eyes. Children! They were acting like children!

Once classes started, we hardly saw our father. He was free of us, for once, and he immersed himself in his studies. He left the house at daybreak and didn't return until after dinner. Our mother slept in, as usual, and then worked late almost every night. Harpo assumed the responsibility of caring for Teddy and me, and he took it seriously. He served our breakfast each morning, and walked us to the bus stop. And while we were at school he devised an intricate schedule of afternoon amusements. Every weekday he waited for us at the bus stop in his black Galaxie 500. When we climbed in the backseat, full of questions, he refused to tell us where he was taking us. We found ourselves at the zoo, where Harpo stood before the cages of fierce animals and taunted them by sticking out his tongue and singing strange songs and performing obscene little dances and reciting, in his most solemn baritone, a poem about a black panther. We found ourselves at the park, where Harpo deposited us on a ride shaped like a flying saucer, and spun us around so furiously that we begged for mercy. We stumbled like drunks when we stepped off the ride, and Harpo mocked us, pointing and laughing and drawing the attention of complete strangers. We found ourselves playing tag at the public library. Harpo forbade us to make a sound, and then instructed us to run through the stacks as fast as we could. He stooped over like a hunchback and chased after us, grunting through reference, through personal growth, through mystery. He was a madman.

We watched television in the evenings, which was nothing new. But watching *The Lone Ranger* and *I Love Lucy* with Uncle Harpo was more exciting than usual because he talked through most of the episodes. Something would remind him of a fix he and my father had gotten into when they were our age, living in the city with their parents, or later, when they were teenagers, after their parents had been killed in a car crash and they had moved in with their grandparents, in the country. Harpo narrated the dazzling highlights of their careers as vandals. In the city, they stole from fruit stands and picked pockets. In the country they stole chickens and attempted to derail trains. They threw rocks through the windows of their neighbor's house, a three-hundred-pound spook of a man who was their own personal Boo Radley, a shut-in who was rumored to keep innocent troops of small children, like the von Trapps, chained in his basement. One night, while we were watching the Three Stooges, Uncle Harpo told us about the two greatest Marx Brothers—Harpo and Groucho—and how he and my father had worshiped them. They memorized the Marx Brothers' wild routines and performed them in the attic of their grandparents' otherwise noiseless and humorless household. "We were brothers," Harpo said. "They were brothers. They were funny and we thought we were funny. We couldn't get over the coincidence, so we stole their names." Harpo recommended that Teddy and I find heroes of our own, men who could teach us how to walk through the world. "Everyone needs a hero," he said. "Which reminds me, I could really use a sandwich."

We had never heard these stories before. Our father had
always been mysterious about his childhood, talking only of its
most peripheral characters, its crazy uncles and neighbors and
vicious teachers. Whenever we asked our father about his immediate family, he always gave the same answer: "Your grandparents
are dead. Your Uncle Harpo is in the army. End of story." All
Teddy and I really needed to know, our father often told us, was
that we were "two lucky bastards." We had it much better than
he ever did.

On  weekends,  while our father was studying at the
library and our mother was at work, Uncle Harpo enlisted us to
help him with the repairs he had planned for our house. "Your
mother has advised me that I need to start earning my keep
around here, since I'm taking such an extended vacation," he
said, in the gentlest voice. "She's a gem, your mother. A precious
gem."

Harpo gave us a formal tour of the house's flaws, pointing out
the bulging, mildewed tiles in the shower stall, the dime-sized
holes in the screen door, the corrosive rust on the bulkhead, the
crumbling plaster at the base of the living room wall, the slow
leak in the kitchen sink. "Lady and Gentleman," he told us.
"Behold the inevitable decay of life!" He explained that the
greatest of human struggles was the ongoing war between
progress and ruin. "Luckily I'm around to help," he said. "Your
parents, I'm sorry to say, are hopeless."

We held his tools as he undid the fixtures of the kitchen sink
and a geyser of water burst forth, spraying him in the face. We

watched as he prepared the new screen door for installation. "It's important to make sure the door is limbered up first," he told us as he danced across the front lawn with it, humming the Tennessee Waltz. He performed several numbers: the twist, the watusi, the fandango. Finally, when he attempted to dip the door in a display of gallantry, he tripped and landed on it and popped the screen out of its frame. One Saturday afternoon we watched in terror as he took a sledgehammer to the base of the living room wall. There was an explosion of plaster, followed by an invasion of fine white dust that settled on our clothes, on our skin, in our hair, and in our lungs. In one swing he had chopped away a hole the size of a bowling ball, and he seemed to regret it. He seemed at a loss for what to do next. "Excellent progress," he said, slapping his hands together. He always liked to call it a day after he had caused more destruction than he was willing to repair.

Just hours after Harpo tore apart the living room wall, it became clear that he had set free a family of mice that had been living there. That night we heard their scurrying and squeaking while watching *The Lone Ranger*, and Harpo stalked through the house, holding a boot in his hand like a gun. When he heard so much as the twitch of whiskers he dove across the room and landed in a belly flop, and banged his boot against the floor with reckless abandon.

By the end of the episode, Harpo had pulled several muscles, and Teddy and I had laughed ourselves sick. It was time for a new plan. "Tonto and Silver," Harpo said to us, in the loud and self-righteous voice of the Lone Ranger. "We must succeed in smiting our rodent enemies." He explained to us that we were in our own personal western. Our very lives were on the line, and we had to work together in order to survive. If our mother came home and found a house full of mice we'd all be goners.

Harpo led us out to the backyard on exaggerated tiptoe. "You may not have realized this," he said, in a tortured whisper, "but I'm an infamous cat burglar." We watched as he hopped the chain-link fence into our neighbors' yard. We followed his shape in the darkness as he moved across the Weatherbees' back lawn, making kissing noises. Then we saw the glowing eyes of the neighbors' cat, Mitzi, as she pranced up to Harpo. He scooped her up with one hand and climbed quite casually back over the fence. Mitzi's collar—which was strung with bells—tinkled faintly, but she showed no other sign of protest.

Harpo set Mitzi down in the bright light of the kitchen. She was a black cat with a white belly and a set of haughty green eyes. She was beautiful, and she seemed to know it. She pranced and sniffed around the edge of the room, unimpressed. Teddy chased after her on his hands and knees, but she was elusive. "Here, Mitzi," he called.

"Mitzi!" our uncle said. "This cat's name is Mitzi? That simply won't do." He picked her up, held her in front of his face, and looked meaningfully in her eyes for a moment. "Your new name is Doreen," he told her, in the kindest, softest voice. "Yes. Doreen. That is your name." He set her down and took off her collar.

Doreen failed to catch a single mouse, but she managed to serve the higher purpose of bearing the terrible burden of our family's previously bottled-up affections. She spent her nights on the foldout couch with Uncle Harpo, curled up on a pile of his dirty clothes. Teddy and I dazzled Doreen with balls of yarn and squeaky plastic toys. My mother watched television with the cat in her lap and stroked her fur for hours. Our father, even our father, took to Doreen. He pretended to shake his fist at her when she clawed at the couch, or sat in his favorite chair, but several times we heard him, behind the closed door of his den, communicating with Doreen in baby talk.

Occasionally we heard the neighbors—a young couple who dressed themselves in nothing but L.L. Bean—calling dejectedly for Mitzi. It was a sad sound, but we weren't about to let her go. This was the world we lived in, Harpo explained. Times were tough. Love wasn't easy to come by. You had to fight for everything you could get, and you had to hold on tight to the Doreens of the world.

It was a bad year. Millions of Americans, including my mother, were swept up in *Dallas* fever. Every Friday night during an hour of prime time a handsome group of Texas oil moguls met in elegant office space hatching plans to overthrow their enemies. They mused, swirling perfectly aged Scotch in crystal glasses. When they quit for the day they dropped in on their blonde mistresses, who surrendered themselves in their living rooms, in their showers, in their satin-sheeted king beds, and in their glistening backyard pools. Meanwhile, the millionaires' wives seethed at home, wringing their hands and plotting revenge in low voices, in empty rooms. That summer eight million people waited in suspense to find out who had shot J. R. Ewing, a man with countless enemies, a man who tended to strut away, tipping his cowboy hat, after causing immeasurable destruction.

The country yearned for its own real-life cowboy, and it turned to Reagan, the B actor who campaigned from coast to coast, waving triumphantly at the huge crowds who had gathered at his feet. Iran continued to hold American hostages while Jimmy Carter struggled futilely for their release. Newspapers published polls that predicted Reagan's landslide victory. A new era was upon us. Whenever Reagan appeared on television—winking, nodding, smirking, cocking his head—my father stopped everything and watched the screen with a crazed intensity. "You dirty bastard," he'd whisper. "You dirty goddamn bastard."

It was the kind of year that people took personally. All that summer our father had suffered from terrible nightmares. Almost every night he'd wake up screaming, and we'd hear my mother try to comfort him. When it was quiet again everyone would pretend to sleep, but we all knew better. No one could sleep after that.

# 3

Our father wasn't the only one with problems. As the weeks passed, our mother's patience wore thin. At first she had been delighted to see the change in our father, and to see us get along so well with Harpo. She was happy that our father was in school, and that there was someone around to care for us in his absence. But soon enough Harpo was all we talked about, and she began to wince as we chattered about our adventures as carpenters and patrons of the public library. She tended to stare despondently at the hole in the living room wall. When Harpo had been with us for six weeks, she began keeping a list of the food he ate, and taped it to the refrigerator door. At the end of each week she tallied the money he owed. One day Harpo left our mother a note. "Child care," it read. "One hundred dollars per week. Minus twenty-eight dollars in groceries. Equals seventy-two dollars owed me."

"Rent," our mother wrote back. "Seventy-two dollars per week."

What had at first seemed charming about Harpo was now farcical. When he bowed gallantly to our mother she simply rolled her eyes. They managed to speak to each other politely, but there was sarcasm in their voices. It was only a matter of time before one of them said the wrong thing and triggered the great fight that would bring this strange visit to an end. In the meantime they smiled and smiled, sick with desire for it.

One afternoon in late October, our mother was enraged when the school principal called to make sure that "everything was all right in the home." Something had only recently caught his attention. The principal was intrigued by the information cards the school had sent home, asking parents to fill in their names, occupations, home and work numbers, and family doctor, to be used in the event of an emergency. Uncle Harpo had filled out our cards. Under "mother's occupation" he had written "sourpuss" on Teddy's card, and "snot rag" on mine. Was this a joke? The principal just wanted to make sure.

That evening my mother went through the unusual and surprising effort of making a sit-down meal. She prepared it with such apparent delight that we knew something was wrong. She sang as she broiled steaks and mashed potatoes and floated two plastic bags of frozen corn niblets in boiling water. Her song was vague, full of "doobie-doos" and "fa-la-las." It was just the kind of song that villains sang in movies as they poisoned apples in bubbling cauldrons.

We watched in amazement as she stacked the table with food. "Oh, this looks good, Gerry," Harpo said, and rubbed his hands together in anticipation. Then he heaped the entire bowl of corn onto his plate. He did the same with the mashed potatoes, and served himself four porterhouse steaks, though my mother had only cooked five. Our mother's eyes bulged.

"What do you think you're doing?" she said. "I mean it, James. I can't take this."

"It's a joke, Gerry," Harpo said.

"Well, it's not funny," she said. "You two always think you're funny, but the sad truth is you're not even close."

Harpo served the rest of us off his plate and then began the unprecedented ritual of saying grace. "O Lord," he shouted. "Thank you for the kindhearted hospitality of my brother's wife, Geraldine, and thank you for the man who discovered peroxide, so that her glorious blondeness can perpetuate itself, forever and ever in your name, amen."

"I don't have to stand for this shit," our mother said. "Who said you could stay here this long, anyway? Do you think I don't know what's going on, here? What kind of a leave is this, James? Does the army give its people *two months* of vacation a year? Do they?" she said, looking at me and Teddy, as if we knew.

"Harpo has saved up a great deal of vacation," my father said quietly. "And he's generously decided to spend it with us."

"It's a reunion tour, of sorts," Harpo said. "Kind of like a revival of brotherhood."

"He's not on *leave*, you idiot," our mother told our father. "He's not on *two months of vacation*. He's been *discharged*. Or he's *AWOL*, for Christ's sake."

"Shut up, Gerry," our father said.

"Oh, excuse me," said our mother. "I forgot. We're not supposed to talk about some things in this family."

"Shut up, Gerry," our father said again. He was almost whispering.

"We're just all supposed to pretend this isn't awkward, right? We're supposed to forget about what happened. Forget you two hardly spoke for twelve years."

"Shut up, Mom," I said, and a silence fell over the table.

Harpo and my father took their plates into the den, and my mother cried silently until Teddy climbed into her lap. "Don't cry, Mom," he said. "You're really pretty. Your hair looks really pretty."

The next morning, Harpo was gone. The couch was still folded out in the living room, and Doreen sat curled in the center of the mattress, licking her fur, tending to herself in the comforting manner animals employ when they find themselves abandoned.

Our father quit school after Harpo left. We found ourselves once again in the backseat of his car, driving around the city between the VA, the pool hall, the Howard Johnson's. When he spoke to us, which wasn't often, he only spoke of our mother. It was as if Harpo never existed.

"Your mother wants me to stay in school," he'd tell us. "She says we can get a babysitter for you two. That I should make something of myself. What do you think of that?"

We shrugged.

"Apparently I'm no good the way I am," he said. "But what's the point? Your mother is always unsatisfied. Your mother would be happier married to a door-to-door vacuum cleaner sales-man, someone with a Cadillac, someone with ambition." He looked in the rearview to see the effect this speech was having on us. But we were used to this kind of talk from him, and we simply stared into our laps. "Your mother thinks I'm from a bad family," he continued. "She grew up with plenty of food in the refrigerator and nice dresses in her closet, and she had braces put on her teeth to straighten them out, and she had her hair cut by professionals in a salon, and she took dancing and singing lessons. She never had to walk through a steaming hot jungle, or carry a buddy who was bleeding to death until she couldn't carry him anymore." He was speaking in a disgusted whisper. "She doesn't like our house. She doesn't like the school you kids go to. She doesn't understand that what you kids have is a hundred times better than what I had growing up. She doesn't understand me."

Our father didn't know that Teddy and I had learned his family history from Uncle Harpo. We had learned about the death of his parents, and we had learned about the significance of the Marx Brothers—the inspiring heroes who had clowned their way out of a miserable existence. We had also learned about the breakup of the brothers. "It was just like the Beatles," Harpo had explained. Harpo and our mother had dated for a month or two while they were supposed to be waiting for our father to return from Vietnam. Later, when our father discov-ered the truth, he stopped speaking to Harpo (presumably he would have stopped speaking to our mother, too, but it was too late—they were already married). "It's the oldest story in the world," Harpo had said. "But it wasn't just your mother's fault. It was everyone's fault."

Our father didn't realize that we knew these things, now. That we knew him.

We watched our father grow sadder and stranger in the weeks after Harpo left. He took over the foldout couch and lay there on his stomach watching movies late into the night. We'd find him in the morning in his clothes, his mouth open, the television still running. When he woke, his eyes were red and bleary. He hardly moved from the couch, where he watched television, stared out the window, and held Doreen. She was still a comfort, but even she had changed. She sulked and pouted, and sniffed about rooms. She seemed to be searching for Harpo, certain of his even- tual return. My father and Teddy and I harbored the same secret wish, though we knew it was futile. But Doreen, stupid Doreen, kept waiting, and we couldn't stand it. One day my father let her out of the house. She came around a few times, scratching at the door to no avail, before she made her way back over to the neigh- bors and their proper L.L. Bean lives. We saw her retreating prints in the snow, and they tortured us for a few days, until our father wiped them out with his foot.

Christmas came and went. Teddy and I bought our father a bowling ball. We had never seen him bowl, but Uncle Harpo had assured us that this was one of our father's favorite pastimes. According to Harpo, our father was a natural, a born winner. He sat and looked at the ball, smiled, then zipped it back in its case and never mentioned it again.

The world iced over. In January, President Reagan took the

oath of office, and this seemed like too great a burden for a reasonable man to bear. Our father's nightmares grew worse. We woke regularly to his screaming. Once, when our mother went out to the living room to comfort him, he broke down. "I can't do this!" he yelled. We heard him sob. "One fucking leg," he cried.

And it went on like this through the bleak winter.

The weather finally turned in April. It was still cold, and the drifts of snow piled along the roadside were reluctant to melt, but it was livable again. Our father started taking walks in the evenings, instead of lying around watching television. He'd return with watering eyes and pink skin. "Lovely night for a walk," he'd say. He'd watch a few minutes of television with us— we'd taken over his place on the foldout couch—and even laughed now and then: a short, awkward bark that seemed to escape against his will. We took this as progress.

One morning he even joined us for breakfast. He entered the kitchen singing and dancing, doing his best Groucho Marx. "Hello, I must be going," he sang, and waggled his eyebrows.

*I cannot stay*
*I came to say*
*I must be going.*
*I'm glad I came*
   *But just the same*
*I must be going.*

He kept advancing toward us, then marching away. It was the best kind of nonsense. We could barely keep up with the ambiguity. We laughed and clapped and begged for more. It had been a long time since we'd seen him like this. He sat down and opened a paper napkin and tucked it playfully into the collar of his T-shirt.

"You know who voted for Reagan?" he said as he spread out the newspaper. "Minnesota. Goddamn Minnesota." Teddy and I laughed. We had forgotten the old joke.

"If you forget your homework, and your teacher asks you where it is, what do you tell her?"

"Minnesota!" we shouted. We laughed and laughed. Our father had returned to us.

That evening, to everyone's delight, he gave our mother twenty dollars and asked her to pick up some takeout, he didn't care what. "I'll go to Chum Lee's," my mother said. There was a cheerful note in her voice. Perhaps she was only pleased that she didn't have to cook. But maybe she also imagined that things were improving. She might have imagined the small happiness that meal would bring us as we sat around the table, just the four of us, like a real family, licking our fingers, laughing, watching reruns of *I Love Lucy*.

"Excellent," our father said, using his vibrant Groucho voice. He actually kissed our mother on the cheek. "Children," he told us. "Would you do me the honor of accompanying your beautiful mother? We can't let her get lonely. You must protect her."

The smell of Chinese food filled the car and Teddy and I swung our legs happily in the backseat. We arrived home and went about the torture of setting the table and filling up glasses with tap water. Oh, we were hungry. "Go get your father," my mother told me, and I ran down the hall toward his den. "Dad," I said. "Supper's ready." The door of the den was open. My father had also pulled up the window shade, and light filled the room, casting everything in an unfamiliar brightness. I saw quite clearly the green of his army jacket, the curve of my father's back. I saw the brilliant red of his blood. My father was slumped at his desk. He had shot himself in the head.

# 4

O nce, while taking our picture, my father
told Teddy and me about certain tribes of Indians
who refused to be photographed, believing that their
souls would be stolen, believing that in a single instant, when the
shutter closed, the life would go out of them. Though they might
go on living and breathing after they were photographed, their
hearts beating like anyone else's, it was only physical. The rest of
them was dead.

These Indians, our father said, would attempt to go back to
their old routines, but everything was strange to them—their
families, their homes, even their own language. They could no
longer understand what the people around them were saying.
When they tried to speak, they found that even their own voices

were unfamiliar, and that their bodies seemed to move against their will, as if controlled by ventriloquists. For a while they'd try to live with their tribes, using sign language to indicate their basic needs. To show the isolation they felt they resorted to the tactics of mimes, pressing their palms against the walls of the invisible boxes in which they were trapped. But no one understood them.

Before long the soulless would decide that their old lives were simply unlivable, and so they'd set off into the dark woods to fend for themselves. There they became fierce and vengeful. They filed their teeth into points and prowled the woods for human flesh, particularly photographers. Our father said that if they caught someone with a camera—some unsuspecting dope from *National Geographic*—they'd kill him in the most painful manner, scalping him, gouging his eyes out, running him through with a stake and roasting him over an open flame.

Then our father had taken what would become his favorite picture. Teddy and I were standing next to each other, bundled in our snowsuits, our hoods pulled up over our heads and cinched tight. Teddy was screaming. We had been sledding in the woods, and it had just occurred to him that we were easy prey for any passing Indians. I was looking down and my mouth was turned up in one corner, skeptical. I had been thinking about all the times my picture had been taken, and it didn't seem possible that a soul—whatever that was—could be captured on film and coiled away in darkness. It didn't seem possible that, in a single instant, you could lose everything like that, yourself and all you knew of life.

But it has since occurred to me that such a thing might be possible. Just the sight of him.

In my mind I have a picture of myself standing in the door-way of my father's den. I said to myself, *He is dead*, and then I felt something go out of me. The force of it leaving was so strong that I fell to my knees. Then it was like I was watching myself from above. I saw myself screaming, heard a sound coming out of me that wasn't quite human, a high and twisting sound, like the call of an elk.

All through that first year of grief I continued to have these moments when I lifted out of myself. My mother called them "episodes," and they came upon me several times a day. All of a sudden I seemed to drift out of my body and regard myself with a strange detachment. In my head I'd start narrating the events of my life as if I were a character in a book, some kind of Frankie in Wonderland, some Frankie Copperfield. The things I said and did in those moments were as much of a surprise to me as any-one else. I could go for hours thinking of myself in this way:

*The day had been going well for Frankie, but then she had ventured outside to get the mail and found an envelope addressed to her father. "Special Offer," it said, "for Randall T. Hawthorne." And the sight of this was painful to her. She felt a tightness in her chest. Her heart flut-tered and she couldn't breathe. It was happening again. Whenever she thought about her father this pain came over her, and she lost herself. She never knew how to find her way back. She stood on the curb for a while, staring off, until she heard her mother calling from inside. "Frankie!" her mother said. "Where's the mail? What the hell are you doing?"*

*"Nothing," Frankie said. She returned the envelope to the mailbox and walked back to the house. "No mail," she told her mother.*

*"Good," her mother said. "Hey, while you're up, can you fix me a drink?"*

*Frankie went to the kitchen and made her mother a drink, Scotch with three ice cubes. For a month now she had been making drinks and fetching slippers and blankets, turning up the television, turning it down, opening and closing windows, answering the phone, walking to the Big G to buy groceries, or to Gino's when her mother had a craving for a meatball sub, all because her mother could not seem to get off the couch. After the business of death was finished, Frankie's mother had collapsed on the sofa bed and surrendered herself to the television. She'd lie there all day watching cartoons and soap operas and game shows and the local news. At night Frankie and Teddy piled on the bed next to her and they watched horror movies until they fell asleep. Sometimes Frankie woke in the night to the roars of giant reptiles who were devouring cities, and she turned the television off. But then, lying there in the dark next to her mother and brother, both of them snoring lightly, she felt very lonely, and so she turned the television on again.*

Sometimes I'd get so lost in one of these reveries that it was difficult to have a conversation. "Frankie," my mother would say. "Can you get me another ice cube? I think it's more of a *four-*ice-cube day today." And I'd have to stop to translate: *Frankie's mother wanted another ice cube.*

"Hello?" she'd say. "Are you *in* there? Are you drunk or something?"

*Now Frankie was being accused of drinking!*

"What the hell is wrong with you?" She'd reach over and slap me lightly in the face. "Snap out of it!"

*Frankie had been slapped!* I'd think.

It was somewhat like watching the news from Russia. You could see someone standing at a podium but only hear his voice faintly. Speaking over him was a British interpreter, who seemed to be losing whole sentences in translation. The Russian would talk for thirty seconds, shaking his fist, and the translator would only say, "Hello? Is anyone in there?"

I kept waiting for this to stop. But even when my mother returned to work and things in our house were somewhat normal again—Teddy and I wasting our mornings bicycling around the neighborhood, then riding out to Lincoln Street for lunch at Gino's Pizza, then returning home in the afternoons to devote ourselves to cartoons—it kept happening. Teddy would be chattering away about something and suddenly he'd realize I was gone. Sometimes he'd try to slap me, like my mother did, but I'd grab his wrist and twist his arm behind his back until he cried. At least, I thought, I was still able to do this.

Eventually I started to think there might be something truly wrong with me. I often thought of the time, in first grade, when Michael Keene broke his right hand and had to wear a cast for a while. As an exercise in sympathy our teacher, Mrs. Smith, had made us go through an entire day using only our left hands. We couldn't do the simplest things. Our handwriting was huge and deformed. At lunch we struggled to unwrap our sandwiches and maneuver spoonfuls of pudding into our mouths. By the afternoon we all gave up and started using our right hands again. We felt blissful in our good health. We felt the pleasure of leaving the lame behind. Michael Keene was on his own.

Something was broken in me, but it wasn't so easy to recognize. I couldn't explain it. I couldn't say to my mother and Teddy, "Sometimes my right mind doesn't work, and I have to use my left." There was no way for them to reproduce my injury and understand what was happening. Even if they could, I had the feeling they'd never stick with it. I had the feeling they'd give up before we finished breakfast.

And so it went on like this, all through the summer.

One morning, while I was pouring myself a bowl of cereal, a small pamphlet spilled out of the cereal box and onto the table. DRAW ME, it said, not unlike the bottle of potion that Alice had found in Wonderland, which was simply marked: DRINK ME. The pamphlet was printed in black and white, on the cheapest paper, but there was something compelling about it. Within its twelve pages the pamphlet showed how everything in the world could be broken down into a series of shapes, and by simply arranging these shapes at the proper angles, a person could draw anything. A dog, a cat, a house, a car, a human face. I went to my room and fished through my backpack, found a notebook and pencil. Then, while eating my cereal, I started drawing. As I drew I felt my mind go wonderfully blank, felt the voice in my head fall quiet. A calm came over me. Starting that day I always kept a notebook and pencil in my back pocket, and whenever I felt myself having an episode, I started drawing. I drew the things that bothered me, the things that set me off. I drew my father's toothbrush, dried out and lonely in the medicine cabinet.

I drew my mother's wedding ring, which she'd set on the kitchen windowsill one night while doing the dishes, and never placed back on her finger.

And when I saw Doreen the cat, escaped from the Weatherbees' yard and roaming loose in the neighborhood, I drew her, too.

My mother was always after me to put the sketchbook away and rejoin what she called "the land of the living." But I couldn't. It was such a comfort, setting things down like that. Though I couldn't express it at the time, I was coming to understand something, something I suppose my father had known: that on paper we could capture things and make of them what we liked, on paper we could pin down the world and take our revenge, on paper we could feel at home, safe in the land of the meek, the lonely, the dead.

# 5

Please believe me when I tell you that my school's psychologist was named Mr. Jolly, and that he was just the kind of person to make the most of this happy coincidence. He was a clown of a man—fat and bald an pink-faced, a man who wore sherbet-colored pantsuits and polka-dot bow ties—and he seemed to be under the impression that all the world was a stage. He walked around the halls of the school winking and whistling, pointing to the students he knew and shouting their names, asking mercilessly for high fives. Mr. Jolly had a habit of bursting into classrooms in the middle of lessons

and exchanging what he considered to be witty banter with our teachers. "I'm so happy for you to see me," he'd tell the teachers, and cackle at his own lame joke. "Bang, bang!" he'd shout, shooting two imaginary pistols into the crowd. Then he'd chuckle for a moment, holding his considerable stomach with both hands, like a person inflicted with appendicitis.

Eventually Mr. Jolly would compose himself and call out the name of the person he'd come to summon. Usually this was Mark Ferris, who lived in a trailer with his mother, and whose father was in prison for murder. But occasionally it was someone else, a new kid who was having trouble adjusting, or a kid who had gotten into a fight. One shocking day it was Jane Corning, a girl who was superior to the rest of us in every way. She was a quiet, flawless student with good looks and rich parents. What, we wondered, could be wrong with Jane Corning? We had hoped for the worst, but in the end it was only a mild case of depression set off by the death of her goldfish.

The day finally came, as I knew it would, when Mr. Jolly called my name. "Frankie Hawthorne," he said, one September afternoon. "Come on down to my office. Let's get Jolly!"

*As she gathered up her books Frankie could feel everyone looking at her. She was mortified. Mr. Jolly put his arm around her and ushered her out of class. "How's it going?" he said to her.*

*"Fine."*

*"How was your summer?"*

*"Fine."*

*"Did you do anything fun?"*

*"Not really."*

*"Well, we're gonna have ourselves some fun, you and me,"* he said. *He kept squeezing her shoulder while he talked.*

*This, Frankie thought, must be a nightmare.*

Mr. Jolly's office gave off the impression of having once been a bathroom. It was small and musty and windowless, with a black-and-white-tiled floor. There were patched holes along one wall that looked like the buried tracks of plumbing. The room was just large enough to contain a desk and two metal folding chairs. The desk was small and battered, its varnish almost entirely worn off, its top like a guest book, carved all over with initials, some of them simply declaring themselves and some of them connected by plus signs, enclosed in hearts.

To fight against the gloominess of the room Mr. Jolly had tacked up a Norman Rockwell print behind his desk, an old woman and a young boy sitting down to dinner at a crowded restaurant, their heads bowed in prayer, the other customers oblivious, distracted by their newspapers and cigarettes, their plates cleared of food they had not bothered to bless. I sat and scrutinized it.

"You like that picture?" said Mr. Jolly.

"I guess."

"I like it a lot. I really do."

I nodded.

"It reminds me of simpler times," he said. "It reminds me to try to do the right thing, even if no one else does."

There was nothing to do but nod again.

"Would you describe yourself as a quiet person?" said Mr. Jolly. He was leaning forward in his chair, smiling, trying to catch my eye, but I'd turned my face down expertly. I could see him without really looking at him, a trick I'd perfected years ago. He had no idea who he was dealing with.

Mr. Jolly stared down at the legal pad on his desk, apparently trying to compose a thought. He kept clicking his pen. Finally he wrote something. "Frances Hawthorne," he whispered, and I added to the list of his flaws the habit of muttering aloud what he was writing on paper.

"You like the Celtics?" he said.

"I guess."

"Who's your favorite? Bird?"

"I don't know," I said.

"Well, you gotta have a favorite!"

"I don't know. I guess I like Archibald." I did. He struck me as thoughtful. Even as he was scoring a basket he seemed to be off somewhere.

"Tiny Archibald!" he said. "Cripes! He's practically a midget!"

"Yeah," I said.

"Don't you wanna go with Bird?"

I shrugged. Mr. Jolly pulled open his desk drawer and took out two stuffed animals, a Donald Duck and a Mickey Mouse, and he waved them happily in front of my face. "Hi, Frankie," he made them say. "Which one of us do you like better?"

"I don't know," I said.

Mr. Jolly made the mouse dance. Its legs swung hopelessly, and its eyes glazed over with a sad complacency, in the fashion of Mr. Bojangles. "Which one of us do you like better?" said Mickey. "Is it me? Is it? Oh, please, please, please. Pick Mickey! Pick me!" A vein bulged in Mr. Jolly's forehead. His eyes were crazed, murderous. I reached very slowly for the duck because his restraint impressed me. I was also a little sorry for him because he had forgotten to put on his pants. Someone had let him out of the house wearing nothing but a blue T-shirt and a hat in the shape of a soufflé. "Aha!" Mr. Jolly said as he stuffed Mickey back in his desk drawer. "So you're a *Donald* person." He scribbled something on his notepad and smiled to himself. "Very interesting."

It was a moment I'd come to know very well—a moment when Mr. Jolly felt he had cracked open a lock and found his way into the clockwork of my soul. He thought it was modesty, my choosing the duck, identifying with the lesser-known character instead of the clear favorite, the animated corporate spokesman. What Mr. Jolly didn't know was that I had a webbed foot. Between my toes was the thin and translucent skin of our ancient amphibian ancestors. It wasn't modesty. When I chose Donald, I chose myself.

Next we played a sudden-death game of twenty questions. Mr. Jolly explained that I should shout out the first answer that came to my mind, without stopping to think. "Go ahead and yell out those answers!" he said, and banged his desk with his fist. "Ready?"

"Ready," I said.

"I can't hear you," he said, and cupped his hand behind his ear.

"Ready!" I yelled. I was trying for sarcasm but it came off in earnest.

We covered it all: what I liked to do in my spare time (draw), my favorite food (peanut butter sandwiches), which superpower I would like if I could choose one (invisibility), the capital of Montana (Helena), my favorite season (fall), favorite subject (history), favorite color (blue), the name of our president (Ronald Wilson Reagan), what I had done with my summer (nothing), the word I would use to describe my mother if I could only choose one (blonde), the word that best described Teddy (annoying), the name of my best friend (Teddy), what I wanted to be when I grew up (a librarian), whether I thought I'd get married (no), or have children (oh, no), the place I went to in my daydreams (Helena, Montana—at this Mr. Jolly reminded me to tell the truth), why I chose to draw in a sketch-book in class instead of listening to my instructors (I didn't know), what I was drawing (cathedrals), why I chose to draw cathedrals (I wanted to be an architect when I grew up), and what happened to being a librarian?

"Things change," I told him, and shrugged.

"What's the most favorite memory you have of your father?" he said next. I took a quick breath, turned away in my chair. It felt like he'd punched me in the chest.

"That's twenty-one," I said.

"Is it?"

"Yes."

"I was sidetracked," he said, "by the cathedral situation."

"Oh."

"Do you mind telling me about your favorite memory?"

"Well," I said. "I thought it was just twenty questions." I sat Donald back on the desk, and he collapsed backwards.

Mr. Jolly sighed, sat back in his chair, tossed his pen on the desk. "Right you are," he said. "We'll just save that favorite memory for next week. Howsabout you write it down? Put your thoughts in a little essay?"

"We're meeting next week?" I said.

"I travel amongst five schools," he said. "I take care of kids all over the west half of the city."

"Oh."

"I've got the elementary and middle schools in my care. In fact I'm seeing your little brother later today."

"Oh."

"Do you think you can wait until next week?" he said. "To see me?" He sat forward in his chair, trying to catch my eye again.

"I didn't think I'd be coming back," I said. Jane Corning hadn't gone back after the single goldfish episode.

"Ha!" he said. "We're just getting started here, Frankie."

"Oh."

"Grief is a complicated process. When someone dies, it takes a year to really process it. We have a lot of talking to do."

"I don't know," I said, my voice phlegmy. "I think I'm doing fine. I don't really have anything to say."

"Let's just start out with the essay," he said, and slapped his desk. "Your topic is, *My Favorite Memory of My Father.*"

"Okay," I said.

*This is going to be a disaster! thought Frankie.*

"Before you go, I have a book for you that you might find helpful." Mr. Jolly rifled through his desk drawer and pulled out something short of a book. It was a mimeographed pamphlet, something you'd expect to find stuck underneath the windshield of your car, left there by some desperate fanatic. Its title was *Oh, Brother!* and it was written by someone named Heathcliff Sloakum, Ph.D. Pictured on the cover, flying an airplane, was a blatant copyright violation: a Snoopy-like cartoon beagle with a roguish smile, a long scarf flapping behind him.

"Thanks," I said. I took the pamphlet and stood up to leave.

"We're going to be great pals," he said, standing up and opening the door, then placing his arm around me and ushering me through. "Right?" He raised his hand in the air and for a second I thought he was going to slap me. "High five!" he said. His pink face was split open in a wide smile, his teeth full of winking silver fillings.

I gave him what he wanted. "Right!" I cried. I not only slapped my hand against his, I jumped up as I did it. Then I ran away down the hall, back to math class, the cheerless territory of Mrs. Gustafson, a woman who had utterly given up on life, who had grown so fat that she could wear nothing but gray sweatsuits, who wore no makeup, who had a tuft of white hair on the crown of her head that she declined to dye. Over the years students had compiled a brief history of her life. Rumors had been passed like batons from one class to the next, and so we knew that once, in the distant past, she had been thin and beautiful and good-natured. But then her husband had left her for another woman. Mrs. Gustafson still wore her wedding band, and the sight of it cinching her finger was painful. It was a matter of occasional debate whether she wore the ring because of undying love for her errant husband, or because she had grown so fat that she could no longer remove it.

When I had almost made it down the hall Mr. Jolly called after me. "Later, alligator," he said.

I had begun to understand that our world was held together by a vast system of unwritten social rules, little conventions that kept people from killing each other, and according to these conventions I was supposed to call back, "After a while, crocodile!" But I didn't. I had my limits.

A t   l u n c h   I flipped through *Oh, Brother!* On the first page the libelous Snoopy was shown in the arms of his best friend, a bald boy in a striped shirt. On the second page, the boy was run over by a car, and from then on Snoopy was pictured in various states of agony. For several pages he lay on the floor, his ears tucked over his eyes. People came up and offered him bones and sticks and balls, but he wouldn't move. Not even a mailman could rouse him. Then, one day, the dog started acting out. He screamed, cried, beat his fists against the ground, smashed bottles, set his house on fire, kicked people, bit them—the works. Once he'd gotten it all out of his system, he was fine. On the last page he was shown sitting in the lap of a new owner—a young, popular boy with a full head of hair.

*This book, Frankie thought, is the stupidest thing I've ever seen.*

M y   s c h o o l   was separated from Teddy's by a giant parking lot, and when classes let out we met in the middle and walked home together. That day Teddy couldn't stop talking about Mr. Jolly. "He's *so* funny!" he said. "There was this joke he told. Listen. There's this duck and he goes to the store. And he goes to buy some Chap Stick? And he says, *Put it on my bill.* When the lady rings him up she says, *That's fifty cents, please,* and he says, *Put it on my bill! Get it?*"

"I get it."

Teddy had to practically run to keep up with me. He was short for his age and I was tall for mine. On top of this, he had made a game of avoiding sidewalk cracks. The pavement in our city had been neglected for decades and it was a tough stretch for him. He was hobbling along, his legs jerking up awkwardly now and then, like a puppet's.

"I ate *so much* candy," he said.

"I didn't get any candy."

"He keeps it in his desk. Licorice and butterscotch. And gum. He said I could go in anytime I wanted and get some."

"Wow," I said.

"I know. *And* I missed math."

"Did you do the questions? Twenty questions?"

"No."

"Did he give you any homework?"

"Nope."

"What'd you do, then?"

"We yelled. He said I could yell as loud as I wanted."

"That's all you did?"

"Yup."

"You just sat there and yelled for half an hour?"

"Yup." He started yelling, "Aaaaaaaaaaaaaahhhhhhh! Aaaaaaaaaaaahhhhhhh!" stopping occasionally to tell me how much fun it was, that I should try it out for myself, that Mr. Jolly thought it was good for the soul.

"Shut up," I said.

"Make me!"

He started screaming again and I shoved him so hard he fell

over onto a section of sidewalk that had bulged up from the pressure of a root and formed, not surprisingly, a crack in the shape of a tree. "Shut up, okay?" I said. But he just scrambled up and started screaming again, all the way home.

I walked ahead of him and thought of the time—back when our mother made us attend CCD classes on Wednesday afternoons—when my class was shown the church confessional, which was lined with brown carpet and supposedly soundproof. The idea was that you could go into this confessional and utter your soul's most horrible secrets, and no one but the priest and God would hear. To prove her point, our teacher asked for a volunteer to shut himself away inside the confessional and scream his head off. Michael Keene—the bucktoothed brute who had broken his hand in first grade—volunteered. He went inside and started yelling, quite audibly, "I hate this stupid fucking class! I hate it! I hate it!" Our teacher was a prim woman who always wore clothes with animals printed on them (sweaters with kittens frolicking in baskets, blue pants embroidered with green whales), and she clutched her chest in horror. In the end, I'd never made the sacrament of confession. We'd stopped going to classes when my father died.

We finally made it home and up the cracked driveway, Teddy doing a jig. Somewhere in our backpacks Teddy and I each kept a house key, but we never bothered to fish them out, just used the emergency key under the doormat. My mother believed this was the safest place to hide a key, as it was so obvious that even the craftiest burglar wouldn't look there.

This was my favorite part of the day. Coming home was like entering a cave, dark and cool and damp, secreted away from the larger world. Our mother was usually working the dinner shift and we were alone, free to do whatever we liked. We'd rifle through the pantry and refrigerator, carry armloads of cookies and crackers and cheese puffs out to the living room, pile them in the middle of the sofa bed, and eat ourselves into a stupor while watching television. We did our homework during commercials. This routine had the effect of entirely sedating us. It was the only time when Teddy and I didn't fight.

Around five o'clock the phone would ring, and we knew it was our mother calling to see if we were alive. Usually we picked up and spoke with her, listened to her instructions about dinner (in the refrigerator there were two lumps wrapped in tinfoil that I was to warm up at three hundred and fifty degrees) and bedtime (teeth brushed and asleep by nine-thirty). But sometimes, like we did that night, we'd let the phone ring, listening to the fierce blasts as they mounted into a panic. She'd keep calling, every twenty minutes or so, then come home in a rage. "Why didn't you pick up the *phone*?" she'd say. "Goddammit! You goddamn kids!" Or some other profanity. She had an arsenal.

That night it was, "Jesus goddamned Christ!" We were still on the couch watching television when she came stomping through the back door. "Do you know how many times I called you?" As she came toward us she kicked off her shoes, pulled her hair out of its bun, peeled off her apron and uniform and panty hose, leaving it all scattered on the floor. In the morning she would pick everything up, put it back on, and go back to work. "You kids!" she said, standing there in her bra and underwear, hands on hips. "You're supposed to be in bed!"

We utterly ignored her, faked an interest in the evening news.

The local anchors, Chet Burns and Mindy Wilson, were covering a story on the city's teachers, who had returned to work without a contract. "Is there going to be a strike?" Chet said, turning to Mindy and flashing his brilliant teeth.

"Well, Chet," said Mindy, "that's the million-dollar question! But one thing's for sure. We've got an angry mob of teachers out there!" The news cut away to footage of a demonstration that some teachers had held that morning in front of city hall. There were about ten of them walking in a small, orderly circle, carrying handmade signs whose print was too faint and insignificant to show up on television.

"Are your teachers on strike?" our mother said.

"Not yet," said Teddy. "They're just an angry mob."

"They're complaining," said Mindy Wilson, "about teaching more classes to more students for less pay."

"I guess we'll just keep an eye on this developing story," Chet Burns said. He shuddered slightly with disgust. No one liked to see teachers like this, as human beings who worked for paychecks, as people who found their jobs—who found us—stressful and unsatisfying. We preferred to think of them as mythical creatures who survived on a diet of glue and chalk dust, who lived in their classrooms and stayed up late each night cutting decorations out of construction paper, pumpkins and Santas and hearts and shamrocks. They were supposed to be fulfilled. They were supposed to be happy.

But that year my teachers were a group of strange, downtrodden creatures. Their clothes were frayed at the cuffs and collars and stained under the armpits, their teeth were crooked and brown, their eyes distorted behind thick glasses. They seemed to live in a constant state of disappointment, and the contract dispute was making things worse by the day. They had lost interest in educating us. Often they wandered off topic and spoke to us of their personal lives, the things they did in their spare time. My English teacher, Mrs. Vandekamp, took ballroom dancing lessons and was practicing for a tournament. Mr. Franklin, who taught history, launched into long descriptions of the model ships he was building on afternoons and weekends. Saddest of all was my science teacher, Mr. Jefferson, who was embattled in a bitter divorce. We knew this because he spoke of his wife in an indirect, slightly educational manner. "This is a highly caustic and erratic chemical," he'd say. "Let's call her Cheryl. Let's put on our protective gear before touching her." Sometimes Mr. Jefferson was able to neutralize Cheryl with a powdered agent he liked to call "the Law Offices of Gary P. Sloan." But sometimes Cheryl got away from him and set off a minor explosion.

"The teachers are still hoping to settle their contract difficulties," said Mindy Wilson, "without having to resort to violence."

"Violence?" said Chet.

"Excuse me!" said Mindy. "I meant to say, *striking*."

"You're supposed to be in bed," our mother said.

"I napped," said Teddy, though this was only half true. After he'd eaten nearly an entire box of vanilla wafers he had fallen into a kind of coma. He'd lain motionless on the couch for an hour in a state resembling sleep, but his eyes were open.

"What the hell am I going to do with you two?" my mother said. She picked up a pack of cigarettes off the TV stand and shook one free, then put it in her mouth and let it dangle. "The summer's over, you know. You've got school in the morning, now. You can't stay up half the night anymore." She left the room in search of a light. The accoutrements of her addiction—cigarettes and matches and ashtrays—were lying all around the house, but she could never manage to put her hands on all three at once. It was always a hunt. Often she enlisted us: *Make yourself useful and find Mommy a lighter.*

"You could at least answer the phone," she said, appearing from the kitchen with a lit cigarette.

"I thought it might be Filene's," I said, another half-truth. For weeks the people from Filene's Basement had been calling about my mother's unpaid credit account. She'd gone on two outrageous shopping sprees that summer, leading us through the store like mules and loading us down with a wardrobe of fancy clothes for occasions which would never arise. Now her closet was full of dresses and silk blouses, with the tags still hanging from the sleeves, and she was more or less a wanted criminal. I imagined her picture hanging in the offices of Filene's Basement, like the mug shots of escaped murderers tacked on the walls of post offices.

"I told you what to say to Filene's," she said. "Right?"

"She's not here," shouted Teddy. "She's indisposed. She's at her second job."

"That's right," she said. "That's all you have to say."

"I don't like talking to them," I said. Which was true. The people from Filene's always sounded desperate, like they were calling from prison, wasting their last dime on the fat chance that my mother would answer.

She sighed. "What the hell am I going to do with you?"

"Nothing," I said.

"I know," she said. "You're just going to do whatever you want and there isn't a goddamned thing I can do about it." She collapsed on the couch and groaned.

We gave in, then, satisfied. We put on pajamas and brushed our teeth, climbed into bed. Before he fell asleep Teddy was always plagued with questions, and he'd lean down from the top bunk and ask me, in a fierce whisper, something he was desperate to know. Usually his questions were about ghosts—whether I thought they looked like sheets or like regular humans in vapor form, whether they could read our minds, why they only came out at night and what they did during the day, whether they traveled the universe and vacationed on Pluto, what they liked to eat, whether I thought they went through the pantry and took small bites of our food, or whether they survived on something else, something we'd never consider ingesting, like the water that collected in the pan of the dehumidifier. At first I told Teddy the truth, that I didn't know and didn't care. But as this never satisfied him I'd started making things up. "Antifreeze," I'd tell him. "They drink antifreeze."

That night, though, Teddy wanted to know about outer space. "How do the planets go again?" he said that night. "I forget how they go."

"Mercury," I said. "Venus, Earth, Mars, Jupiter, Saturn, Uranus, Neptune, Pluto."

And he kept asking me to repeat them. Then he strung them together in a song, which he sang over and over again in a tiny voice until he fell asleep.

I got up then, as I often did, and went out to the living room and stretched out on the couch next to my mother. She'd already smoked three cigarettes down to their filters and crushed them out in her favorite ashtray, which she kept balanced on her stomach. It was a green ceramic souvenir in the shape of Nantucket, where she and my father had spent their honeymoon. The whole settlement was covered in ashes, like a little Pompeii.

"You're going to fall asleep someday and wake up on fire," I said.

"Good."

"I mean," I said, "you'll be dead."

"How was your day?" she said, and lit up another cigarette.

"Okay. The usual."

"How'd Teddy do?"

"Good."

"Did he do his homework?"

"I made him."

"Good," she said.

We watched TV for a few minutes. Channel 38 was going through some sort of identity crisis, and you could never tell what they'd be playing. We always hoped for the Classics, as my mother called them—romantic movies starring Rock Hudson and Cary Grant. But more often they played movies we had no interest in, westerns and B horrors. That night there were cowboys riding around the desert on horseback, stopping occasionally to exchange threats with their Indian enemies. When we were in the mood, we turned this sort of thing to our advantage. While the cowboys and Indians spoke we'd voice over their dialogue with ridiculous statements. "I wish I wasn't in this stupid movie," one would say.

"Me also," the chief would answer. "But me have to pay bills. Me have squaw at home."

"Why does life have to be so disappointing?"

"It is great mystery."

"I wish I could get cast in something decent."

"How."

"How indeed."

But we were in no such mood. I lay there wondering what Mr. Jolly was up to with me and Teddy, prying into our lives, trying to usher us through grief now that our father had been dead for months. We'd already made it through the worst, the absurdity of those first few days. We'd seen it all. Instead of returning to school we'd skipped the last two weeks and stayed home with our mother, who was on the phone almost constantly. All day she talked with people about the most bizarre things—my father's cremation, his obituary, the certificate of death, the switching of names on bank accounts, the transferring of pensions. While she was talking she kept looking around, looking for someone who might help her. She circled through the kitchen, dining room, and living room, stretching the long phone cord behind her as far as it would reach, then reversing directions and circling back again. "I don't know," she kept saying, turning her head this way and that. Sometimes her eye would fall on me. "It's the cleaners," she said to me once. "They want to know when to come. I don't know," she said. "I don't know what to tell them." She had a pained expression. Her right hand was pressed tight against her forehead, as if to prevent it from splitting open.

"Right now," I'd said. "Tell them now."

"What's our address?" she said then. "They want to know our address."

*Frankie's mother could not even remember their address!*

An hour later a van pulled up in front of the house. Two fat men emerged, wearing blue coveralls and knee-high black rubber boots. They wore yellow dish gloves, white paper masks over their noses and mouths. One of them was dragging a wet vac behind him, the other a trash can filled with various potions and scrub brushes. They'd come into the house and gone to work in the den. They'd switched on the vacuum and the sound of it, the screaming sound of it, had filled up the house. We'd huddled together on the couch, pretending to watch television, the volume blasted, but really we were just holding ourselves together, just breathing.

This was the worst.

But we'd survived it. Slowly we'd found our way back to the world. Teddy and I started playing outdoors again. And our mother went back to Friendly's, just a couple of shifts a week at first, then full time. The weeks passed, and before long it was time to start school again. It had been awkward, falling back into old friendships, the old routine of our lives. We were like rich kids who had spent the summer in a distant land, seeing things and speaking languages that other kids had never heard of, and it was hard not to be disappointed by the smallness of everything. But we'd done it.

Now, after all of this, Mr. Jolly wanted to talk. I considered telling my mother about him, having a laugh, but decided against it. Sometimes I kept important things from her so that later, when she discovered them, she'd be struck down by the feeling that she didn't really know the first thing about us, her very own children.

"I almost forgot," said my mother. "Let's do the ticket."

"Right," I said. I got up and took her apron off the floor, fished around in its pocket for the scratch ticket that my mother received each night as a tip from one of her regulars. His name was Clyde Snavely and he was a resident of a halfway house for mentally disturbed adults. Clyde harbored an intense phobia of being poisoned, and had convinced himself that the food at Friendly's was the only safe food in the world. He was eccentric about his meals and the way they were presented to him. He didn't like his hamburger to come into contact with his french fries; he wanted his coffee diluted by an exact third with luke-warm water. My mother was the only waitress willing to put up with him.

"Here," I said, and handed the ticket to her. She scratched off a square of silver film with her thumbnail, then returned it to me. We traded back and forth until we'd lost.

"Another loser," I said. "What a surprise."

"Thanks a million, Clyde," my mother said. "You cheap bastard."

But the truth was we both loved the ticket, the little thrill it gave us. We loved to talk about the things we'd do with a hundred thousand dollars. My mother wanted to buy a new house and car, and I wanted to move to London and live in a hotel, ordering room service three times a day, plus high tea, occasionally going out for walks in the rain or rides atop a double-decker bus, stopping once a week outside Buckingham Palace to stare down the Queen's stoic guards. Considering all that the ticket did to enrich our imaginary lives, the fact that we rarely made so much as a dollar didn't matter.

"I'm going to bed," I said.

"Would you make me a drink first?"

"Okay."

"Just a splash! Three ice cubes!" she said, as if I didn't know this, as if I hadn't been fixing her drinks every night for months.

In the kitchen I poured her an inch of Scotch into a fat plastic cup, plunked in the ice cubes. I knew she'd protest, say I'd poured her too much, but I also knew that she'd drink every last drop and then pass out on the couch, which was exactly what happened.

# 6

I remember this day the way you remember the quiet, careless moments before a car accident. When you think back on how you were driving along, utterly without suspicion, perhaps even singing along with the radio, it always seems as though you should have known what was coming and done something about it. I often wished I could go back to that day and rescue Teddy from Mr. Jolly and his hysterical cure for grief. But of course it was too late.

Over the following weeks Teddy developed a habit of throwing violent tantrums. They came out of nowhere. We'd be in the grocery store and suddenly he'd be screaming—*I want it! I want it!*—while he clutched something, a bag of potato chips or a box of cereal, protectively to his chest. Sometimes he clutched things that he couldn't possibly want. Once it was a 1982 calendar with a different kitten featured each month. *I want it, I want it, I want it, I want it!* he screamed. People would look up from the cartons they'd been examining, and when they saw that Teddy was eight years old, not the toddler they'd expected, they looked disgustedly at my mother, glaring over the tops of their half-glasses.

"Did you hear something, Frankie?" my mother would ask me, tossing back her long blonde hair with a calculated nonchalance, examining her fingernails. She'd look around, puzzled. "I thought I heard something." Teddy would keep on screaming, squealing, approaching a frequency only dogs could hear.

"I think it's your imagination," I'd say. "I can't hear a thing."

Sometimes when we ignored Teddy he'd stop on his own. If not, my mother would yank his arm viciously, which often jolted him out of his tantrum. He'd look around, stunned, instantly calmed. But when this didn't work, when Teddy couldn't be stopped, we'd have to abandon a full cart in the middle of the store. We'd speed out of the parking lot like criminals, thinking of the poor stock person who'd have to unpack our groceries: the family-sized bags of potato chips, the packages of marshmallow cookies, the frozen pizzas, the liters of cherry soda, the half-gallons of mint chocolate chip ice cream, the boxes of individually wrapped cupcakes, the cans of frozen juice concentrate, of pale, veiny pears floating in lite syrup, the loaves of white bread, jars of crunchy peanut butter and marshmallow fluff, the sacks of potatoes, the tubs of brilliant yellow margarine.

My mother and I didn't know what to do. Of the three of us, Teddy had been doing the best, and we had taken solace in the fact that something, at least, was the same as before. Teddy was still safely within childhood, and so he had been easily distracted from whatever sadness he felt about our father. He was a collection of small desires, and he gave voice to everything that entered his mind. We'd be watching television and a commercial for fast food would come on, a hamburger rotating slowly on-screen, and Teddy would say, "Mmmmm. I wish I had that hamburger right now." There was a strange comfort in this. All summer Teddy had been the only person I knew who didn't make me nervous, the only person I really talked to. Now he was no longer himself. The house was filled with his screams, or the echoes of them, or the heavy dread of screams to come.

Things were getting bad for Teddy at school, too. His second-grade teacher had started sending home notes that detailed, in perfect penmanship, the troubles he was having: how once, in music class, during the singing of "America the Beautiful," his voice had soared beautifully from sea to shining sea; but then, as the rest of the chorus stopped, he had kept singing—wailing, really—holding a fractious, disconsolate note longer than anyone could believe, with his eyes closed, his shoulders shaking. "Kind of like Pavarotti," Miss Trotta wrote. Another time she sent a letter describing how Teddy had run out of science class when confronted with a scale model of the solar system. "Teddy seemed troubled by the smallness of the Earth, and the length of time it would take to travel to Pluto." She wrote that she had followed him into the hallway and found him standing in his locker, humming, in a kind of trance.

In a third note Miss Trotta discussed a sock Teddy had brought in for show-and-tell—one he had found on the side of the road all by itself, one he had made into a puppet and named Eugene

Franklin. Teddy had worn the puppet on his hand and talked through it all day, using it to answer questions. Miss Trotta had sent a note suggesting that Teddy might be having *difficulties*, that he might consider seeing the school psychiatrist.

"No shit, Sherlock," my mother said when I read her the note. Teddy and I liked to read the notes out loud to our mother when she got home from work. We did our best to imitate Miss Trotta's voice, which was goosey and breathless. We tried to make light of her complaints, to cast her as the villain: a sour old woman, ridiculous and demented, a fussbudget, a fink.

And it worked. "He's already *seeing* the school shrink," my mother said. (As it turned out, she'd known about Mr. Jolly all along, and my attempt to keep something from her was pointless.) "What did she, like, *forget* that? What kind of a teacher is this?"

"Miss Trotta's kind of old," I said. "She's not the sharpest knife in the drawer."

"She's not the brightest bulb on the tree," said Teddy.

"Not," my mother said, "the fastest slut on the cheering squad."

It was hard to know what teachers hoped to accomplish by sending home notes. They were always written in tiny script, the letters curled up with embarrassment. They were like things whispered at dinner parties, polite reminders that there was spinach in our teeth, that our flies were down. But it was never just a matter of flossing our teeth or zipping our pants. The teachers tended to call attention to flaws that couldn't be changed—we were painfully shy, we tended to walk around with our heads in the clouds, we often lost control of our emotions—

and so we could only continue showing up for school each day with the usual difficulties, accompanied now by the knowledge that our teachers found them offensive.

My teacher, Mrs. Pearson, had sent me home with a note once, too. "Frankie tends to keep to himself," she'd written. "Though his grades are excellent (the best in the class, as a matter of fact), he never volunteers to answer questions. At recess he likes to sit under a tree, away from the other children, drawing in a little notebook. While we do not consider this *abnormal* behavior, it does cause us some concern, especially in a boy, as boys tend to be more physical and energetic at this age."

"Jesus Christ!" my mother had said. "What a moron! You've been in her class for *two months* and she still thinks you're a boy!" She'd grabbed the note out of my hands and crumpled it up, tossed it over her shoulder in a dramatic imitation of despair. But then, as often happened, her attempt to pass something off as a joke backfired, and her throat started quivering. She'd gone into her room for a few minutes and sobbed.

It had been obvious for years that my mother was disappointed in me, that she vaguely suspected some kind of maternity-ward blunder. One day we'd all find out the truth, that I was in fact the daughter of a pale, dark-haired Amish couple, two unfortunate people who were currently struggling to reform a feisty blonde who hiked up her skirt and refused to tuck her hair away under a bonnet. Meanwhile my mother kept waiting for me to change, to utterly reverse my thoughts and looks and habits. She'd hoped that junior high would work some kind of magic on me, but it hadn't. I still wore my hair cut short, still dressed in jeans and T-shirts. I hadn't developed in the traditional sense. I was gangly, hipless, flat-chested, pale, freckled. I tended to slouch, to walk with my head down. I tended to trip and fall. There were bruises up and down my legs and arms, in various shades of green and states of soreness. I looked like one of those kids that charitable organizations were always showing on their television ads. Just a dollar a day could feed and clothe a child like me.

Worse, I hadn't gotten involved in a legitimate group activity. Instead of cheerleading for JV football, I had chosen to play the clarinet in the marching band. "The band!" my mother had said. "The clarinet! Oh, for Christ's sake. I give up."

My mother seemed to think of herself as the victim of a life-long practical joke. I heard her on the phone, once, talking to her best friend, Little Dora. "A freak and a mute," she said. "What a pair I got. What a royal flush." She told Little Dora that she sometimes fantasized about the arrival of a prize committee on her doorstep. Instead of a giant check, this committee would award her with a new family. The husband would be one of the handsome doctors from *General Hospital*, instead of a suicidal Vietnam veteran. The children would be charming and well behaved, with beautiful singing voices and matching outfits, like the von Trapps. "I'm only kidding," she said, eventually, but I wasn't so sure. Some of my mother's habits were suspicious: the way she raced toward the phone whenever it rang; the way she ran to look out the window whenever a car drove by the house. She seemed constantly to be expecting someone who never arrived.

Once, when it was late and she thought we were asleep, my mother's conversation with Little Dora took a dreadful turn. She'd started sobbing, and her words came out in a squeal. "I just don't know how this *happened* to me," she said. "I was prom queen, for God's sake. I was Scarlett O'Fucking Hara. You should have *seen* me!"

It occurred to me then—perhaps for the first time—that my mother was a person, someone with a history that preceded mine. I lay in bed for a long time trying to piece together what I knew of her life. I knew that she had been an only child, and that her parents had been in their forties when they had her. From a single picture I knew that they had been prim and gray-haired and unsmiling, almost expressionless. And from the way my mother spoke of them so tersely—which she only did when Teddy asked her questions—I knew that their house had been dull and quiet, that it had been loveless. My mother had been raised in the house we lived in now—and she had slept in the very room Teddy and I slept in. The wallpaper on those walls had once been her wallpaper, and she had probably lain in bed counting its tiny pink and green stripes, like I often did.

It seemed to me then that my mother must have felt trapped. She was a person who loved to drink and smoke and laugh, who liked to curse in a loud voice, who liked to dance and sing and strike up conversations with complete strangers, and it must have seemed a cruel fate that she had been brought into the world by such serious parents. Her father had been a bank manager, her mother a teller in the same bank. Once my mother had told me that her parents had expected her to work in the bank after graduating high school. Instead she had enrolled in—and later dropped out of—a series of professional schools. Finally she had given up on school and become a waitress at Friendly's, which was where her life had truly begun. At Friendly's she had met Little Dora, who was twenty years her senior, who was fat and loving and irreverent—the mother she had always wanted. And at Friendly's she had met our father.

My mother loved to talk about that first year of waitressing, when everything was new and exciting, when she felt alive for the first time. "It was like I was in a movie," she often said. "I felt like everyone was watching me and I was a big star." Customers were always asking her on dates, and that year she went out with more boys than in all the previous years of her life combined. She stayed out late almost every night, and at two in the morning she would sneak down the hall to her bedroom and hear her parents snoring behind the closed door of their room. When she woke in the mornings her parents were already at work.

It was a nice life. She was independent for the first time and saving her money for even greater independence—an apartment and car of her own. In the meantime she even enjoyed riding the bus in her uniform, the attention she got.

Then it seemed as if the world changed just as she had started to live in it. It was 1968 and suddenly the war in Vietnam was real. Suddenly the draft was real. People were going overseas, people she had known in high school. People died on television, right there on the evening news, while she was trying to eat her supper. There were protests and rallies in the streets. Once she watched from the bus window, staring at the people gathered in groups on the side of the road, chanting and holding signs. They were older people who supported the president, supported the war. Across from them, out in the middle of the road on the median, was a group of hippies calling for withdrawal, and the bus driver seemed determined to run them down.

At work everyone was always talking about it. It was nearly

impossible to wait a table without overhearing something, a mother telling her children to eat and be glad they weren't in Vietnam, teenagers wondering about the extent of the draft, older men remembering their time overseas fighting Germans. The war was on the covers of all the magazines she browsed through at the drugstore. It was no longer possible to ignore.

Finally the draft became so sweeping that even the college boys she knew couldn't defer. Our father was one of them. At the time he was called up she knew him only slightly. He was a regular who spent his evenings sitting in a back booth reading giant, uninteresting books—biographies of President Lincoln, ten-volume histories of the United States—and he was so poor that he could afford nothing but coffee. Each time she filled his cup he seemed to be on the verge of asking her out, but he never did.

When he told her one night that he was going to Vietnam, she had burst into tears. It didn't seem possible that this shy boy— with his pale skin and rosy cheeks, with his dark hair parted neatly to the side—could be given a gun and sent off to defend himself in a distant jungle. She'd sat down across from him, setting the coffeepot on the table between them, and wept. He had seemed surprised at this, flattered. Why did she care? Even she couldn't say. Still she felt they had come to know each other over the past few months, in the smallest increments, and she was devastated.

She thought of him often that winter, watched for him on the news. She sat in the cars of luckier college boys pretending to listen to them talk about their fathers and professors and fraternity brothers. But really she was thinking about that boy, that quiet boy who had gone off to war.

Then a bizarre turn: while everyone was talking of war, both of her parents died. Both of them! Her mother of stomach cancer, her father of a heart attack. It seemed impossible. Too many people were dying in the world already. For a while she lived alone in her parents' house. She sat on their furniture, ate off their plates, watched their television. She worked as usual, continued to sneak home quietly after a late night, though there was no one home to disapprove.

Now and then the quiet boy's brother—James—came into the restaurant. Though he looked nothing like his brother, James sat in the same booth, reading and drinking coffee in much the same manner as the quiet boy. One night he introduced himself. "I believe you know my brother," he had said. He took a letter from his jacket pocket and read a section out loud. "Please tell my beautiful blonde waitress that I am alive and doing well. If I ever get back home I think I'll marry her." Marry! How strange, she thought. They barely knew each other. But the idea began to settle in her mind. Marrying the quiet boy. And so when James asked her to the movies, when they started going around together a few nights a week, driving all over town in his car, parking by the lakefront, it felt like a terrible betrayal.

Then one day the quiet boy returned. Limping, bearded, shaggy-haired. But safe. He had come in and sat at his usual seat and she had run over to him. They had embraced, kissed each other. Within a month they were married.

Now she was crying to Little Dora, terrible sobs of confusion and regret. "I wish I never met him," she was saying.

# 7

Every week I saw Mr. Jolly, who seemed determined to torment me. He wanted to set off some kind of hysterical confession, some tearful yearning for days gone by—but I wasn't about to break. He'd gotten to Teddy and cracked him open like a Russian doll, and now Teddy seemed smaller and more helpless with each passing day. He lost friends with every tantrum, with every word uttered from the mouth of Eugene Franklin. Soon he'd be a total outcast. As time went on he'd be turned away from group sports and forced to join up with less popular enterprises, like the band. He'd never be able to find a date. In the world of childhood there was no forgiveness. One of the kids in my class, Brandon Fraser, was still paying for a minor infraction he'd committed five years ago. He'd wet his pants in the middle of a dodgeball game, and no one had really spoken to him since.

I wasn't about to start talking to Mr. Jolly about my father. I *couldn't*, even if I'd wanted to. I could hardly stand to hear my father's name or see it printed on an envelope. I still felt a tightness in my chest whenever Teddy or my mother mentioned him, still drifted out of myself when I saw something that reminded me of him. There was no way I could talk about my memories of him, least of all to Mr. Jolly.

And so I'd been writing fake essays about my father. In the first essay I wrote about a scene in which my father and I were walking across a bridge and I accidentally dropped my childhood teddy bear, Hoppy, over the railing and into a lake. "My father jumped over the railing and dove into the water," I wrote. "Hoppy had sunk to the very bottom of the lake but my father swam down and saved him. I felt very proud that he would do that for me." In reality my childhood teddy bear was named Boris, and I'd lost him long ago during a fight with Teddy. We'd been in the backseat of my father's car, driving over a bridge, when Teddy unrolled his window and threw Boris out. Boris had cleared the side of the bridge and plunged to an icy death in Lake Quinsigamond.

After reading this essay Mr. Jolly had asked me to write about another memory for our next visit, and then the next. In the following weeks I had written about the time my father ran into a burning house to save a cat, the time he'd gotten up at dawn the morning after a blizzard and shoveled every driveway in our neighborhood, the time he'd chased down the masked thief who had stolen the pocketbook of a feeble old lady. And though it was impossible for anyone to believe these things, Mr. Jolly pretended to go along with it. Each week he read them aloud, almost shouting his way through the sentences in enthusiastic little bursts, and it often sounded like he was playing the kazoo instead of speaking.

"In conclusion, I feel optimistic and filled with purpose when I think about volunteering," he read, the Tuesday before Thanksgiving. I'd written an essay about my plans to spend the holiday serving turkey and mashed potatoes to the poor, just as my father and I had always done on previous holidays. "That's fantastic!" he said. "And your writing is quite mature and stylish."

"Thank you," I said, though it was hard to believe anything he had to say about style. He was wearing a pink suit and a lime green shirt. His bow tie was canary yellow.

"You seem to be doing very well," he said. "Before long I won't even need to see you anymore."

"That's good," I said.

"We'll just see how the holidays go. The holidays can be tough on people. Sometimes they can stir up feelings we didn't know were there."

"I know."

"I mean, people can really lose it. You think you're fine and then, BLAM! You explode! You're down for the count!" He pounded his desk with his fist.

"Boy," I said. "That sounds pretty bad."

"Sometimes it's good, though," he said. "To let it all out."

"It doesn't sound so good," I said.

"Trust me," he said. "It's the only way to move on." He reached in his desk drawer and rifled around for a bit. I couldn't see what he had in there, but I imagined it was filled with dime-store wares, whoopee cushions and X-ray glasses, false teeth that chattered in perpetuity.

Finally he pulled out a deck of flash cards and started shuffling them. "Let's play a game!" he said. "I want you to shout out the first word that comes to mind, okay?" He held up a card with a picture of a white house on it.

"House?" I said.

And the cards kept coming: refrigerator, table, bed, stove, sink, bathtub, baseball, couch, desk.

"Are you reminded of anything?" said Mr. Jolly, his eyebrows arched hopefully. He waved the picture of the desk in front of my face.

"No," I said.

"This desk doesn't get you thinking, free-associating?"

"No."

We sat there staring at each other. These were the critical moments of our meetings. Every week, after going through another ridiculous essay, Mr. Jolly presented me with some new game, hoping to set off some terrible reaction, some torrent of horrible memories. He'd sit forward in his chair, drumming his fingers together and anticipating the destruction, like a cartoon villain who had just lit the wick of a bomb.

"It's okay to talk about the times in your life that weren't so great," Mr. Jolly said. "It's okay to be angry. It's okay to be sad."

But I just sat there. A long moment passed.

"If you're having any problems adjusting," Mr. Jolly said, "it can help to talk about them. You don't have to go around pretending. Do you have any problems you'd like to talk about?"

*Frankie's throat was very dry. Like Alice in Wonderland, she wanted to drink something, to shrink down to a millimeter and run away. She wanted to fall down a hole and disappear entirely.*

"Well," he finally said, and sighed. "Maybe next time." As I left I heard him mutter to himself, writing on his notepad. "Zip," he said.

# 8

For the second year in a row, my mother volunteered to work on Thanksgiving Day. In the car, on the way, she tried to make it sound like an adventure. "You guys can have a booth to yourselves," she told us. "And you can keep track of all the customers, decide who's the most pathetic. It'll be like a contest." Only the loneliest and most desperate people, she explained, would be caught dead in a chain restaurant on Thanksgiving Day.

"Doesn't that include us?" I said.

"No," she said, "it does not." She shot me a look in the rearview.

"Why not?"

"I don't like your attitude, Frankie," she said. "You have no sense of humor. No sense of adventure."

"You said only losers are caught dead in restaurants," I said. "That's where we're going. We're going to Friendly's."

"Because I'm getting *paid*. Other people are *paying* to be there. There's a difference."

"I was just asking."

"Have you ever noticed that the only time you open your mouth is to say something smart?" she said.

"Fine," I said. "I'll never talk again."

"We're lucky I have this job," she said. "We're lucky I can take you two to work with me all the time, and my boss doesn't care. If I had a job in an office we'd be screwed right now. We'd be up shit creek with no paddle." This was her favorite expression. Occasionally she modified it, saying that we were up shit creek without other critical supplies, like toilet paper. Either way, the message was clear. We were adrift in a slippery ship, in a world of shit. Life stunk.

"How'd you like it if I left you home alone on Thanksgiving?" she said. "How'd you like to spend the whole holiday by yourselves? How depressing!"

I shrugged.

"You wouldn't last a minute," she said. "You'd be bored to tears. You'd be in deep shit."

My mother was on time for work, for once. But she spent five minutes in the car putting on lipstick, putting her hair in a bun. Then she spent another five minutes singing along with her favorite radio station, Oldies 103. I'd heard all of the songs before, dozens of times, but I could never keep them straight. They all seemed to be parts of a single, larger song, about finding a lover, stealing him away from a rival, sharing a milk shake at a soda fountain, then crying later at a party after hearing about the lover's infidelity and subsequent death in a motorcycle accident.

"You're late," I finally said.

"I know." She leaned her head against the window and sighed.

"We should go in."

We all sat for a moment staring at the restaurant, watching the workers inside as they wiped off tabletops and set out little caddies of sugar packets, bottles of mustard and ketchup.

"Maybe I should find a real job," my mother said, softly.

"This is a good job," I said. "You like it. You get to work with Little Dora."

"That's true," she said. "Thank God for small favors."

My mother and Little Dora always scheduled their shifts together. They liked to talk to each other while they worked, nonstop, talking as they set down hamburger platters and ice cream sundaes in front of their customers, talking as they cleared tables, as they waited for milk shakes to thicken in the blender, talking the whole time about the scoundrels they loved so pointlessly, so unprofitably—the greatest loves and sorrows of their lives, their families.

"Charlie was in jail last night," Little Dora said that day. "And I had to go bail him out."

"Again?" said my mother. "You're a saint!"

"I told him last time, I said: *This is the last time.*"

"But it wasn't."

"Of course not."

"And when he called, you couldn't just ignore him."

"I should've. But I couldn't."

"Of course you couldn't."

"Who could sleep at night, their kid's in jail?"

"What'd he do now?"

"Bar fight."

"That's not so bad," said my mother. "You know, by comparison."

Business was slow, and they were standing behind the counter, pouring salt and pepper into shakers.

"I don't know why I keep doing it," Little Dora said. "I got nothing left in the bank."

"Because you're a saint," said my mother.

"*You're* a saint," said Little Dora.

"Not compared to you. What you put up with."

"You've got a load on your shoulders, too, you know. I don't know how you do it. You're a tough kid."

"I just think of you. How hard you have it."

"I think of *you*."

"It's a good thing our kids have mothers like us."

"We're saints."

"Someone should give us a prize."

"We should win the lottery."

"We should win a trip to Atlantic City or something. At least."

"But we won't."

"Of course we won't."

"They never give us a break."

As usual, my mother had tried to put us in a booth, in the back corner of the restaurant, but Teddy had insisted on sitting at the counter. He couldn't stand to be away from the excitement. He liked that the counter was on a foot-high platform, from which he could observe every table in the restaurant. He liked to swivel on the vinyl stools, liked to say hello to the waitresses whenever they walked by to pick up their food. He knew all their names, Tracy and Stacy, Karen and Sharon. "Hi, honey," they always said. "You being good?" Most of all Teddy liked to watch the cooks, who worked right in front of the counter, frying and flipping hamburgers, garnishing plates with parsley and pickle chips. He liked their uniforms, their tight blue pants and white T-shirts, the long white aprons they tied around their waists, the white paper hats they wore, which were shaped like ocean liners. Teddy wanted to be a cook. "Seven more years," he always told them, "and I'll be old enough to work. I'll be back there with you guys."

"That's right, buddy," the cooks said. Though everyone knew—everyone in the world except Teddy—that it would never happen. That none of the cooks stayed working at Friendly's for even a single year, that it was the kind of job you left without notice, right in the middle of a shift.

When business was slow the cooks tried to entertain us. They'd turn around every so often and offer us their failures— their overcooked burgers—which they decorated with mustard, squeezing out smiley faces and fanged monsters. They'd show us their green tattoos—the anchors and skulls and hearts and snakes that ran down their forearms—and tell us the stories behind them. "Got this one in the navy. Got this one at the Cape. Got that one right there," they'd say, pointing to a heart, "that's from when I used to be married." One of the cooks had a belly dancer tattooed on his stomach. "Watch her dance," he'd say, and roll his stomach, setting the girl in motion. "A belly dancer on a belly. Pretty sharp, right?"

I liked it best when the cooks were busy, when they had

orders lined up all along the grill, when there were so many hamburgers hissing under metal weights that you could hardly hear anything else. When it was busy like that, the cooks were so preoccupied that they forgot about me and Teddy, and they talked uncensored about their boss, and what a *fucking asshole* he was, how they wanted to *fuck his wife right in front of his fucky little face*. They talked about *fucking child support, fucking parole officers*, and all the *fucking whores* who pretended to give away their phone numbers at bars, but who really gave away the numbers of *fucking pizza parlors*.

I liked to draw the cooks in my sketchbook and write down the things they said. They were always making plans for themselves, plans to *quit their fucking jobs and get out of this fucking place*, take jobs on cruise ships or move to the Grand Canyon and work as guides. I kept hoping to show up one day and find they'd actually done it.

That day it was slow and the cooks were complaining about working on Thanksgiving.

"Boy, I'm really thankful I'm working today," one said. "Thanks a *lot*."

"I'm thankful there's a case of beer waiting when I get home."

"Time and a half. That's good."

"I'm thankful I'm getting a new job soon."

"I'm thankful I'm not that guy," one said, and pointed to a customer whose shirt and hat read *Jimmy Carter for President*. "What a loser."

"I'm thankful I'm not *that* guy," said the other, and pointed to Clyde Snavely, who was sitting alone in a booth as usual, drawing cathedrals on napkins.

"Holy shit," said the other. "Me, too."

"Holy shit. Me, three," said Teddy.

Then there was an awkward moment when I could sense people were looking at me. What they saw was a person who kept her head down, who scribbled so intently that she appeared not to notice what was going on around her, a person very much like Clyde Snavely.

"Hey," said Teddy. "Whatcha drawing?"

I didn't answer. All morning we'd been going through the same routine. Teddy would ask me what I was drawing and I'd tell him nothing. He'd act like he was mad, and he'd spin away from me on his stool and stare out the window. But a few minutes later he'd ask again, this time as Eugene Franklin. "Whatcha drawing?"

I could never figure out why Teddy cared so much about my sketches. That year I tended to draw cartoons of all the popular kids in my class, kids Teddy had never even met. "Who's that?" he always said, whenever he caught sight of a sketch. "What's his name?"

"I don't know," I'd say. "Abraham Lincoln."

That day Teddy caught sight of a sketch I was drawing of George Benson.

"Who's that?" he said.

"What *difference* does it make? It's not like you're close personal friends."

"Where's he live?" he asked. "How come he has a cast? Does he play football? Did you sign his cast? How come you didn't sign his cast?"

The worst part was when Teddy read the captions, the little catchphrases I included with each drawing. "I *might* take Patty Connors to the dance," George Benson was saying. I'd noticed lately that this was one of the ways the popular kids expressed themselves. They always said the opposite of what they meant. I *might* do my homework, they'd say, meaning they wouldn't in a million years, on pain of death, even *consider* doing their homework.

"I might take Patty Connors to the dance," Teddy read. "Who's Patty Connors?"

"She's in a wheelchair," I said. "She's the smartest kid in school." This was sadly true. There was a handful of us at the top of the class whose only amusement was studying for tests and comparing grades, but none of us could catch Patty Connors. We consoled ourselves with the notion that, really, she had nothing better to do.

"Are they going to the dance?"

"No."

"Lemme see another one. *Please?*"

"Forget it," I said. "Leave me alone."

We did this until it was time for Little Dora's break, when she asked us to join her in the backmost booth of the restaurant. "Let's go, you two," she said, lighting up a cigarette. "Come tell Little Dora what you've been up to." Teddy raced after her, but I took my time, dragging my feet like all the world's gas station attendants, whose insolence and lack of enthusiasm my mother could never stand.

"Why the long face?" Little Dora said when I settled in the booth.

"Nothing," I said.

"How do you like the clarinet?"

"Okay."

"It sounds like a dead duck!" said Teddy. "And sometimes it sounds like a goose who's dying." He started laughing. He always stood outside the door of our room and laughed when I tried to practice, ruining the mood, making everything I played sound to me like circus music.

"That's very impressive," said Little Dora. "It takes a lot of talent to sound like that." She winked at me.

"It sounds *exactly* like a dead goose," said Teddy, still laughing.

"Dead geese don't sound like anything," I said. "They're dead."

"You stick with it," Little Dora said. "It builds character to play an instrument. If I had it to do over, I'd make Charlie stick with piano."

"Charlie played piano?" I said. This surprised me.

"Like an angel," she said, and released a cloud of cigarette smoke into the air between us.

Little Dora was always talking about Charlie, her Charlie, Charlie who had dropped out of high school at the age of sixteen, Charlie who disappeared for months at a time without word of his whereabouts, Charlie who returned home wanting a place to sleep and a short-term loan, Charlie who drank away these short-term loans and got himself arrested for drunk and disorderly, for barroom brawls, for driving under the influence, Charlie whose very name brought tears to her eyes, Charlie for whom she lived and breathed, Charlie, her Charlie.

"You should've heard him," Little Dora said. "He could've played Carnegie Hall."

"How come he quit?" said Teddy. But Little Dora didn't seem to hear him. She had gone into a wistful trance, as she often did when she thought about Charlie. I tried to study her face while  she wasn't looking. I'd been trying to draw her, but I hadn't been able to get it right. I knew how to draw her hair, which was thin and gray, and which she swept into short peaks, like meringue. She had a round face that was easy to capture. And her uniform was easy—the black apron and checked dress. Little Dora's dress had a few crooked seams, as she had sewn it together from the fabric of two regulation-sized uniforms. The thing about Little Dora, she wasn't so little.

I couldn't find anything in particular that I was doing wrong when I drew Dora. What I couldn't quite capture, I realized, was her *expression*, which was exhausted and hopeful at the same time.

"I can play piano," Teddy announced.

"No you can't," I said. "You've never seen a piano in your life."

"Yes *sir*. I played it at school."

"No you didn't."

"Did so!"

"I bet you're *wonderful*," said Little Dora, who had returned from her daydream. "And you know what else? I have something for you." She started rifling through her giant purse.

"What is it?" Teddy said. He leaned across the table, reaching his arms out, wriggling his fingers.

"Voilà," Little Dora said, producing a small plastic bag. It was filled with tiny green plastic soldiers, a whole platoon of them, each no more than an inch high.

"Wow!" said Teddy. He emptied the bag on the table and started looking them over, one by one, inspecting them carefully. They were all the same—anyone could tell that they were all the same—but he held each one in front of his face. "This one's name is Bobby," he said. "And this one is Wally. And this guy is Leonard."

"How can you tell them apart?" I said.

"Because."

I picked up Wally and Bobby and Leonard and mixed them up in my hands. "Who's this?" I said.

"Leonard," he said, instantly, and snatched him out of my hand.

"These were Charlie's, right?" I asked.

"Yes," said Little Dora. "I found them in the closet the other day. I thought you two would like them." She was always bringing us old things of Charlie's—baseball cards and board games and comic books. I kept a pile of his stuff in my closet, and I looked at it whenever I wanted to scare myself. I tried to imagine Charlie playing with these things, as a kid, oblivious to the troubles that awaited him. Sometimes I imagined scenes in which I appeared from the future to warn Charlie, as he was organizing his baseball cards or flipping through comic books. "Don't grow up," I'd tell him. "You're not safe."

"Go away," he'd say.

"You should be careful. You don't want to end up in jail."

"I know," he'd say. "I'm not *retarded*." He just didn't get it. He was still young, still the kind of kid who allowed Little Dora to hug him to her chest, as she was doing to Teddy now that her break was over. She had him pinned tight, folded under her arm. "You be good for your mother," she said to him. "Don't you run off like Charlie." Like Charlie, Charlie, her Charlie.

"I *might* let you look at my sketchbook," I told Teddy when my mother's shift was winding down.

"Really?" he said. He was so excited, leaning toward me, that he knocked over his glass of milk.

"Oh *great*," said my mother, swiping at the milk with a rag. "This is just *great*." She had been popular all her life. She never said what she meant.

Then Teddy started crying, working himself into a tantrum, and all the cooks and waitresses gathered around trying to distract him. Even Clyde Snavely seemed for a moment to come out of himself. He put down his pen and stared at Teddy, his mouth open slightly, as if he were a ventriloquist and Teddy his dummy—the smaller version of himself that channeled his true feelings. Finally my mother had to carry Teddy to the car, past all of the staring customers, whose hamburgers were growing cold in all the excitement.

# 9

The weeks between Thanksgiving and Christmas were, in a public school, just a formality. Our teachers had grown tired of us by then, and they were just counting the days until vacation. That year was even worse than others. The teachers were still working without a contract, and the mere act of showing up to school seemed to them like a concession. Every day they passed out stacks of holiday-themed worksheets—still wet from the mimeograph machine, their text purple and blurry—and told us to work quietly. Occasionally one of the more conscientious students would raise a hand and ask for clarification. "On sheet two," Jane Corning asked one day, "is the second word in the third column *Santa* or *Satan*?" Mrs. Vandekamp, who had a smudge of purple ink on her nose, looked up from her romance novel and sighed. "I don't know," she said. "It doesn't matter. Just skip it."

Even Mr. Jolly had given up. On our last visit before Christmas break, when I sat down across from him and presented him with the week's essay, he skipped the usual routine of reading through it and pretending to believe what I'd written. Apparently I'd gone too far with my imaginary memories. The previous week I'd invented a little brother named Chum Lee, whom my father had adopted through the mail. Before my father adopted him, I'd written, Chum Lee had been forced to work in a circus, traveling across China performing dangerous stunts, like blasting out of a cannon, or diving from a high ladder into a tiny bucket of water. But now, with my father's sponsorship, Chum Lee was living in a nice home for boys and even going to school. "My family looks forward to continuing to sponsor Chum Lee," I wrote, "in my father's memory. It's very cheap to sponsor a child in China. For just ten dollars a year, Chum Lee lives like a king."

"Tell you what," Mr. Jolly said. "How about this? If you feel like talking today, go right ahead."

"Okay," I said.

"You can talk about anything you want. Anything at all."

"Okay." I sat and examined my shoes. For the first two minutes I counted off the seconds in my head—this was a nervous habit of mine, something I did while talking to people, and also while brushing my teeth—but then I gave up counting and just sat there. After another long moment I untied and retied my sneakers. Meanwhile Mr. Jolly sat back in his chair, his hands folded over his stomach, whistling. He kept changing his tune, cycling through various moods, from "Nobody Knows the Trouble I've Seen" to "Ol' MacDonald Had a Farm" to "The Girl from Ipanema."

Mr. Jolly broke first, like I knew he would. "Do you know why I'm not going to read your essay?" he said.

"No."

"You don't?"

"Not really."

"Maybe you should think about it. What possible reason would I have for throwing this lovely essay," Mr. Jolly said, stopping for a moment to pick it up by one of its corners, "in the trash?" He held the essay over his trash can and dropped it. But it swirled in the air and missed the basket, skidded to the floor. I was sad to see it lying there. I had put a lot of time into describing the dazzling lawn displays that my father created for us each Christmas. There was a life-sized manger complete with a menagerie of adoring animals. On the roof, even bigger than life, there was a glowing Santa waving from his sleigh, pulled by eight luminous reindeer.

"I don't think you've been telling me the truth," Mr. Jolly said. "And I'm good and tired of it."

I sat in my chair, stared at Norman Rockwell's praying family.

"Before you can move on," he said, "you need to grieve." He was speaking slowly and sadly, less like a kazoo and more like a trombone. He looked wan. It was as though he'd been wearing makeup for the past few months and I was only now seeing his real face. "You're never going to get over this death unless you start talking to me. This is serious business, Frankie. You can't just go around pretending everything's fine. You're headed for big trouble. You're in deep shit, if you want to know the truth."

I fought off a smirk. Deep shit! He sounded just like my mother.

"I've never had a kid I couldn't reach," he said. "I don't know what I'm doing wrong. I really don't. I've gone through all my books. All my tricks." He was almost whispering, now. His head was bent and his hands were folded, as if in prayer. I began to realize that I had sparked some sort of personal crisis in Mr. Jolly. I hadn't taken him seriously, hadn't appreciated his efforts. I was part of the larger problem that was driving all the city's teachers to the edge of reason. "I've tried everything to help you," he said. "But you keep shutting me out. I don't know why. I just wish I knew why. Is it me? Is it something I said? What is it?"

Sometimes I wondered the same thing. I didn't really know why I was writing all those fake essays. Or why I lied when he asked me questions. I always claimed to see the most innocent and childish things in his Rorschach blots—flowers and puppies and balloons, butterflies and kittens and teddy bears. I sat stoically through the little plays he put on with hand puppets that, Hamlet-like, were meant to parallel my innermost secrets and send me into fits of sobbing. "Sometimes I keep things bottled up inside," one of the puppets would say. "Because I don't want to be a burden to my mother and little brother." Or, "I'm thinking of letting my hair grow longer. It would be much more flattering that way."

"It's not you," I told him. "It's just that I'm fine. There's nothing wrong. Really."

"When you come back from vacation," he said, "I'd like to start over, okay? I want you to start telling me the truth." He extended his hand for me to shake, but I just sat there.

"That's more like it," he said. "Now get lost."

S o m e t i m e s   i t  seemed to me that our television was more of a person than an appliance. It was the best member of our family, the older sibling I'd always wanted—the bright one, the pretty one, the one who kept up with current events, the one who told all the jokes. We were happier when the television was there. When it wasn't—when we were in the car, at school, at Friendly's—things weren't the same between us. We fought. We drifted off into our own dull thoughts. We felt the smallness of our lives.

That fall our television had developed an ailment. It started as a line of static that rolled continuously up the screen, but then progressed into a type of palsy, where the whole screen would shudder, and sometimes the reception would blank out altogether. We felt betrayed. We jerked the antennae around like abusive parents yanking at limbs. We smacked the cabinet, twisted the dials. When that failed we resorted to begging. *Please*, we said. *Don't leave us! Oh, please, please, please.* But things only got worse. We started missing the forecasts and the punch lines of promising jokes. It was becoming difficult to tell whether the people on-screen were laughing or crying.

But that night, on the eleven o'clock news, I saw quite clearly the face of my science teacher, Mr. Jefferson. He was surrounded by police officers who were escorting him from a squad car toward some vague but doomed destination. Though they were flickering across the screen, there was no doubt about it. I recognized Mr. Jefferson's glasses—the square plastic frames—and I recognized his walk, slow and springy, like the walk of an ostrich.

"In jail, tonight," said Chet Burns.

Mr. Jefferson's hair—which at school was always slicked back—was puffy and out of control, alive with static. He wasn't wearing his usual blue shirt and brown corduroy suit. He was wearing a white T-shirt and tight jeans. His first name, I learned, was Samuel.

"Allegedly soliciting a prostitute," said Mindy Wilson. "At an adult theater."

"What's *soliciting a prostitute*?" said Teddy. But my mother, who was exhausted after her shift, ignored him. I ignored him. "What's an adult theater?"

"Jefferson is a teacher at West Middle School," said Chet.

"Holy shit," said my mother. "That's your school."

"That's my science teacher," I said.

"Holy shit," she said again. Then, softly, "Oh my God."

"I imagine this comes at a bad time," said Chet Burns, "for the teachers who are trying to negotiate higher pay."

"What's he like?" my mother said. "Is he a weirdo?"

"In other news," said Chet Burns, "a local man has broken the Guinness record for the world's longest fingernail!"

"I'm talking to you, Frances," my mother said.

"Yeesh," said Mindy Wilson.

"It's the custom in this country," my mother said, "that when someone talks to you, you say something back." She slapped me on the back of the head, apparently hoping to improve my reception. "Hello?" she said. "Are you in there?"

"No," I said.

"Did you know anything about this teacher of yours?"

"No."

"It kind of gives me the creeps," she said, and stroked my hair for a moment. "Holy shit."

Teddy was full of questions when we went to bed. "How come your teacher got arrested?" he said, leaning down from the top bunk. "How come?"

"Shut up," I said. "Go to sleep."

"I just wanna *know*," he said. His hair looked funny, hanging straight down. "You never tell me anything."

"Just shut up, okay?" I said.

"Fine," he said, and pulled himself back into bed. "But the next time you need to know something, don't come crying to me."

"Don't worry," I said. "I won't."

Then Teddy started playing with the soldiers Little Dora had given him. He had separated them into small platoons and kept some everywhere, in the pocket of his coat, underneath the couch, under his pillow. "Psh, psh, psh," he said, which was the language of gunfire. "You're dead."

"Aaaaaaaah," said one, in a whispered scream. "I'm dying!"

"Oh no!" said another. "Me too!"

When they were all dead Teddy held a burial service, lined them under his pillow, hummed taps, and went to sleep.

The next day at school, everyone was talking about Mr. Jefferson. There were two groups: those whose parents had called the principal and the school board with complaints, who had sat their children down and explained the evils of adult theaters and prostitutes. Then there were the others, like me, whose parents had more or less ignored the subject, knowing that Christmas break was just days away, that the school would hire someone new and we'd forget all of this, because we always forgot, kids would forget anything. This was the response favored by our teachers, who walked around the halls looking especially cheerful, giving big waves, giving high fives, occasionally giving what they called nookies, lighthearted attempts to drive their knuckles into our skulls.

Our science class was monitored by a Latin teacher, Ms. Sullivan, who arrived pushing a television cart. "Movie time!" she called out, almost singing. There were three days left before Christmas break, she told us, which was the perfect amount of time to show *Ben-Hur* in its entirety. "It's *perfect*, how this happened," she said. "Sometimes everything just comes together. Sometimes things just work out so well in life."

Before showing the movie, Ms. Sullivan took a few moments to acquaint us with the life story of one of her distant relatives— the uncle of a third cousin—who had died during the filming of *Ben-Hur*. "He was an extra who was killed in the chariot scene," she said. "Trampled by a horse. Just a poor dreamer who was hoping to become a star. Trampled by a horse." She stared out the window for a moment, her chin quivering. "They decided to leave the trampling in the film," she said. "Even though it's gruesome. Because if they took it out, he would have died for nothing." Ms. Sullivan stood for a moment in a trance. Then she seemed to spring back to life. "Ready?" she said, smiling. She started the movie, and stood to the right of the screen for the whole class, her hand held over her heart. "Oh, he's so handsome," she said, whenever Ben-Hur flexed his muscles. "Isn't he handsome?" She looked to us for approval, but we were unimpressed with the image of Charlton Heston, wearing what looked like bedsheets and metal tennis skirts.

I couldn't follow the movie. I kept looking around the room: at the chalkboard, where Mr. Jefferson had written *Happy Holidays* and *For Friday—Organize Your Organelles!* with his favorite orange chalk; at all the glimmering glassware he had always handled so tenderly—the neat rows of test tubes and beakers that were tucked away on their shelves; at the periodic table of elements, which he often bowed to with a religious reverence; at the posters he had hung on the walls of Elvis Presley, young and old, with and without muttonchops, always pictured in mid-song, in a state of ecstasy so intense he was propped on his toes. Like Elvis, Mr. Jefferson had believed in shock value, in the power of performance. He was the kind of teacher who hoped to interest his students by producing small explosions, by running an electric current through himself until his hair stood on end, by lighting his hands on fire.

"Thank you very much," he always said, in his best Elvis impression, whenever he inspired our applause.

"Young man," said Ms. Sullivan, "you might want to stop drawing for a moment and pay attention. The big scene is coming up."

"Busted," somebody said.

The trampling scene—when it finally arrived—only lasted half a second, and Ms. Sullivan kept rewinding it and showing it again. "See how he's running to safety?" she said. "But at the same time he knows he's doomed?" She showed it again, raising the volume, the thundering hoofbeats. When she backed up the tape, we saw the horses run backwards, saw her distant relative spring up from the ground, from the dead. Then we watched him meet his fate once more. "Does this bother any of you?" she asked. "I hope not. Because if we don't watch it, then he died for nothing." It was becoming clear that there was something truly wrong with Ms. Sullivan, something beyond the fact that she was a strange woman with bad style, with thick glasses and orthopedic shoes and homemade dresses that snapped together down the middle, like smocks. Ms. Sullivan, I realized, was having *difficulties*.

"I wonder if he thought he had died for nothing," she said. "In the few seconds it took him to die. He must have thought no one would remember him."

The bell rang. "I'd love to stay and watch that again," people were saying to each other. "But I've got an appointment. Back on *Earth*."

# 10

For Christmas my mother bought us a new television. She brought it home on the night of the twenty-third and presented it to us, plopping it down on the foot of the foldout mattress, unwrapped and unboxed. "Ta-da!" she said. "Merry Christmas!" She was breathing heavily, and her skin was flushed. Presumably this was from the exertion of carrying the set in from the car, but it seemed like something else, like she'd broken into a neighbor's house and stolen the television right off their stand, then run all the way home. "It's used," she said. "But it's bigger than our old one. And it's color!" Already we were unplugging the old set, moving it aside, settling the new one in its place. We switched on the knob and watched as Chet Burns and Mindy Wilson came to life, in glorious color. "Ew," said my mother, making a face. It was a face we knew well, the disapproving face that natural blondes reserved for bottled ones.

My mother spent the entirety of the next day lying on the foldout, under a pile of blankets, watching the Doris Day movie marathon on Channel 38. Teddy and I wandered aimlessly around the house, reading and drawing, snacking, playing board games, getting in little fights and hiding away from each other, then making up, then fighting again. In a remarkable display of restraint, we didn't ask if we were going to be doing anything special for Christmas Eve.

"I really lucked out today," my mother said when it was getting toward evening. "They're playing five of her movies in a row." Doris Day was my mother's favorite actress, the woman whose platinum hair was an inspiration, whose sense of style—the way she matched her purses and shoes and hats to her satin dresses— was the gold standard of fashion. My mother also admired the way Doris said just the right thing in all situations. "She's like an *angel*. I don't know how she *does* it!" My mother seemed to believe that Doris did all of this single-handedly, without the help of screenwriters and directors and stylists, without the benefit of a fictional world designed to revolve around her.

"Wouldn't it be great," my mother said, "if there was a movie about me? With her playing the lead, playing me?" In some ways this was easy to imagine, as my mother and Doris looked very much alike. But on the other hand it was hard to picture Doris Day living my mother's life, waving a small flag as she watched her lover go off to Vietnam, showering him with kisses when he returned with an amputated leg and a case of depression that worsened over the years, no matter what she did to help. I imagined the way a director would choose to represent my mother's long-term suffering, the mundane routine of her life. Perhaps a silent scene picturing Doris washing dishes, her famously blonde hair tied back in a kerchief. She'd stop for a moment to stare meaningfully out the kitchen window, then wipe her brow with the back of her hand, and then, very cinematically, shed a single tear. The camera would pan back; the music would soar. The director would let the camera roam through the house, lingering on the small details of Doris's miserable life: the ashtrays filled with the crushed ends of cigarettes, marked with red lipstick; the amber-colored glasses scattered on the coffee table, half filled with flat ginger ale, their rims also marked with lipstick; the preponderance of half-finished crossword puzzles on the couch, on the floor, on the dining room table, with wrong answers drawn boldly in capitals, in ink; the perfume bottles clustered on her dresser, with their gold spray pumps. The director would make us understand that this was an unappreciated woman who sought to make a mark. Who wanted desperately to leave a print, a scent. Somewhere. Anywhere.

"Coming up next," said the Channel 38 announcer. "Who would want to kill Doris Day? Find out in *Midnight Lace*."

"Oh, I can't *stand* this one," she said, clutching the blankets with her fists. "She gets married and she's living in London and everything's happy, and then someone starts threatening to kill her in this weird little voice. He calls on the phone and hides in the fog and tells her how he's going to kill her. But he always does it when she's alone. And no one believes her. They think she's making it up for attention. But it's real, and the voice is so spooky. It's *awful!*"

"Don't watch it," I said.

"I *have* to!"

The movie started. The opening showed Doris Day walking through the park during a thick London fog. Out of nowhere came a creepy little voice, high-pitched, puppetlike. "Mrs. Preston," it said, calling Doris Day by her fictional name. "Yes?" she said, turning around in the fog, terrified, as the voice made a number of threatening innuendos.

"It's the husband," my mother said. "Her own husband's doing this to her. Isn't it awful? Poor Doris! She's really up shit creek. With no Pepto-Bismol."

"You kind of ruined the suspense," I said, and started off toward the basement.

"Don't leave me!" she cried. "It's too scary!"

"Turn it off," I said.

"Stay!" she said. "Be a girl for once! Stay and watch Doris with me!"

"I'm gonna go see what Teddy's doing."

"Where's Teddy, anyway?"

"I don't know."

"Go find him, will you?"

"That's where I'm going. That's what I just *said*."

"Oh," she said. "Can you bring me my headache pills first? Can you bring me a drink?"

I brought them.

"Can you bring me my slippers? Can you bring me another pillow?"

I brought her pillow and slippers, delivered them with a bow. "Your highness," I said.

"Hey," she said, as if the thought were occurring to her for the first time, "where's Teddy?"

I went down to the basement. Teddy was hiding in the laundry room, playing with his soldiers again. He'd filled the collection pan of the dehumidifier with water and he was floating the soldiers in it. "Oh no!" he had them say, when he heard me. "Hurry! Get across the river! Intruder!" He didn't look up from his game.

"Hi," I said.

"Leave me alone," he said.

"Do you wanna play a game or something?" I was feeling generous, Christmas and all.

"I *am* playing."

"We can play Monopoly," I said. This was his favorite. In the form of a dog he liked to round the board, buying real estate with reckless abandon. He never planned, never saved up for the future, but even so he tended to win more than he lost.

"Go away," said Eugene Franklin. "I'm busy."

I went to my room and stretched out in bed on my stomach, pulled my sketchbook out from under my pillow. I drew a picture of Doris Day.

And I drew Teddy in various moods.

The whole time I was drawing him I was thinking about what had happened to us. We had always been allies—kids joined together against the larger world—but lately things were ruined between us. There were days when Teddy only spoke to me through his sock puppet. And some days he wanted nothing at all to do with me. I'd wait around for him after school, watching all the other kids come running out of the building, filing onto their buses, watching all the while for his little blond head, the hair overgrown and hanging in his face. But he wouldn't show. The next day, when his mood had changed and he wanted my attention, I was mean to him. "What are you doing?" he'd say, looking over my shoulder when I was doing my homework. "What does it *look* like I'm doing?" I'd say. Or I'd push him away from the sink when he was brushing his teeth, having decided that I, too, wanted to brush my teeth at that exact moment. "Hey!" he'd say, toothpaste running down his chin. "Let me in!" He'd punch me, and I'd punch him back, and tears would well up in his eyes. There was always a moment when he seemed to be looking for someone to console him. I was the person he had always turned to, but I was also the person who had hurt him. He'd stand there for a moment, bewildered, before he realized that he was on his own.

Now it seemed the only time Teddy and I were allies was when we joined together to torture our mother. She'd be trying to get us out the door for school and we'd thwart her every effort. "You're going to be *late*, you two!" she'd say, standing over us as we sat watching cartoons. "Get dressed! Get going! For Christ's sake, get going!" We'd just sit there staring ahead at the television until she turned it off. Then, very lazily, we'd go about the business of dressing and gathering up our books. When there was a bake sale or costume party or field trip, we'd tell her about it at the last possible second, just before we left the house. "You kids!" she'd say. "Jesus! Why didn't you tell me sooner!" And she'd rifle through the pantry for a bag of unopened cookies, the kind we refused to eat because they didn't contain chocolate, the kind she continued to buy nonetheless, on the belief that they were vaguely nutritious, there being pecans ground into them somewhere, or so the package said. Then, when she dropped us off at school, she had to endure the sight of other kids climbing out of other cars with pans of freshly baked brownies and cupcakes, some of the kids even stopping to blow kisses to their mothers, and she'd say again, "Jesus Christ! You kids!"

Eventually I started drawing pictures of my father. I still couldn't get him right. It had been eight months since I'd seen him, and I was starting to forget his face. It hurt, looking at him. Every time I finished a sketch, I had to wipe it out with my thumb.

When I ventured back out to the living room, Doris Day was fighting with Rock Hudson. They shared a telephone line and he was always on it, tomcatting. "What happened to Mr. Preston?"

"He went to jail," said my mother. "The creep. He could have just lived with Doris, happily ever after. They had it good. But it wasn't enough for him."

"What's this one about?"

"Oh, I *love* this one," she said. "They get married. Her and Rock Hudson. I *love* Rock Hudson. He's such a hunk."

"He doesn't look like a hunk."

"Trust me," she said. "He is."

Little Dora came over a few minutes later. Apparently she and my mother had made plans, but my mother had either forgotten about them or neglected to mention them to us. "Let's see some holiday cheer," Dora said when I opened the door. She was wearing a red sweat suit and a Santa hat, carrying a gallon of pink wine.

"Ho, ho," I said.

"It's Doris and Rock," my mother said.

"Jeez," said Dora when she saw my mother lying on the couch in front of the television. "Where's the tree? Where's the presents?"

"I meant to go out this afternoon," said my mother. "But I just didn't get around to it. I couldn't tear myself away from Doris. Doris and Rock are on."

"Doris and Rock?" said Little Dora. "What luck."

"They have such good chemistry."

"I bet they were really in love."

"You can tell."

Little Dora settled herself on the bed and I sat on the floor. We watched as Doris and Rock became entangled in a series of misunderstandings. In alternating scenes they hated and loved each other. Rock was pretending to be a Texan, but this didn't seem strange. Little Dora kept pouring me little splashes of wine, and everything was starting to make sense to me. I was okay with everything.

Finally the Doris Day marathon ended and we switched over

to the local news. *Action 13* was using its second-string anchors, who were fat and unattractive and unable to read their copy without stumbling. It was a harsh transition back to the real world. "Where's Chet and Mindy?" said my mother. "I want Chet and Mindy."

"I don't know," said Little Dora. "Where's Teddy?"

My mother looked at me, and I shrugged. There was a terrible silence. For weeks Teddy had been hiding himself away in the basement, in closets and cupboards and underneath the bed, but my mother hadn't thought much of it. "It's a phase," she said to me once, after she'd served him his dinner in the boiler room. But now, in that silence, in front of Little Dora, the usual affairs in our household seemed to embarrass her.

"Teddy!" my mother called. "Where are you?"

"I'm in *here!*" Teddy yelled, from the dining room. We all struggled up from our places and walked over to the archway between the living and dining rooms. Teddy had made a fort by draping the table with the sheets from our beds—his featured Spider-Man, mine the characters from Peanuts—and he was presumably hidden under there, behind a curtain of cartoon characters. "I've been in here *forever*," Teddy said. "You didn't even notice I was gone!"

"Oh, honey!" my mother said. "We noticed! We missed you!"

There was a long silence, during which my mother and I stared at each other. We could feel it brewing, another horrible tantrum.

"You didn't even notice I was *gone!*" he said again, yelling now.

"We missed you!" my mother said. She looked at me. I was supposed to verify this, supposed to say something nice, but as usual I was at a loss.

Little Dora was the one. She went over to the table and knocked on it. "Hello?" she said. "Can I come in?" There was no answer so she got down on her hands and knees and crawled through the sheets, under the table. "Did I ever tell you," I heard her say, "about the first time I met your mother?"

This was not a story my mother wanted to hear. She turned and slouched away, started prowling around the living room for cigarettes.

"Frankie," she said. "Be a love, would you?" She was combing through the blankets on the sofa bed, overturning pillows. "I really need a cigarette," she said. "Can you find me a cigarette?"

I didn't want to leave the living room, wanted to hear Little Dora's story. But between the two of us, my mother's need was greater. We searched the living room. The newscasters were signing off. "Santa's gassing up that sleigh right about now," said the fake Chet.

"And with the price of gas these days," said the fake Mindy, "look out!"

I saw a pack of cigarettes under the TV stand. There was no explanation for how it got there, how anything in our house wound up where it did. When there had been a cat living with us, there was someone to blame for all the things we mislaid. Now, I supposed, we blamed my father, either his absence or his ghost, when things went awry.

As a kind of Christmas surprise, this pack of cigarettes happened to have a book of matches tucked inside. "Here," I said, and tossed the pack to my mother. She had given up the search and was lying on her stomach on the sofa bed, her head under a pillow.

"Oh, thank God!" she said. "I thought I was going to have to send you out to the store!" She sat up and lit the cigarette, closed her eyes and took a deep drag. Smoking like this seemed to have the effect of transporting her out of the known world, into some solitary, blissful confinement. Those days there was nothing else she liked so much as smoking.

Suddenly we heard Teddy laugh from the dining room. At first just a few giggles, and then a laugh that overtook him entirely.

"Oh, great," my mother said. "I'll never live this down."

"What's the story?" I said.

"It's about my first day at Friendly's."

"What happened?"

"I wasn't so friendly," she said. "I almost got fired. My boss was gonna fire me but Dora convinced him to give me another day."

"Wow," I said. Teddy was still laughing. It occurred to me that I hadn't heard him laugh in a long time.

"I don't know," she said. "Sometimes I wonder what might have happened if he just went ahead and fired me. What I'd be doing now, you know?"

This was, I realized, the same as wondering what she'd be doing if Teddy and I didn't exist.

"Maybe I would've gone back to secretary school," she said.

"You'd hate being a secretary."

"I know," she said. "But sometimes I wonder."

Little Dora appeared in the archway and I saw her in a new light. Now it seemed to me that this short, fat woman in a Santa suit was the reason my parents had met. It could even be said that I owed my life to her. I wasn't sure how I felt about it.

"Well," Dora said, "I'd better get going if I'm going to make the midnight mass." I had the feeling that this was just an excuse to leave. I had the feeling we'd become so depressing that even Little Dora couldn't stand it, Little Dora whose life consisted of working at Friendly's and bailing her criminal son out of jail.

"Drive safe," my mother said. "Say a prayer for me." Her voice was weak and raspy. If I hadn't known better, I would have thought she was about to cry.

As always it was my job to walk Little Dora down our sloping driveway to her car. We were both drunk, leaning against each other, wobbling a bit. "I almost forgot," she said when we got to the car. "I have something for you." She opened the trunk and pulled out a Polaroid camera. "It was Charlie's," she said, and handed it to me. "He only used it once. I thought maybe you could take pictures of things and then draw them in your notebook. I don't know, that's what I thought."

I nodded.

"I know you don't like me," she said. "Or anything else about your life right now." She grabbed me and pressed me against her, held my head down to her chest. I could smell her sweat, her rose-scented perfume. "But you can't hide away forever. You can't hide away forever."

*Then Little Dora released Frankie and drove off. Frankie stood and watched the car disappear down the street. "I like you," she said, knowing she couldn't be heard.*

*When Frankie turned back to the house she saw her mother and little brother standing in the window. She could just see their silhouettes, lit up in flashes by the blue light of the television. They waved to her, and she waved back. For a moment they seemed like perfect strangers waving from the window of a Greyhound bus, like people who were just passing through town on their way to some far-off land.*

*Frankie walked back up the driveway, unsteady on her feet. She was drunk for the first time in her life. Instead of the giddiness she'd hoped for there was only a weightlessness, the terrifying sensation that she might suddenly lift up from the ground and drift off, as she did sometimes in dreams, floating high above the house and the trees and through the clouds, up and away, with no means of coming down.*

# 11

Teddy and I spent the rest of Christmas break hoping that our teachers—who were supposed to either settle a contract by the new year or go on strike—would walk out on us and school would be cancelled for the rest of the year. We watched the local news, hoping for disaster. The teachers had a spokesperson—a woman named Glenda Robertson who was always wearing an orange sweater, and whose hair and eyebrows were a wild, Einsteinian disaster—and she gave nightly interviews to *Action 13*. She was a high school chorus teacher, and she had a flair for the dramatic. She was like a character in a musical, shouting things that should have been spoken, using exaggerated gestures and postures, shaking her fist, wagging her finger, pulling her hair. "We want an eight percent raise!" she yelled. "We want smaller classes! We want to preserve the arts! We'll rot in jail before we settle for the contract on the table!" For their part, the city was offering early retirement to the higher-paid teachers. "A raise is out of the question," said a young official, looking dour and sane next to Glenda Robertson. "The money just isn't there. We're just trying to avoid having to lay people off."

It seemed that they would never reach an agreement, but on the last day of the year the teachers signed a contract that increased class size, forced dozens into early retirement, and cut the "nonessential" faculty in half, but offered a two percent raise. "We consider this a victory," Glenda Robertson told *Action 13*, in a lackluster wheeze. There was no trace of her former aggression. She was taking early retirement.

Teddy and I were crushed. We had imagined a full strike with picket lines and the National Guard, our teachers arrested and thrown in the slammer. But now everything had been peacefully settled without our missing so much as a single day of school. "This *stinks*," Teddy said. "This is so unfair."

"We have the worst luck," I said. "I can't believe this is happening to us." I knew this was a ridiculous sentiment—that the strike had nothing to do with us and its settlement wasn't some divine plan to punish us. But still, I felt cheated by the whole deal. What good had any of it been—all the strife and excitement—if it didn't amount to anything?

But I didn't yet know the full story. I didn't know that, under the terms of the new contract, Teddy and I had been named beneficiaries.

Mr. Jolly, it turned out, was leaving. When I showed up to our next meeting I was still turning things over in my mind, trying to decide whether I was going to start telling him the truth. I had expected some ridiculous scene. I thought I'd walk in and find him wearing a silver party hat, blowing into a noisemaker, saying something like, "It's a brand-new year! Are you ready for the new you?" And though I would have *wanted* to be kind to him, to level with him, I'd decide that it was necessary to punish him for the hat and continue with my usual antics.

Instead, when I walked in, he was hunched over his desk, his head lowered. When I sat across from him he only looked up for a second, then bowed his head again. "I'm sorry to have to tell you this," he said, "but it seems that my job has changed with all this contract nonsense. My counterpart, who works at the high school, is going to retire. I'll be taking on all her cases, in addition to my usual load." He glanced up at me to see how I was doing, if I'd collapsed in despair. "There's a lot of troubled kids over there at West High," he said. "They have some serious problems. I'm going to have to spend a lot of time over there. I'm going to start transitioning this week."

"Oh," I said.

"Perhaps you can see where I'm going with this." He held his hands out toward me, wriggling his fingers. Apparently he wanted me to give him my hand. I did, and he sandwiched it between his sweaty palms. "I'm only going to have time to see kids who are really in trouble. I'm afraid I won't be able to see you very much anymore," he said. "If at all."

*Frankie was being dumped by Mr. Jolly! She couldn't believe it! For months he'd been telling her that she was on the brink of a serious break-*

*down, that she needed his expert guidance through this thing he called grief. Now he was dumping her!*

"I know this is going to be hard. These are hard times we're living in. But you're tough," he said, and squeezed my hand. It felt wilted, a lettuce leaf trapped between two hamburgers. "You wouldn't believe what those high school kids are like," he said. "Drugs, suicide, pregnancy, grand theft. You name it." He let go of my hand and sat back in his chair, sighed. "I just don't see how I'm going to handle it. I just don't see how."

I tried to imagine it, Mr. Jolly walking the halls of West High in his sherbet-colored pantsuits and polka-dot bow ties, his skin flushed with hypertension. I imagined him asking complete strangers for high fives, getting kicked in the shins. "You'll be fine," I told him.

"I don't know. I think I might be too old for this kind of thing."

"You're not so old," I said.

"I suppose I should be glad I didn't get laid off."

"That's true. You should look on the bright side."

"I could be standing in a soup line, you know? Who'd take care of my mother? She's eighty-three and she doesn't see well. She's got bad arthritis. She needs a lot of care." He was hunched over his desk, now, head in hands, lost in an imagined disaster.

"It's a good thing she has you."

"I know. You're right. I'm just going to have to make the best of it. It's just such a big change," he said.

"Sometimes change is good."

"I guess." He was still sulking.

"You should make a list," I said. "Of things you're looking forward to. Write an essay or something."

It was then that the irony of our conversation struck him. He sat up and regained his composure, cleared his throat. "I'm not going to say goodbye," he said, "because I'll be seeing you around. I'll probably see you when you get to West."

I didn't know what to say to this. In a way, I thought, he was telling me that I was destined to turn into a pregnant criminal. "Well, see you around," I said, and stood up to leave.

Before I knew it Mr. Jolly had stood up and closed his arms around me. He started shuddering slightly, and a few seconds later he gasped, sniffled. "I just wanted to help you," he said, in a stifled sob. "I hope I was able to help you in some small way."

I stood there, flattened against the rough polyester of his orange suit, my neck turned up awkwardly. I could barely breathe.

"I just wanted to help," Mr. Jolly said.

"I know," I told him, and realized with surprise that it was true.

And so, just like that, we were released from the good intentions and bad style of Mr. Jolly. In the following weeks I felt a weight come off me. I no longer had to come up with fake essays, or read *Oh, Brother!* or replay my visits with Mr. Jolly over and over again in my mind, as I did each week. I no longer had to show up late to math class and endure Mrs. Gustafson's hopeless attempts at kindness. "Hello, Frankie," she'd always said. "How was your appointment?" Right in front of everyone. It was a relief to be left alone, to be given up on, to sit unnoticed in a corner and fall quietly out of tune, like a piano. People were always saying that kids my age couldn't get enough attention, that we spent most of our time trying to make ourselves noticed, but I found there was nothing so satisfying as being lost, faceless and nameless, utterly unknown.

For this reason my new favorite class was science. Mr. Jefferson was gone and our class was being taught by a permanent substitute named Mr. Milton, who for some reason was under the impression that my name was Emily. Mr. Milton was old, bald, liver-spotted, with a hoarse voice and a chronic cough. Behind his left ear he wore a hearing aid the size of a pea pod. He seemed to know nothing about science, and often looked around in a confused manner, as though he'd found himself in our classroom by mistake, having taken a wrong turn on his way to a shuffleboard game. To pass time in class he had us read aloud from our textbook, one paragraph per student, while he paced back and forth in front of us, jingling the change in his pockets. "Miss Emily," he always said when it was my turn to read. He said the name with such confidence that people laughed. "Why are you laughing?" he asked once. "Let's all settle down and listen to Emily read the next paragraph."

*Emily liked her new name! It was fun to be someone else, to let Frankie disappear entirely. Emily was different from Frankie in every way. Her life was interesting and glamorous. A girl named Emily, for instance, might have seen London. She might have taken a trip there once and returned home with an accent. "Hallo," she would say when George Benson approached her. "Ever so sorry, love. I simply cahn't go to the dance with you. I've already committed to another chap." A girl named Emily did not feel the need to scribble constantly in a notebook, and could simply stare out the window like everybody else. Oh, it was nice being Emily, if only for an hour a day, Monday through Friday.*

**Things were** turning around for Teddy, too. He started having fewer tantrums, and they were less violent. Sometimes he even lost interest in them right in their midst. And one day Eugene Franklin met the fate of all other socks, disappearing completely, escaping into another world from some secret vent in the dryer.

Within a few weeks Teddy had stopped his fits entirely, and in fact seemed to have no memory of them. My mother and I often found ourselves exchanging baffled glances behind his back, shrugging and raising our eyebrows. "Beats me!" we said to each other, walking out of the grocery store with a full cart, Teddy running ahead to the car without a care in the world, having declined to throw a tantrum even though he had been denied a box of assorted donuts, and several species of candy bar. In the age of witch trials, people would have said that a demon had been cast out of Teddy. Some man of God would have pronounced it a miracle. And perhaps it was. In our time miracles were hard to recognize. Angels didn't swoop down from heaven on rays of light, fairies didn't appear in clouds of dust. We weren't transformed by the word of God, or the touch of a wand. Never had I found myself in the sudden possession of grace or of fancy shoes. But still, there was this. Teddy given back to us.

**Winter dragged** on in the way that it always did, so bleak and cold and endless it seemed that time had stopped. It seemed we would always live that way, under that colorless sky, senseless, mummified in our thick coats, clumsy in our giant boots, struggling to turn doorknobs with our fat mittens. Every day we marked off a box on the kitten calendar. Right before our eyes there was proof that we were moving forward through time, that one day soon it would stop snowing and we would be released into the world again, but we couldn't feel it. We lay around the living room like hibernating bears, hardly even breathing, watching a sickening amount of television. Each night our mother came home and we cycled through the same questions and answers in a nonsensical loop, like Abbott and Costello.

"Why aren't you in bed?" our mother said when she got home from work.

"We're not tired," we said.

"Why didn't you answer the goddamned phone? I called you fifty times."

"We didn't feel like getting off the couch," we said. "We're too tired."

"Why aren't you in bed, then? Jesus Christ!"

When she saw us in the light of morning she always said the same thing. "Look at you two!" she said. "You look terrible! You look like you're forty-five years old!" This was true. We were ghostly pale and there were dark circles under our eyes. Our eyes themselves were dead from watching so much television.

This was winter. As always it hung around so long that we eventually gave in to the idea of it, forgot that spring was even possible. Then, when it had us where it wanted us, pinned down and hopeless, it packed up and left.

# 12

The weather turned and brought the usual luxuries of spring: greenery, the pleasure of walking outside without a coat, the ability to start a car on the first try instead of sitting there for ten minutes cranking the ignition, flooding the engine. My mother, who despised winter, was encouraged. She was going through some kind of spring cleaning of the soul. She put herself on a diet, joined an aerobics class, vowed to lose twenty pounds. In the mornings she made us eggs instead of leaving us to our usual sugared cereal, and she resumed her old habit of reading "Dear Abby" aloud at the breakfast table. "Listen to this!" she'd say, and narrate the letters in the voice of Betty Boop. "My mother-in-law often stops by without warning. I'm afraid that if I ask her to call first, I'll offend her *and* my husband. What should I do?" She'd lower the paper and look at us, to make sure we were properly appalled. Then she'd dispense her own advice in neat little snippets, things that could fit in a fortune cookie. "Get some balls!" she'd say, our very own Confucius.

Later, instead of driving us to school in her housecoat, as had been her custom, she dressed in an old sweat suit of my father's and insisted that we walk together. When we reached the road that led to our schools, she shooed us away and kept going. I'd stand for a moment and watch her walk away from us, her arms pumping, her ponytail swaying from side to side. She had a determined step. She seemed to be walking in the direction of the person she had once been.

A new family moved to the neighborhood and filled it with commotion. Their names were the Brownings, and they had five boys. Teddy started spending most of his free time with them. Like Teddy, they were all blond and blue-eyed, and when I looked out on them from the window it was hard to tell anyone apart. The Brownings thoroughly adopted Teddy, taking him into their games of kickball and stickball, of tag and keep-away, of cowboys and Indians. They played their games according to a complicated system of rules. Often there were disputes over boundaries or the legality of certain kills. There was shouting and shoving. Then, inevitably, the matter would be decided by calling for a *do-over*. I could hear them shouting it—*do-over, do-over!*—and in those moments, with everyone scrambling into place, rushing back to the positions they'd occupied before things had gone wrong, everything seemed quite simple.

After a few weeks of playing with the Brownings, Teddy

started applying the concept of the *do-over* to our daily lives. There were so many things we could change, so many ways to improve ourselves, if only we'd try. He was full of suggestions for me: I should go outside and get some fresh air, I should change my clothes and do something with my hair, I should cheer up and enjoy life. It was like living with Mary Poppins.

Teddy had suggestions for my mother, too. For an entire week he spoke of nothing but the money my mother spent on cigarettes. He calculated her weekly total, multiplied it by fifty-two. With a year's worth of cigarette money, he claimed, we could take a vacation to Mexico, buy a new car. "You should quit, Mom," he said, every time my mother lit up a cigarette. "That's another ten cents down the drain." He often described to her, in excruciating detail, the preserved smoker's lung he had seen on a field trip to the hospital. Every time she smoked, he told her, she was turning our lungs black and hard, killing us slowly, not to mention denying us an inground swimming pool.

This new Teddy had the effect of turning my mother and me into allies. Teddy was breaking one of the unspoken rules of our family—that certain things weren't to be discussed, that we were supposed to carry on with certain bad habits without acknowledging their wickedness—and he needed to be reined in. "You're really turning into a little brat," I'd say. "Why don't you get lost? Why don't you go find someone who cares?"

"Who died," said my mother, "and made you king of the universe? Get lost! Get out of my hair! Go get a job or something!"

"I just think it's for the best," he'd say, and shrug. He was so reasonable, so unflappable. For months we'd hoped for him to get better, to be free from those seizures of grief. And now here he was, cured to an obnoxious extent, the thing we'd wished for without being careful.

More than anything else, Teddy wanted his own room. He was ruthless about it. "Please, please, please, please, please, please, please," he'd say, all through breakfast, and every night when my mother came home. "I'll be good. I'll never ask for anything again as long as I live!" My mother kept putting him off, claiming she had a headache, that she wasn't in the mood, that she'd think about it later. Though we had been due to move into separate rooms, anyway (our parents had fought about it in the months before my father's death, my mother saying we were getting too old to share a room, that if I was ever going to turn into a proper girl I would need my own space), the prospect of clearing out my father's den was overwhelming. There was his desk, so monstrous it was a wonder he'd ever fit it through the doorway. There were all of his books and records, his typewriter, the posters on the wall. There was the rug, which, despite having been cleaned, was still stained with blood, and would have to be taken up. Most of all there was the idea of my father, the vague feeling that, so long as the room was left intact, he might still be there behind that closed door, sitting at his desk, reading and daydreaming, hiding himself away for days at a time, as he had done that last year.

But Teddy was relentless. He raised a number of valid points. We couldn't, he said, keep the den like it was forever. Eventually we'd win the lottery and move to a new house, or we'd die, and someone would have to clean it out for us. Second, if we let him have his own room, he'd stay in it and leave us alone and stop harassing us about everything. Third, he was about to start a paper route, and he'd be getting up very early in the morning, all summer long. The alarm would be going off at six. Was that what I wanted? To wake up at six? Finally, he wanted to have the Brownings for a sleepover, all five of them, and where else would we put them?

"In a million years," said my mother, "you're not having those kids for a sleepover." She hated the Brownings. She felt there was something fishy about them—something about the fact that Mrs. Browning was even blonder than my mother and married to a doctor, something about the way Mr. Browning turned to Mrs. Browning each morning before getting into his car and blew her a kiss. It really turned her stomach.

"It's up to Frankie," my mother kept saying.

*It was up to Frankie. She knew she was going to have to give in to her brother eventually. Every day she told herself, This is the day. Today I will go into the den and have a look around. I will say my goodbyes. Then Teddy can have it. But every day after school she stood in the hall, looking at the closed door of the den, and she couldn't go in. She wanted to. She wanted to move on like her mother and brother had, to let things go like Mr. Jolly and Heathcliff Sloakum, Ph.D., had said she should. She wanted to be able to have a memory of her father that didn't seize her with pain. But she couldn't yet. She was still waiting for something. She didn't know what.*

# 13

Finally the day arrived, the anniversary of my father's death. *Oh, Brother!* had recommended that families come together on that day to mark it in some way, with a ceremony or even a party. But as my family was not particularly good at grief, we just went about our business as if it were any other Friday. At breakfast my mother gave me a quick pat on the back and said, "What a day." Teddy seemed not to notice at all. After school he went out to play with the Brownings.

I was alone in the house all afternoon. I tried to pass the time reading and watching TV, but my thoughts kept drifting. Around five o'clock I started thinking, *It was now that he sent us for dinner.*

I thought of how we'd all gotten in the car and driven off. I wondered if my father had stood at the living room window and watched us, if he'd waved to us, if he'd been waving and we hadn't seen him. I wondered what might have happened if I'd looked up and seen him and waved back, if things would be easier for me now. The worst part of his death, I realized, was that I had never said goodbye.

I turned from the window and walked through the living room, down the hall to the den. I stood in front of the den's closed door, rested my forehead against it for a moment, thinking, *It must have been now. He must have done it now.* My heart was pounding.

Finally I opened the door and went in. I spent a few minutes walking around, just looking. The room seemed small. Dust was everywhere, a fine covering on the desk and bookcase, motes floating in the air. I sat at my father's desk and examined the treasures he had always kept there. His pale blue Smith Corona that said *Silent-Super* in white lettering on its side. A picture in a plain wooden frame, my father and two other men leaning against a jeep, their shirts off, cigarettes dangling from their mouths, looks of utter disdain on their faces. A paperweight replica of the Iwo Jima memorial. And another picture, unframed, propped against the paperweight, me and Teddy in red snowsuits, our hoods cinched tight and just our faces peeking out, Teddy screaming, me smirking.

I got up and stood in front of the bookcase, skimmed through the titles. Most were history books. Biographies of Lincoln and Washington, multivolume histories of the United States. There were Hawthorne's and Hemingway's books in paperback, and books by some writers I had never heard of. One of the books was out of line with the others, pulled forward a bit, and it seemed to me that this might have been the last book my father had ever touched. It was called the *Illustrated Manual of Amputations* and it was bound in red leather, its title stamped on the spine in gold. On the bottom of the spine there were library markings. I took the book from the shelf and opened it. There was a placard glued inside, where the book could be stamped when it was checked in and out of circulation, but there were no marks. It appeared that the book had never been checked out. It appeared my father had stolen it.

I flipped through the book. Each chapter was a tour through a different type of surgery. My father had dog-eared a chapter dedicated to below-knee amputations. "*Indications,*" it read. "*Advanced ischemia, gangrene, acute infection.*" The first illustration was of a surgeon's gloved hand, shown pressing a scalpel against the skin of a leg, just below the knee. The artist had taken great pains to approximate the texture of latex over the surgeon's hands, as if to emphasize that this was the person who wasn't being amputated, who had a protective layer between himself and this kind of misfortune. There were several drawings showing the skin and muscle being cut away. Then the surgeon was pictured holding an oscillating saw. The book recommended that saline irrigation be used during sawing to "alleviate frictional heat."

The next page was particularly gruesome, picturing the sawed-through bone, and the cutting off of the remaining muscle and skin. Then the surgeon was pictured smoothing the end of the tibia with a rasp. He used a harsh-looking file and he worked it against the remaining bone. The picture was disturbingly casual about the whole procedure, this filing of bone with a sharp instrument. To the surgeon it was nothing more than a tedious, repetitive motion, like the nail-filing of millions of gum-chewing secretaries. Finally there was the suturing of the posterior flap over the end of the now smoothly filed tibia. This time the surgeon's hands weren't even pictured, as if the tweezers and scissors and sutures were magically suspended, doing their jobs without assistance as in cartoons—like the talking brooms that swept themselves, the good-natured teapots that filled up with water, lit their own fires, and brought themselves to a boil.

After the procedure the patient was shown lying in bed with a carefully wrapped stump. The illustrator had detailed the stump with lots of shading and crosshatching, but the rest of the patient was just an outline, much like the outline of a dead body traced by police at a murder site. The patient had no face, no features. He wore a hollow gown over his hollow body.

It was then that I drew my father. I sat down at his desk, took a pencil from the drawer. I started filling in the patient's features, giving him my father's stubbly beard, his unruly dark hair. I drew circular lenses where his eyes should have been, thick lenses with nothing behind them.

Then I put the book back in its place.

I went into my room and retrieved Little Dora's Polaroid. Then I went all around the den taking pictures from every angle. I took close-ups of the bookcase, the desk, the posters on the walls. Finally, with the last picture in the camera, I stood in the doorway and took the whole room into view and pressed the button. There was a flash and a grinding of gears, and then the picture rolled out of the camera with a wheeze. I stood and watched it develop, the den copied in miniature down to the smallest details, even the slender red spine of the *Illustrated Manual of Amputations*.

*This is it, Frankie thought. She felt a lump in her throat, the familiar tightness in her chest. Hello, she thought, I must be going.*

We spent the entire next day transforming the den. We hauled armloads of books down to the basement, untacked the posters, carried the chair and the bookcase down the stairs. We made dozens of trips until there was nothing left but the desk. Once we took out the drawers we found the desk wasn't too heavy to move, and we managed to push it out of the room and down the hall. Then, when we reached the basement stairs, we realized we had no good means of getting it down, and so we simply left it there. "I'll get someone from work to come move it sometime," my mother said. Which meant that the desk would sit there in the hall for a year or two. We'd have to squeeze past it all the time. I kind of liked the idea of it.

But Teddy was unsatisfied with this. He seemed to want all evidence of the den to disappear immediately. He went down the street and retrieved Mr. Browning, who was wearing his usual scrubs and white coat, and who brought a sense of the professional into the house. "What seems to be the problem?" he said, with the confidence of someone who was accustomed to fixing things.

"We're sorry to bother you," my mother said, "but I can't get this down the stairs by myself."

"It's no trouble at all," said Dr. Browning. He was so pleasant. He and my mother lifted the desk and carried it down the basement stairs. Then Dr. Browning came up the stairs, smacking his hands together. "Piece of cake," he said. And I knew then why my father had hated his doctors. For them everything seemed so easy. With no apparent effort they were able to lift weights which ordinary people found unbearable. Life, for them, was a goddamned piece of cake.

Teddy and I had spent the next day together, the Browning boys having driven to New Hampshire to have Sunday dinner with their grandmother. We bicycled through the neighborhood like we always used to, stopped at Gino's for lunch. Teddy was full of plans for the summer. He talked almost constantly about the fort he was going to build in the woods with the Brownings, the vacation they'd invited him to go on, to Martha's Vineyard, where they were going to rent an entire cottage all to themselves. He talked about his new paper route, all the houses he delivered to, the tips he made. "That house," he said, "that house right there. That house gave me two dollars!" He had plans for his new room. He was going to save enough money to buy himself a new television, and he'd place it on his dresser, facing the bed. "I can watch whatever I want," he said. "I can watch TV all night and no one can stop me."

"That sounds good," I said.

"You can't come in," he told me. "It's my room."

When we returned home in the afternoon, our mother was beside herself. Something was loose in the house, some flying animal. "I think it's a goddamned bat," she said. She had seen it come flapping out of the fireplace while she was watching *Gone with the Wind.* "It was all such a blur," she said. "I mean, you're sitting there minding your own goddamned *business*, and look what happens!" She had gone through the house carrying a large pot and its lid, hoping to trap it, but it had flown from room to room so quickly that our mother saw nothing more that a blur of blackness. She couldn't get close enough to catch it. She'd given up a while ago and now had no idea where it was. "One of us has to be the man of the house and catch this thing," she said. "I'm counting on you, Frankie." She gave me the pot and lid, and handed Teddy a tennis racquet.

I took the pot and walked around the house, trying not to make a sound. I looked in the kitchen, the bathroom, my mother's room, my room. Teddy was only willing to search his room, which was the only room he cared about. He stayed in there for the longest time, pulling open all the drawers of his dresser, going through his closet, opening and shutting the windows. "It's not in here," he finally reported, then shut his door on us.

"I don't see anything, either," I told my mother. "Maybe it flew back up the chimney or something."

"Oh, God," my mother said. "We have to find it. We can't just walk around with a goddamned *bat* in the house. God! I can't *believe* this!"

My mother and I sat on the couch and waited. Melanie Wilkes was in labor, and Scarlett was picking her way through a field of groaning Confederates, in search of Dr. Meade. Even with a thousand men dying on the ground in front of her, reaching out to grab the hem of her dress, it had not yet occurred to Scarlett that some people had bigger problems than she did.

Later that night I was brushing my teeth and saw the bat in the mirror. It was behind me, perched on the shower curtain rod. Though it was peaceful and minding its own business, I screamed and went running out to the living room. The bat came flying after me, swooping through the room, and my mother and Teddy, who had been watching TV, started running around screaming. "There it is! There it is!" my mother shouted. "Somebody *do* something! Where's the pot? Get it! Get it!" At one point the bat landed on the arm of the sofa bed and we all stood still, watching it. Then, without really knowing what I was doing, I went to the front door and opened it. I stood there holding the screen door open and the bat—as if it knew instinctively the difference between inside and out, between captivity and freedom—lighted from the couch and flew toward me. It flew right out the door and over the yellow light that lit up our doorstep as if to welcome the world, though no one ever came to our house, though the sole purpose of the door was to keep people out, to prevent exactly this kind of disruption. As it passed over this yellow light I saw its skin—the black, translucent skin of its wing stretched tightly over its intricate bones. I flexed my toes.

And it came to me: a gift, a memory long buried. It was a memory of my father sitting in the office of my pediatrician, who was explaining the procedure for removing the webbing between my toes. "It's a simple matter," the pediatrician said, but my father was already standing, picking me up, marching out. "No, no, no, no," he said. "I'm offended by the very suggestion." Afterwards my father took me for an ice cream and explained, as we sat outside on a bench underneath a tree, as I licked the ice cream that was melting down the sides of the cone, that was running down my chin and hands and down the front of my shirt— all this time he was explaining to me that we were two of a kind, me and him, that we were fine just the way we were, deformities and all, that we wouldn't want to join any club that would have us as members, that I was his glorious girl and there was nothing, nothing wrong with me.

part two

# 14

Every day of her life my mother wore a silver bracelet whose charms represented the passing fancies of her youth. The charms were arranged chronologically, starting with a teddy bear she had bought as a twelve-year-old girl. Next there was a tiny pair of ballet slippers from her year as an aspiring dancer, and a set of pom-poms from her season as a football cheerleader. There was half of a silver heart split jaggedly down the center, the other half belonging to a girl named Sheila, who had been my mother's best friend for three months before a fight over a boy named Rick Ferris turned them against each other. There was a graduation cap with the smallest of tassels, a miniature typewriter from her first semester of secretarial school, which she dropped out of in order to attend nursing school. To represent her time there she had too hastily purchased a thermometer, which became obsolete just six weeks later when she realized that she held the sick and lame in the lowest possible regard, that she in fact wished them harm, and that even the sight of them was enough to turn her stomach. Finally there was a small silver ice cream cone representing the beginning of her career as a waitress at Friendly's Restaurant and Ice Cream Parlor. She had taken the job on a whim, as something to do while she considered her next move. But Friendly's had turned out to be the final charm, the affair of her life, outlasting even our father.

For my sixteenth birthday my mother bought a bracelet for me, a fat chain of charmless silver links. "I didn't know what kind of charms to get," she said. "I figured we could go to the jeweler together and you could pick something out. I didn't know." This was the same as saying that she didn't know anything about me. Or, more to the point, that she disapproved of the lonely charms that defined me: a book, a clarinet, a television.

"These bracelets are real conversation starters!" she said. "You wouldn't believe how many people stop and ask me about mine. Every day someone asks!" I had seen this with my own eyes. My mother had developed a speech that explained the entire history of her life and she loved to give it, fingering each charm like a spokesmodel. She didn't seem to see the bracelet in the same way that I did, as a chain of abandoned dreams cobbled in miniature.

We never went to the jeweler's, and the bracelet sat in its box. But sometimes I liked to think about my life as a series of unusual charms. I imagined a question mark dangling from my wrist, making a constant tinkling sound every time I moved. I was about to start my senior year of high school and the question of what I intended to do with my future couldn't be put off much longer. Sometimes I imagined a small cash register as the answer to the question that was my future. I was working as a cashier at the Big G Grocery on Lincoln Street, and for some reason I couldn't see past this minimum-wage job. I couldn't see myself in college, or working as a professional. I just saw myself standing behind that register, scanning merchandise, all day every day, forever and ever, amen.

To represent the depression our city had fallen into I imagined a tiny FOR SALE sign. That year two of the city's major employers had relocated south and west, following something referred to on the news as "the high-tech revolution." No one seemed to know what this revolution was about, except to say that it involved a generation of younger, smarter people who lived in better climates and spent long days sitting in front of computers. It involved the skyrocketing of the unemployment rate in our city, the total collapse of the housing market, the failure of dozens of local businesses, the steep rise in drugs and crime and prostitution. According to the local newscasters, half the people walking the streets of our city wanted to sell you something illicit and potentially fatal. The other half just wanted to mug you.

Everything was up for sale now. In our neighborhood alone there were five houses sitting empty, the owners having moved away without even waiting for buyers. Everyone was using the same realtor. Her name was Midge Durdle and her picture was printed on all of her FOR SALE signs. She was an older woman with gray hair that was curled tight against her head. She wore a red jacket and red lipstick. Her smile was forced, as if she knew that she was beat, that she was trying to sell outdated houses in a city that people were fleeing in record numbers.

The signs depressed me. Every time I saw one I thought of our old neighbors and wondered what had become of them. Poor Mrs. Weatherbee, whose husband had gone ahead to California without her, then sent word that he was in love with another woman and wanted a divorce. Poor old Mr. Fletcher, who was always out walking his wife's dog (a miniature poodle named Snowball that had its own wardrobe of hand-knit sweaters) and who always waved to me and Teddy, sometimes even stopping to fish pieces of butterscotch from his pocket. For years Mr. Fletcher had endured the humiliation of walking this ridiculous dog, but then he had lost his job and his wife had left him, taking Snowball with her. Shortly thereafter he had suffered a stroke and moved to a nursing home, where he was lying even now, all alone, without so much as a poodle to keep him company.

As an amalgam of the four men my mother had dated in the last few years, I pictured a charm in the shape of a gorilla. These men were all more or less the same—people she had met at work who called themselves "businessmen," but who really sold electronics out of the backs of vans. These men were red-faced, acne-scarred. They stank of cologne and wore their thinning hair slicked back with pomade. They had loud, violent laughs and they were prone to reaching out and enthusiastically slapping people. They wore gold rings and bracelets and necklaces. They showed up at the door bearing flowers bought at gas stations—single roses wrapped in cellophane, their small heads shut up tight.

N e x t I imagined a life-sized silver capsule, representing the "oral supplements" my mother had started taking. That summer, on the advice of Little Dora, she had begun making weekly pilgrimages to a man named Dr. Woo, who operated a covert pharmacy out of his efficiency apartment on Lincoln Street. There he concocted various pills and potions out of foul-smelling herbs. My mother was always coming home with different bottles of pills, each marked with a handwritten label. Her favorite pills were labeled with the words *For female troubles*. There were also bottles that claimed *To help with sleep* and *To feel awake*. Each had the same set of instructions: *Take as many as necessary.*

Once my mother had brought a bottle home for me labeled with the words *For the relief of sadness*.

"Just try one of these puppies," she said. "I promise you you'll feel like a million bucks! Dr. Woo is a *genius*! I've never felt better in my life!" I had to admit that this appeared to be true. My mother was unusually animated that summer, sometimes even dancing around the kitchen while shaking the bottles of pills like maracas. Worse, she had turned into a manic optimist, one of those happy people who believed that everyone else should feel the same way.

"I don't want a puppy," I told her.

"Well you need *something*," she told me. "You need some god-damned thing, that's for sure."

To  r e p r e s e n t  the time I had spent with a boy named Nathan West I imagined some human organ other than a heart—an expendable organ no one ever saw or talked about, perhaps a spleen. Nathan was a year older, a trumpet player in the marching band, and after a series of football and basketball games we had snuck off into the woods that bordered our school. There we had set up a blanket and lain on our backs looking at the sky while Nathan talked of his strategy for get-ting into Princeton. We had smoked cigarettes and sipped bour-bon from a flask. We had kissed and groped each other, our hands slipping underneath each other's band uniforms, roaming about wildly, recklessly, doing the most we could manage to do to each other without removing our clothes. We had done all of this because Nathan—who was popular and successful, who was liked by all his teachers, who was president of his class and an altar boy—had something he called "a dark side," and this dark side was attracted to me. I was a quiet, skinny girl with family problems, a girl with black eyes he claimed to find haunting. I was nothing like his proper girlfriend—a senior named Jennifer Brooks, someone he drove home from school and took to the prom, someone he allowed himself to be seen with—and this was what he loved about me. Our "love," as he called it, was something he kept secreted away in his heart. It was something so special he couldn't describe it, couldn't dare speak of it to anyone, anyone at all. Which was why, I could only assume, he had gone off to Princeton without so much as a goodbye.


**T h e   c h a r m** for Teddy took the form of one of his favorite childhood toys, whose name was Troy. At first glance Troy was a regular plastic boy. But with a few twists of his head and joints, Troy could be turned inside out and transformed into a vicious monster named Rex. Rex had sharp, bloodstained teeth, and his sole desire was to destroy everything in sight. Now and then, when I wasn't home, Rex would go on a rampage, disrupting the pristine order I kept in my bedroom, knocking all the books off my desk and onto the floor, taking all of my folded clothes out of my bureau drawers and throwing them about, unmaking the bed, snapping all the heads off my sharpened pencils. "What the fuck is your fucking *problem*?" I'd say when I found my room like this. I'd stomp out to the living room, where Teddy was watching cartoons. I'd dive for him, and we'd roll around on the sofa bed launching punches at each other, driving our knees into each other's ribs. "Don't look at *me*," he'd say. "*I* didn't do anything." We'd fight until I got the better of him, had him flat on his back. Then I'd kneel on his chest and strangle him.

"Ow!" he'd say. "You're *hurting* me. I can't *breathe!*"

"Just admit it was you," I'd say. This was all I really wanted.

"I don't know what you're talking about!"

"Just admit it!"

"You're not supposta *hurt* me! You're supposta be my *sister!*"

"You're not supposed to trash my room," I'd say. "You're supposed to be my brother."

"It must have been Rex," he'd finally say, and I'd let him go. It was pointless to punish him further. By that time Rex had turned back into Troy, just an innocent kid who was collapsed on the sofa, watching cartoons.

Eventually Troy was lost or thrown away, Teddy having abandoned all his toys, having abandoned, for the most part, our entire house. He was always off on his bicycle, going places and doing things I couldn't even imagine. He was a teenager now, and like most teenagers he was living two lives. Inside the house he was Teddy, our Teddy. But when he left he was someone else, someone entirely different, someone so mysterious to us we didn't even know his name.

And of course I imagined one last thing: not my father, but something representing what little was left of him, perhaps his Buick Skylark, which I had started driving as soon as I got my license. After six years this was pretty much all that was left of him, the only evidence of his existence that hadn't been relegated to the basement. He was more or less gone from our lives. We hardly spoke of him, and when we did it was as if we were poor people sending a telegram, wanting to reduce our memories to the shortest possible phrases.

It was the same with all the dead. I'd learned this in high school English: that no matter how spectacular a person had been in life or even in death, their existence would eventually be summed up in a few phrases on a book jacket. Publishers had reduced Hemingway to just a few sentences, saying that he had traveled extensively, fought in wars, written a few books, and died in 1963. There was no mention of violence or suffering. Time passed and the details fell away, and soon everything was whitewashed. Sylvia Plath was only said to have "died prematurely," as if by some accident, as if she'd slipped on a child's roller skate and fallen into an oven. The truth was too difficult to mention. Oh, we were all afraid of Virginia Woolf.

I wondered why anyone had bothered to counsel me out of my grief, why people focused so much on "letting go" of their loved ones, when the truth was that, given time, we censored ourselves almost completely. We simply couldn't hold on to certain things—the sound and smell of them, their gestures and laughs, even their faces. It was a struggle to keep my father's memory alive, to remember the small things. His pet peeves, for instance: animals dressed in sweaters, fat people wearing white pants, the spelling of *nite* instead of *night* on the signs of cheap motels, the enunciation of the *t* in *often*. Some of his peculiar habits: the way he bit the inside of his mouth when he was thinking, the way he cracked his knuckles so slowly and methodically. How the skin of his left arm was sometimes covered in cartoons drawn in blue ink—the smiling, chubby faces of young friends who had been killed in the war.

I knew now that the trouble with the dead wasn't that they overwhelmed you, that they haunted you and stifled you with memories. The trouble with the dead was that they packed up and left you, and there was nothing you could do to bring them back.

Or so it seemed until that year, when Teddy started his infamous career at West High School. It was the year that Teddy discovered his uncanny knack for impersonating the adults in our lives, the year that he disguised himself with wigs and fake beards and tortoiseshell glasses. The year that he filled his closet with a hopelessly outdated wardrobe, a platoon of polyester. The year that he was anything and anyone but himself. After that year, nothing was the same.

# 15

My mother was thrilled when Teddy started at West High. Finally, after years of going to separate schools, her children would be roaming the same hallways. She imagined us giving each other high fives, tossing a football around in the mornings before school started, like the Kennedys. She was particularly taken with the thought of us playing in the same marching band. "I bet you'll be the only pair of siblings in the whole band!" she said, while driving us to our first day of school.

"I think that's true," I said, though it was a blatant lie.

"My kids!" she said. "The only siblings in the marching band!" Already I could see her telling this to her customers at Friendly's. Because of this one innocent lie, hundreds of unsuspecting people would have to endure my mother's bragging, though they wanted nothing more than to eat their hamburgers and ice cream sundaes in peace.

We stopped in front of the school and my mother turned to Teddy, who was sitting beside her in the front seat. "Oh, my little boy!" she said. She licked her fingers and then reached over to smooth Teddy's hair.

"Get a *life*," Teddy said, and scrambled out of the car. My mother and I sat and watched him walk toward his new high school career with a nonchalant strut I had seen him practicing all summer.

I climbed out of the car and my mother called after me. "Bye, sweetheart!" she said. "Go get 'em! Be all you can be!"

I felt sorry for my mother. Recently she seemed obsessed with the idea of finding something exceptional about me and Teddy. She thought, for instance, that I was going to win full scholarships to several colleges. And she thought that the cartoons I was always drawing—though they were nothing more than careless sketches of people and things—would be syndicated in the funny pages. "Like *Cathy*," she said. "I love *Cathy*! Today she was trying on swimsuits again! You should do something like that! Have a character, like me for instance, who's on a diet and trying to resist eating an ice cream sundae. People *love* that!"

Where Teddy was concerned my mother thought that he was a lover of nature, that he was always going out for long walks because he was secretly a deep thinker. But the truth was that Teddy had started spending his newspaper money on pot, and he was always walking to Lincoln Street to meet his supplier, a dropout who worked at a gas station, who smelled so strongly of gasoline that he always seemed in danger of bursting into flames. When Teddy came home from these walks with bags of cheese puffs and Ding Dongs and Ho Hos and Crumb Cakes and Twinkies, with bouquets of shriveled beef jerky, with liters of cherry-flavored soda, with sticks of licorice and bags of pork rinds—all of which he ate in his bedroom while watching TV— our mother thought he was merely *spoiling his appetite*, he was such a bad boy.

Teddy started high school in much the same way I did—wandering the halls with quiet, anonymous disdain. In grade school, Teddy and I had been used to a certain degree of fame. *Our father had killed himself! We were troubled!* But high school was wilder, more chaotic. There were, quite simply, *more exciting things going down*. Our teachers were busy keeping students from killing each other, from overdosing on drugs, from impregnating one another in the toilet stalls. During the first week of Teddy's freshman year, two juniors—Pete Jones and Kenny Larson— fought in the cafeteria. Pete forced Kenny's face through a plate-glass window, and when Kenny returned to school, his face looked like it had been stitched together from scraps. He walked the hallways with a cross-eyed stare and a spooky brutality, trading insults with our school's most popular outcast, David Wells, who had Tourette's. The hallways were full of *fuck you*s and *cocksucker*s and *shitdick*s, and for the first few weeks Teddy faded reluctantly into the woodwork, just as I had done. It was easy to lose yourself in our high school, which was so hopelessly overcrowded it had resorted to holding some of its classes in mobile homes. Fourteen of these unheated "portables" had been set up in neat rows behind the gymnasium, away from the road, where the townspeople couldn't see them. They were said to be temporary solutions to a temporary problem, but they had been there for years—permanent, rusting reminders of our overabundance, our superfluousness, our youthful extravagance.

But this was not Teddy's fate—this herding, this wall-hugging. He took after our mother, who had been popular and newsworthy in her day, and who had, she liked to remind us, significantly lowered herself by marrying the likes of our father. Notoriety was in Teddy's blood. No one would point to *his* picture in the yearbook and say, "Is this guy in our class? I've never seen him before in my life." Teddy was built for popularity, and it only took him a few weeks to figure out how to claim it.

I'm proud to say that I witnessed, along with the one hundred and fifty-six other members of our marching band, Teddy's first impersonation of a West High School faculty member. We were practicing one morning when our long-suffering director, Mr. Chase, threw Teddy out of the classroom. Mr. Chase had *had it up to here* with Teddy, who couldn't restrain himself for more than thirty seconds at a time from rolling his drumsticks on his snare. "Hey, snare drum," Mr. Chase was always saying. "Cool it. We're trying to practice the trumpet solo." But Teddy was restless. He was always tapping, tapping, tapping—with his drumsticks, with his pencil, with his fingers. He was forever bobbing his head and tapping his foot to some internal beat. He couldn't stop himself from giving off a tic, a pulse, like radium.

"Get out!" Mr. Chase finally said. "Get the hell out of my classroom!" Murmuring filled the room. This was Mr. Chase's first eviction of the year, only three weeks into the term. It would all be downhill from here. Once Mr. Chase started throwing people out, he couldn't stop himself. My fellow clarinets looked over to see what I thought, and I shrugged. We watched Teddy exit through the swinging doors. Unlike the other players, who always trudged out of the room with their heads down, Teddy gave Mr. Chase a long, insolent stare. "I've got your number now, you punk," Mr. Chase yelled. What was Teddy doing? Hadn't I told him that Mr. Chase had suffered two heart attacks in the last three years, and we weren't supposed to upset him?

A few minutes after Mr. Chase composed himself and continued conducting, Teddy came walking back through the swinging doors. He stood behind Mr. Chase, whose back was turned, and he began to imitate the way Mr. Chase conducted, the way he stabbed his baton furiously at the sections he was disappointed with, the way he cut us off from whatever phrase we were butchering as though he were slicing his way through a jungle with a machete. When Mr. Chase slouched at the end of a song, letting his arms hang limply in front of him, Teddy did the same. He creased his forehead and shot up his eyebrows and shook his fist, all in unison with Mr. Chase, who was oblivious. "You think this is funny?" Mr. Chase yelled at the band. We seemed to be laughing at everything he said and did. "You think this is funny? Just wait 'till you get out there on that football field and you fuck up 'America the Beautiful' in front of the *whole town*! You won't be laughing then!"

It didn't take Teddy long to figure out that he could expand his repertoire, as our high school was a wasteland of embarrassing afflictions. There were teachers with lisps, with limps, with

crossed eyes and facial tics. "Do Mr. Jolly!" people would yell, and
Teddy would stand in front of the cafeteria, in crowded hallways,
in band practice, and amidst the fog of smokers who stood huddled outside the school before class, their jean jackets decorated
with pins picturing the jagged logos of Van Halen and with the
lascivious pink tongue that represented the Rolling Stones. "Hey
there," Teddy would say, and make a gun out of his right hand.
"Howsabout we turn that frown upside down!" He'd pull the
trigger and wink. He had Mr. Jolly's walk down pat—the walk
of a man in high-heeled ankle boots, in tight-fitting polyester
slacks, a man with a bad hip who favored his left side, a man who
had taught himself to move in the way he thought teenagers
related to by watching the host of *Dance Fever* swagger beneath
a disco ball.

As someone who had been raised in front of the television,
Teddy understood that he needed to keep evolving his act in
order to survive. After he had mastered the gestures and speech
patterns of the school's most unpopular teachers, he was left with
no choice but to advance to mocking their appearance. Most of
our teachers had stopped buying new clothes in the mid-seven-
ties, and there was gold to be mined here. Their bell-bottoms and
their knit ties, their pink shirts with stained underarms and
threadbare collars, their orthopedic shoes and their thick, owlish
glasses—Teddy set it all in his sights. He raided the Salvation Army
store and started walking the halls in secondhand bell-bottoms
and rainbow-striped shirts and—most famously—three-piece
leisure suits. He strutted down the halls giving impromptu lectures. "Polyester is back and it's better than ever! Everyone's gaga
for this vintage look updated in fall colors. Mark my words, ladies

and gentlemen, 1987 *is* the year of the leisure suit." Students applauded when he walked by. "It's Teddy Hawthorne," they said, and stood on their toes to catch a glimpse of his purple paisley shirt, his lime green vest.

"He's your brother?" people would say, their foreheads creased. I couldn't blame them. Teddy and I were nothing alike. I was overly thin and tall and pale, like my father. I had his dark hair and black eyes. Teddy took after my mother. He had her dirty blond hair, blue eyes. They shared a dark complexion that could tan in five minutes of winter sun. He was short and well muscled and steely-looking, like her, and he had her bone structure, her hawklike face. Even when they slept, their expressions were fierce, focused on some distant prey.

"He's your brother?" people said. "Are you sure?"

# 16

That fall my mother sent off for applications to several colleges. When they arrived, she read through them and highlighted the passages that seemed particularly interesting. She'd leave them at the foot of my bed with notes of encouragement. "This could be the place for you!" she wrote. Or, "It's time for you to get the hell out of the house!"

"Did you see that one from Lowell that come today?" she said one night at dinner.

"*Came* today, Ma," Teddy said. "You retard."

"Fine. *Came* today, smart-ass. Who's talking to you anyways?"

"Any-*way*," Teddy said, laughing, sending a spray of food

across the table. His mouth was always full of food. He was an eating machine.

"I'm talking to Frankie," our mother yelled, slapping her hand down on the table. "So," she said, and turned to me, all smiles. "Did you see it?"

I had seen it. Along with the ones from Boston, Worcester, Springfield, Amherst, and even New York. Lowell's was yet another brochure that pictured students walking in racially mixed groups, strolling across green lawns without a care in the world. They wore colorful sweaters and polished loafers. Their backpacks were slung casually over their shoulders and they smiled and smiled, amazed at their good fortune. The only thing different about Lowell's brochure was that it featured a small section on the historical aspects of the city and the educational benefits a student stood to gain from studying in the very place where thousands of millworkers had lived horrible lives, bent over their looms and sewing machines. Those factories were still standing, their windows boarded over, right beside the river that they once polluted!

"The application says you have to type it," I said.

"Uh-huh?" she said, leaning forward as though I had just promised to tell her a great secret.

"So, our typewriter's broken." I shouldn't have had to remind her of this. For years my father's beloved typewriter had been missing its *h* key. His manuscript was pocked with missing letters, and sometimes even his speech was affected. "Our 'ouse," he'd say, "is really going to 'ell." He couldn't even write his name.

"So what? Big deal! We get a new typewriter!"

172 • Christie Hodgen

"I don't want to have to buy a whole typewriter just for a stupid application."

"So we borrow one."

"But I don't know anyone with a typewriter."

"You don't know anyone, period," Teddy said, through a mouthful of ravioli.

"Dora's got one," said my mother.

"But even if I applied," I said, "it's expensive."

"So what! You *have* to go. Your father went to college, for God's sake. He wasn't exactly a road scholar. He couldn't even keep a Christmas tree tied to the car!"

"Rhodes," I said. I was trying to be nonchalant, though she had committed, right before my eyes, the unforgivable sin of mentioning something from the last months of my father's life. What the hell was wrong with her? She wasn't supposed to talk about certain things. Especially not that Christmas Eve, when we were driving our discount five-dollar tree home in my mother's hatchback, which *someone* had stuffed in the back without tying it down with string, and then the tree had started slipping and slipping, and Teddy and I said, "Hey, the tree's falling out!" and someone said, "That's impossible. A little thing called physics," and we watched in amazement as the tree slid right out of the car and onto the highway, and *someone*, we're not saying who, had to pull over and dodge traffic and risk his life to carry our cheap, last-minute celebration of the season back to safety while we all watched from the car, laughing ourselves sick.

That was the rule in our house. No one was supposed to talk about those last months. We were supposed to carry them around in the privacy of our hearts, like always.

"You just need some confidence!" she said. "Maybe you should start taking some of those puppies. Why not just try?"

"Ma," I said, "don't start."

"What?" she said. "I only want you to self-actualize!" In addition to taking Dr. Woo's pills my mother had been reading paperback self-help books that gave her an optimistic vocabulary for talking about the ways in which we suffered and failed. "You have a bright future!" she said. I could hear a trembling in her voice, a pleading and earnest quality that only appeared when she spoke of my wasted potential. Otherwise she preferred to cackle and shout her way through dialogue, pretending that life was a ball, a riot, that she wasn't the least disappointed with how things turned out. "*You're the one*," she said. "Teddy and me, we're not college material. But you are, darling." She actually reached over and patted me on the head, tried to smooth down my hair. "And you could be so *beautiful* if you tried. Look at Mia Farrow! She grew her hair out, and boy, what a difference!"

"I object!" Teddy said. He pounded his fist on the table. "I object to this perjury! This witness-badgering! I want it stricken from the record, that part about me not being college material!"

"Overruled," my mother shouted.

"Your honor, I *strenuously* object!" Teddy said. "This case is purely circumstantial."

"Fine. Sustained," my mother said. "But I'm putting out an APB on your brain."

This was a favorite act of theirs. Teddy and my mother spoke to each other almost exclusively in the dramatic language of prime-time dramas. Each night they watched actors speak the lingo of policemen and doctors and lawyers and businessmen.

These people were always trapped in the most exhilarating circumstances—having police wires taped underneath their shirts, meeting with drug lords, performing intricate surgery on innocent children, signing international corporate mergers, and hiding their mistresses in coat closets when they heard their wives' high heels clicking against the marble foyers of their mansions. My mother and brother spent almost every evening lying side by side on the sofa bed, my mother chain-smoking, Teddy reaching over to take a drag whenever she rested her cigarette in the ashtray between them, my mother scolding him.

They watched *Hill Street Blues* and *St. Elsewhere* and *Dallas* and *Miami Vice*. Their favorite was *L.A. Law*. My mother swooned whenever the blond and tanned Arnie Becker appeared onscreen. He was the character of characters—the sexy and successful divorce lawyer, the man who knew the business of breaking up better than anyone else and who therefore couldn't find happiness for himself. Teddy loved that the show featured a retarded office assistant who walked around filing and delivering mail and making innocent chitchat that unfailingly threw meaningful light on the plights of the show's anguished stars. Teddy did a great impression. During commercials he got up to refill my mother's glass of diet soda, and he came back into the room shuffling, breathing through his mouth, jerking his head slightly. "Here, pretty lady," he said, in a slow and flattened voice. "I brought a drink for the pretty lady." His eyes darted frantically. "Why is a pretty lady like you all alone in the world? I wonder," he slurred. "It doesn't seem fair."

Teddy had developed our father's old fondness for quoting famous movie and television characters. His personality was a jumble of impressions. The longer he sat in dark rooms, before glowing screens, the more characters he swallowed. He eventually stored up so many famous one-liners, like "Dynomiiiiiiite," like "Aaaaaaaaaay," like "To the moon, Alice," that he hardly needed to form words of his own. He often weaseled out of trouble by borrowing lines from our mother's favorite film. "I don't know nothing about birthing no babies," he'd say, when accused of stealing money from my mother's purse, of smoking her last cigarette. Our mother never had the heart to pursue him as he ran away from her, down the hall, scurrying with all of that prissy terror. "Frankly my dear, I don't give a damn," he'd say when she lectured him about the poor quality of his latest report card. When she was feeling down he'd put his arm around her and stare off hopefully toward the horizon and cry out in a silvery, hopeful voice: "After all, tomorrow *is* another day!"

I couldn't tell if Teddy realized how similar he was—at least in this regard—to our father. He was only seven when our father died. Did he remember?

# 17

By mid-November I had caught the attention of my guidance counselor, Miss Clapsaddle. Everything about Miss Clapsaddle suggested that she was a person who wanted to escape notice. She was short and incredibly thin. Her eyes were gray, her skin pale. Her voice was high and thin, just above a whisper. While other guidance counselors had pictures covering their desks, and tacked up on the fabric walls of their cubicles, Miss Clapsaddle's workplace was entirely unadorned. I had trouble imagining her outside of her office, as a person walking through the world, grocery shopping and such, going to the post office, buying clothes, seeing movies. It seemed to me that at the end of the day Miss Clapsaddle crawled into the bottom drawer of her filing cabinet and fell asleep.

I had hoped that Miss Clapsaddle, of all people, would appreciate when someone wanted to be left alone. But instead she called me into her office one afternoon. I sat across from her while she showed me various colorful brochures. In addition to the state schools, she told me, there were some private schools in distant locations that offered "exciting educational landscapes."

"This one doesn't even give grades," she said. "There are no tests and they don't even have classes. It's a one-on-one system where you just do your own work and then meet once a week to talk with your professors. It's very experimental and cutting-edge. I think you might like it."

"Well," I said. I often said this, as though I were preparing to say something else. But the something else rarely materialized.

"I know you're probably concerned about money," she said. "I've read your file and I realize your circumstances." She nodded her head, indicating a thick manila folder that was stuffed with paper, a bouquet of yellow and pink and blue carbon copies. I wondered what the hell was in there. I wondered what anyone at West High could possibly have to say about me. "You may not be aware of this, but there are a number of scholarships available that I think you'd qualify for. Especially with, you know," she said, nodding to the file again, "the obstacles you've overcome."

I stared at the folder. Suddenly West High seemed far more dangerous and organized than I'd ever realized. Suddenly it no longer seemed to be an asylum run by monkeys, but some kind of tricky Orwellian universe in which privacy was only an illusion. I wondered if Miss Clapsaddle could read my mind. She appeared to be eating her lunch, a small container of cottage cheese, but perhaps she was translating my thoughts.

"I know what you're thinking," she said. "You just don't want to deal with this application business. You don't want to have to make a decision right now. But it's my job to communicate to you one very simple fact: you've got to move-it-or-lose-it." It was funny to hear Miss Clapsaddle use an expression like this. She wasn't much of a hustler, much of a move-it-or-lose-it type.

"I'm just not sure I want to go to college," I said.

At this she set down her cottage cheese and straightened her posture. I'd offended her, questioned the very reason for her existence. I'd sneezed in the middle of her opera house, walked right into her temple with my shoes on. "May I ask," she said, "what other options you're considering?"

"I haven't really thought much about it," I said.

"Unfortunately you don't have the luxury of time on your side."

"I know."

"I'm expecting you to meet with me each week from now on," she said. "Kids like you go to college. They just do, and that's that."


Kids like me. What Miss Clapsaddle was referring to, I assumed, was the handful of kids in West's "honors track," a strange and isolated group brought together not so much by our superior academic skills as by our failure to thrive in all other aspects of teenage life. We were the kids who played the clarinet, ran unopposed for student council, joined the French club. At lunch we sat and discussed, in French, our upcoming tests and concerts. We talked about protractors and metronomes and scientific calculators, about the stupidity of our school's popular kids, who didn't even bother to show up for lunch anymore, having instead raced their sports cars out of the parking lot and disappeared to places so cool we had never even heard of them.

That year all the people I called my friends spoke of nothing but their college applications. They were fighting each other for scholarships and incremental changes in class rank. The fight for valedictorian was particularly gruesome. For years there had been a statistical dead heat between Patty Connors and Ben Simon. Both had straight A's, and already there was fierce debate over who would be allowed to give the big speech at graduation. It was thought that Patty Connors had a slight advantage, as she was a true senior, while Ben had been accelerated several times and was only twelve years old.

But then something unexpected had happened. In October a girl named Wei Zhu had transferred to West, bringing with her from Michigan a transcript of straight A pluses, even in gym. (She was rumored to have choreographed some kind of Olympic-medal-winning rhythm gymnastics routine, involving hoops and scarves and flags.) No one knew how this was possible, as Wei was the size of a fourth grader and seemed unable to speak English. She always sat by herself at lunch, eating elaborate meals she had brought from home—steaming brown soup in a small thermos, a bowl of rice, a container of some mysterious pink meat some people claimed was flamingo breast. The only sound Wei ever made came from her gold bracelet, which had a single charm in the shape of a heart, and which tinkled faintly as she wrote.

For weeks Patty Connors had waited for Wei to collapse in

despair, unable to take the pressure of West High. "I don't see how," Patty said, "someone who doesn't even speak *English* is going to make it through *Anna Karenina*." But Wei made it through and turned in an essay on Tolstoy that, our teacher told us, was the best she had ever read. Ms. Flores read us long passages of Wei's writing, barely able to speak in places because she was choked with tears.

Now Patty Connors and her mother were making inquiries about the legality of allowing grades from another school to enter into the battle for valedictorian. The stage seemed to be set for some kind of scandalous news story. Soon Wei would be mysteriously poisoned and unable to attend school for the rest of the year. Or Mrs. Connors would work out some arrangement with one of the gym teachers, a trade of ten thousand dollars for a B plus. In the end the truth would be discovered and Mrs. Connors thrown in jail.

These were my peers, my friends, the *kids like me*. "You haven't *applied* yet?" Patty Connors said when I returned to study hall from seeing Miss Clapsaddle. "*Zut alors!*"

I knew what I was supposed to do, that the only sensible thing was to go to college and make something of myself. The problem was, I just couldn't see it. There was nothing I really wanted to do. I didn't think I'd survive long in an office, or any kind of environment where I had to show up at a certain time and *do* something for eight hours. Maybe, I thought, I'll be a college professor. I pictured myself sitting in a book-lined office, asleep in my chair with my feet propped on my desk.

This was the closest I came to imagining a real future for myself. But even that was fleeting. Most of the time I saw myself wandering around Lincoln Street like the rest of our city's home-less people, who my mother referred to as *the Crazies*. She liked to point them out whenever we drove past them. "Look," she'd say, "there's Crazy Eddy." She had named all of them after the celebrities they resembled. Crazy Eddy was her favorite, a man who looked very much like Ed Sullivan. For a time Crazy Eddy had made his living by walking around wearing a sandwich board marked with advertisements for local businesses. But then the city had fallen on hard times and the businesses had failed, and Eddy had taken to wearing a sign that simply said "The End Is Nigh." His face always seemed to be frozen with terror.

"Wunnerful, wunnerful, wunnerful," my mother called out whenever we drove past him, sometimes splashing him with water from a puddle.

# 18

Most people thought of football season as the time of year when the school's most popular young men strapped on shoulder pads and shimmied into skintight pants and attempted to injure one another each Friday night in front of hundreds of adoring fans. Our band director, Mr. Chase, was of the opinion that football season existed for the sole purpose of showcasing the marching band. These football games gave music lovers a chance to leave the comfort of their homes and stand shivering in the cold, enduring the monotony of the actual game itself, so that they might catch a glimpse of our band as we took the field at half-time. This was Mr. Chase's solemn belief. *He actually believed this.* Each week it was his duty and pleasure to put together a masterful eight-minute medley of patriotic and popular songs, and to choreograph coordinating steps for all one hundred and fifty-seven members of the band so that we marched about the field in perfect time, forming snowflakes and crosses and hearts. No one could decipher the logic of Mr. Chase's medleys. "Louie, Louie," we played. "This land is your land. Tequila!"

Mr. Chase woke up each morning knowing that his job rested in the fickle hands of the school committee, that he'd be the first to go when it came time to make further budget cuts. Art was gone, and music was next. So he tried harder, day after day, to make our band into something special. Something he could point to with pride when the time came to defend himself. But we refused to make it easy for him, and the stress was killing him. Over the years his hair thinned and turned gray. He put on so much weight that he grew out of every pair of pants he owned, except for a pair of rust-colored corduroys, which he wore every day. He started smoking so much that he couldn't make it through a forty-minute practice without a cigarette. Several times during each rehearsal he'd turn his back on the band and light up a smoke. He'd take one drag and then stab it out on the chalkboard. "I'll stop smoking the day you go for *one minute* without screwing up!" he always said.

The more we failed, the more it seemed as though we were personally, with our own bare hands, killing him. He'd make the smallest, most precise gestures with his baton, indicating that he wanted us to play pianissimo, with a profound delicacy, but all we did was blare. Oh, the years we took away from his life. The graying hair, the circles beneath his eyes, the arthritis in his hips and elbows. It was all our fault.

A few mornings a week, our band braved the cold and practiced our formations on the football field. We did this for the sake of the Thanksgiving Day game, our most important performance of the year. Mr. Chase chain-smoked and screamed himself hoarse when we turned right instead of left, swinging our lines in such a way that *they made the whole formation look like a swastika!* "Goddamn you kids! You goddamn kids!" he'd scream. He screamed until his face was purple, until he lost his voice. "Go *left, left, left!* How many goddamned times do I have to tell you! You think this is funny? You think this is funny? Just wait till it's Thanksgiving Day and you're standing in front of the whole town and you can't tell your head from your ass! You won't be laughing then!"

There was a particular rivalry between Mr. Chase and the drummers. The percussion section was full of long-haired punks, pot-smoking know-nothings, and one of them always continued drumming after the rest of the band had stopped, sending out a few awkward beats, like coughs in a library. Teddy was the worst offender. "Teddy Hawthorne, you good-for-nothing punk!" he'd yell. "You think you're something? You think you're something? Well let me tell you something, Mr. Hotshot. Mr. *Ironic Pantsuit.* Punks like you are a dime a dozen. A dime a goddamned dozen, Mr. Big Shot, no matter what you wear. And wipe that smirk off your face!"

Teddy got kicked out of practice more often than not. He and Mr. Chase were developing a relationship that mystified the rest of the band. It was plain to see that they hated each other. Teddy often gave Mr. Chase the finger as he walked off the field, and Mr. Chase gave it back. They'd stand there, hopping up and down, giving each other the finger with all their hearts. Later, after practice, Teddy always sat in Mr. Chase's office, awaiting his daily reprimand. As we filed out of the band room we strained to see into the office through the small glass window, but it was clouded over with smoke, the commingling smoke of two cigarettes, of two people gratefully letting off steam. They got along famously.

It was strange having a brother who was so noteworthy. Every day I heard people talking about him—his latest impressions, his latest eviction from a classroom. More and more Teddy was spending his days in the purgatory of West's in-school suspension program. This was where students went when they were being punished, when they weren't allowed in the classroom but also weren't allowed to stay home. The suspension room had glass walls. When I walked by the room I could see Teddy, asleep on his desk, his head resting on a pile of books. When he was asleep he breathed through his mouth, and he looked so young, like a baby in a nursery.


It snowed all through the Thanksgiving Day game. All around us, turkeys were cooking slowly in warm ovens. Men were waking, reading their morning papers, then crumpling them in their fireplaces and striking matches and blowing tenderly on weak flames. Women stood in front of the television, watching parades, all of those ridiculous balloons and floats. They stood there hoping for nostalgia, hoping to feel the magic of the season stir inside of them, hoping that the announcers would stop their banter and talk like normal people. But they never did. "What's that sound I hear?" the announcer would ask, oh-so-cheerfully, almost maniacally, and she would actually cup her hand behind her ear, miming someone trying to hear. "Well, that's the proud beat, beat, beat of the Marching Colonials from Franklin High Band, silly!" said Mitch, her trusty counterpart. "Look at those Minutemen go!" And the women stood in their kitchens and watched for a moment as teenagers swayed their brass instruments from side to side. Then the women turned down the volume, turned away from their televisions, and basted their turkeys. This was what normal people were doing.

But Teddy and I and the rest of our high school marching band were sitting in the bleachers in our thin polyester uniforms, watching the home team take a beating. We sat next to the fourteen rusting portables and watched as flakes of snow landed on our instruments and as Mr. Chase wrung his hands, thinking of our instruments, which weren't supposed to get wet, thinking perhaps that a mouthpiece might freeze to the lips of an unfortunate band member. He paced in front of the bleachers, deciding whether to pack it in, to give up the ghost, to "call it." But he never called it. In downpours, in subzero temperatures, and on that Thanksgiving Day, in the midst of a snowstorm, Mr. Chase sat and stalled, asking the flutes if they thought he should call it. They shivered and held up their beautiful silver instruments, which were spotted with snowflakes. "Oh, you're right, I know, I should call it," he said. "But it's so close to half-time, everyone's here to see the performance."

Finally it was half-time. We marched, for once, in perfect formation. We played in tune and in time. Mr. Chase stood before

us, conducting with a light hand, with a look of utter astonishment on his face. We formed a circle, a triangle, a rhombus, a star.
And finally, as we played our finale, "I Wanna Be Loved by You,"
we marched ourselves miraculously into the letters *W, H,* and *S,*
the initials of our school. Or, as Teddy always said, Wasted, High,
and Shit-faced. And perhaps because he was for once not wasted,
not high, and not shit-faced, Teddy even managed to stop drumming when Mr. Chase gave his triumphant swoop through the
air, his cutoff.

We stood in silence for a moment and watched the first smile
we had ever seen break across Mr. Chase's haggard face. "You
sons of bitches!" he yelled, in his raspy voice. "You did it! You did
it!" And for the briefest of moments our adolescent hearts were
filled with pride. Until, of course, we turned to see that we were
utterly alone, that the game itself had been called, that everyone,
everyone had left, returning home to their crackling fires, their
browning turkeys, their Macy's Thanksgiving Day parades, to the
televised marching bands which they could silence with the flick
of a switch.

By the time Teddy and I walked home—the Buick having
refused to start that morning—our feet were numb and our
cheeks pink, which was just the way our mother liked us. We
grumbled as we walked up the driveway, expecting her to call us
her "tiny, darling *babies*," expecting her to force preventive tea-
spoons of cough medicine down our poor little hatches. We
expected to find her in the kitchen, mashing potatoes or jiggling
a cylinder of cranberry sauce out of its can. Lately she'd been
reading aloud to us from one of her psychology books. It was
important, she'd said, that we start celebrating holidays again. For

years we'd ignored them, sitting around the house watching television, like any other day. We'd endured the holiday commercials in which happy families were seated around long tables piled with food, in which prodigal sons returned home from distant lands and rang the doorbell just when their mothers had given up hope. Now it was time, my mother said, to *be* one of those families. "This is a time that can fill certain families with mental anguish," she read. "The best way to fight against this is to celebrate, celebrate, celebrate!" And so she'd filled the refrigerator with food. She had been planning on cooking enough food on Thanksgiving to last us until Christmas, on Christmas to last us until Easter.

But we returned home to an empty kitchen. We found a frozen turkey thawing on the counter, sitting in a puddle of water in its shiny plastic jacket. The oven was on, but there was nothing in it.

"What the fuck?" Teddy said. He stomped through the house. "I want something to eat!" he cried. I heard him open the door to our mother's bedroom, then slam it. "What the fuck?" he yelled.

I found my mother in the dark basement watching the Thanksgiving parade on the old black-and-white TV, which wasn't even hooked up to cable. Lines of static were running up the screen, and the sound was going in and out, but she didn't seem to notice. She was sitting on the floor, wrapped in a blanket. She was still wearing her housecoat and slippers. She didn't seem to have heard me come down the stairs.

"Ma?" I said, and she flinched.

"Oh!" she said. "Frances. I didn't hear you."

"What's going on?" I said.

"I didn't realize it was so late." Her face was expressionless. I hadn't seen her like this in a long time.

"I'm sorry, honey," she said, still looking at the television. "I'm not feeling so well." In the dark, I could see little else but the gleaming blonde of her hair. I stood there staring at her for a moment. I didn't know what to say. Finally I went upstairs and told Teddy.

"I think there's something wrong with Mom," I said. "She's just sitting downstairs watching TV. She's not even moving."

"Jesus Christ," he said. "I'm starving."

"I mean, I think there's something really wrong with her."

"What are we gonna eat?" he said.

"Teddy!" I said. "I'm serious. She's acting like Dad."

This seemed to get his attention. He sighed deeply. "Gimme a minute," he said. "I'll handle it."

Perhaps there was something to be said for being raised in front of the television, for Teddy had become an expert at navigating life's more dramatic moments. Over the years he'd watched his favorite characters deal with unwanted pregnancies, false arrests and convictions, cheating spouses, failed businesses, and the sudden appearance of evil twins. A mother in the basement—a sad widow having a bad holiday—this was nothing.

I went back downstairs and sat next to my mother. She was crying quietly, stifling herself as if she were in a public library, afraid of disturbing someone. The Rockettes were on-screen—dressed in red leotards and Santa hats—doing their big finale. They kicked and kicked. They formed a long line and rotated like the second hand of a clock. There was a band playing, and cymbals were crashing every time they lifted their legs. It was ridiculous.

"I coulda been a Rockette," my mother said. "I had the legs for it. I coulda moved to New York and lived a life of excitement and adventure. When my parents died I coulda sold the house and gone anywhere and done anything I wanted."

"I read somewhere," I said, "that the Rockettes don't make any money. I mean, it looks glamorous and everything. But they barely make enough to eat. They all live together in this tiny apartment."

My mother sighed. I was always ruining her fantasies with the factoids I'd picked up from the newspaper.

"I don't feel so good," my mother said. "I think I took too many puppies. I was feeling a little blue so I took a whole handful. They're really barking in there."

"I don't think you should take those anymore," I said.

"I *have* to," she said. "I can't live without them. I don't know how I ever lived without them." She was trembling.

We sat there as Santa paraded around New York in his giant sleigh, waving. Kids were lined in the streets, waving, jumping up and down, calling out to Santa, presumably naming their innermost desires. We watched their jubilance, their folly.

Then I heard my father's voice booming from the top of the stairs. "Frankie, Gerry," he said. "Get your fannies in the car." It was Teddy. Dressed in my father's old fatigues, wearing his old canvas hat, his black boots, his round gold-rimmed glasses. He spoke from behind a fake mustache, which looked just like our father's. My mother and I stood at the bottom of the stairs, stunned. "I mean it," he said. "Let's go. Hup two. Chum Lee's is waiting."

It was spooky, the way that Teddy had brought to life the exact tone and expression of our father's voice. He remembers, I thought. He hasn't forgotten a thing. My heart pounded. We followed him to the Buick, and climbed in reluctantly as he settled behind the wheel and adjusted the rearview exactly as my father used to. He swore elaborately as the car cranked and stalled, as he flooded the engine. "You goddamn nag," he grumbled. When the engine finally roared to life he gave the dashboard a triumphant smack, then put the car in reverse. Was he actually going to drive? Would my mother let him? She simply sat, clutching her blanket around her—she was still wearing her housecoat and slippers—as he backed down the steep driveway without looking, as he wound through the neighborhood singing "Like a Rolling Stone" through his nose, drifting carelessly all over the road, just like my father. I stared out the back window, watching the dark tracks we left in the snow, just as I had always done as a child.

We followed Teddy into Chum Lee's, where he bowed to the hostess and requested a booth, where he used my father's voice to read us the menu, joking around at first. "Shredded kittens in a savory garlic sauce," he read. And, "Sweet-and-sour hamster." Just as our father had done, he ordered spareribs and chicken fingers and beef fried rice and shrimp lo mein and a scorpion bowl, and we sat in silence under the glow of a red paper lantern and stuffed our faces and licked our fingers and leaned down to sip our liquor through long red straws, just as we had done on the last holidays our father was alive.

# 19

After her Thanksgiving breakdown my mother started taking more puppies. Litters of them. She brought home bottles marked *For the relief of headaches* and *For joint pain*, and—unbelievably—a bottle full of red capsules marked *For good luck*.

One night, when my mother asked me to fix her a drink and fetch her a headache pill, I'd taken one of each of her capsules and split them open. The headache capsule was filled with a brownish powder. The pill for joint pain contained something that looked like black honey. Good luck, apparently, came in the form of a fine white powder.

"I don't think you should take these anymore," I said, and handed her a pill.

"Dr. Woo is a very brilliant man. In China he was famous. He was like royalty!"

"I guess that explains why he's living in a studio apartment on Lincoln Street."

"You're such a pessimist," my mother said. "You should really have a puppy!"

"I don't need a puppy."

"You're about to miss all your admissions deadlines!" she said. "You're letting your whole life pass you by! It's such a waste! It's a sin!"

Sometimes I considered trying a puppy. I had to admit that my mother seemed happier. But then again, there was a shakiness to her. Her hands were always trembling. And the desperation in her voice—the strain of it, the warbling—was worse than ever. "Go away!" she'd say. "Please, go away!" And though she was supposedly instructing me to move on, to make something of myself, it sounded like something different. It sounded like the cry of someone who wanted to be left alone, fearing herself contagious.

I arrived at my last appointment with Miss Clapsaddle and found that she had arranged for Mr. Jolly to sit in on our session. When I saw them sitting together in her cubicle I stopped dead, like a person who had walked into a glass door.

"Frankie!" Mr. Jolly said. He stood up and smiled, raised his hand in the air. He wanted me to give him a high five, which I hadn't done in years, having studiously avoided him in the hallways. But I couldn't. I sat down across from Miss Clapsaddle and turned my head away from both of them.

"I've asked Mr. Jolly to join us," Miss Clapsaddle said, in the softest voice. "I hope you don't mind."

"Miss Clapsaddle tells me you're dragging your feet about college," Mr. Jolly said, settling into his chair. "Do you know why that is?"

"I don't know," I said.

"Is there a good reason you're not applying? Can you think of one good reason?"

I was staring into my lap, unable to look at Mr. Jolly. He was exactly the same, wearing one of his old classics—a purple suit with a yellow shirt and bow tie. All the old feelings started swirling around in my chest, the confusion and the crushing sadness of that first year of grief. *Frankie felt terribly betrayed by Miss Clapsaddle*, I thought. *Suddenly Miss Clapsaddle seemed like a little Napoleon, someone small but vicious, someone determined to get her way no matter what the cost. Instead of climbing into her filing cabinet after school, Frankie thought, Miss Clapsaddle probably ducked into some secret underground catacomb and spent the evening practicing judo.* I hadn't thought about myself like this in years, but now I saw that it was the kind of bad habit that stayed alive in a shallow grave, just waiting for the chance to escape.

"Are you afraid of leaving home?" Mr. Jolly said. "That's not uncommon."

"No."

"Are you acting out," said Mr. Jolly, "because you feel overshadowed by your brother?" From his breast pocket he fished out a plastic toothpick in the shape of a miniature sword, and he started slicing it between his teeth. "Teddy's pretty famous around here. Everyone's always talking about him. Do you think this is maybe your way of getting some attention?"

"No," I said.

"Don't you think it'd be nice to go off and make a new life of your own?" he said.

"I don't know."

"Don't you think it's time to seize the brass ring? You know, be a winner? Make something of yourself? Pull yourself up by the old bootstraps?" He was pointing the sword at me now, making violent little stabs in the air. "Don't you want to feel like Mickey instead of Donald? Don't you?"

*Was he still using this Mickey and Donald stuff?* Frankie wondered.

"I spent a lot of time on your recommendation," Miss Clapsaddle said. "And Mr. Jolly has written one too, at my request. The least you can do is send them in."

*Frankie tried to imagine these letters. "Frankie Hawthorne is a special case," they probably said. "For someone whose mother is a blonde waitress, and whose father killed himself, she's done pretty well in school. Though she has the personality of a saltine cracker, we think it's possible that she has hidden depths just waiting to be discovered in a wonderful university setting like yours."*

"Do we understand each other?" said Miss Clapsaddle. "Mr. Jolly and I just wanted you to know that we care about you, and that we think you have a bright future ahead of you, if you could only make some small changes."

"Try to take a more enthusiastic approach to life," said Mr. Jolly. "You know, get up each morning and jump out of bed and say: *Hello, world! Here I am!*"

"*What do you have in store for me today, world?*" said Miss Clapsaddle, in the loudest voice I'd ever heard her use. "*Whatever it is, I can make it shine!*"

"*Bring it on, world!*" Mr. Jolly said.

*"I'm somebody special,"* said Miss Clapsaddle. She was almost shouting now.

*"I, Frankie Hawthorne, deserve to be happy!"*

*"I deserve to be successful!"*

*"I have so much to offer!"*

Mr. Jolly and Miss Clapsaddle were lost in each other, shouting back and forth like lovers in a musical.

*"I've been afraid to open myself up to you, world!"*

*"But now I'm ready!"*

*"I'm excited about jumping in headfirst!"*

*"Look out, here I come!"*

For a second I thought that, if I was careful, I could escape unnoticed. But then Mr. Jolly turned to me and said, "What do you think? Are we gonna give it the old college try?" Then he reached over and punched me in the shoulder. "Whaddaya say?"

*Fuck you, Frankie thought.*

# 20

The week before Christmas Little Dora had a massive stroke. No one found her for two days. When she didn't show up for work my mother called the apartment, then stopped by on the way home from her shift. She had to get the super to unlock the door, and they found Dora on the bathroom floor. While the super called the ambulance, my mother knelt down beside Little Dora and stroked her hair. "I couldn't believe she was alive," she said. "She had peed all over herself and was just lying there helpless. She couldn't focus her eyes and she was just moaning and moaning. It was the worst thing I ever saw."

We both knew that this wasn't exactly true. We were in an elite group of people who had seen worse than that.

Little Dora had been admitted to University Hospital and would stay there until she stabilized. After that, she'd be moved into a state-operated nursing home. "Those are real shitholes," my mother said. "She doesn't have any savings, though. There's nothing else to do." Doctors were trying to determine the extent of Little Dora's brain damage. She was having trouble talking and couldn't see out of one eye. She would probably never walk again.

"Maybe," I said, "you should stop seeing Dr. Woo."

"What does Dr. Woo have to do with anything?"

"I don't know. Don't you think, I mean, I don't know. The pills? Wasn't she taking his pills, too?"

"Don't you *dare* blame this on Dr. Woo," she said. "If anything he's been keeping her alive!"

"Fine, keep taking them. Take a whole bottle! See if I care."

"Maybe I will," she said. "Now that you mention it, I really have a headache."

On Christmas Day I went to the hospital with my mother while Teddy stayed home playing the video games he'd begged my mother to buy him. She'd asked him to come along with us but he was too engrossed in his fictional war, guiding his GI—whom he'd named Rex—through a dark, enemy-infested jungle. "No way," he'd said, without even looking away from the television.

"It seems to me," my mother said, "that Little Dora has been very nice to you over the years. And the least you can do is take an hour out of your life to visit her."

Teddy didn't say anything. Rex was in mortal danger, firing a machine gun while swinging across a swamp on a vine.

"It seems to me," my mother said, "that in addition to being obnoxious you also used to be cute sometimes. You used to be nice."

"In addition to being annoying," Teddy said, "you used to be cool sometimes."

"Theodore James Hawthorne," my mother said. She had a hand on her hip and was trying to be authoritative, but it was difficult to pull off. She was wearing a matching hat and mitten set, pink with a giant pom-pom on top of the hat, and a smaller pom-pom dangling from the cuff of each mitten. It was a gift I'd made her in a weekly craft class West High liked to call "enrichment."


University Hospital welcomed us with the usual stench of hospitals—a mix of iodine and harsh solvents and something faintly metallic, like fear. They'd decorated for Christmas, put up a tree in the lobby and draped a garland around the nurses' stations, but the effect was more depressing than cheerful. From the time I'd spent in the VA with my father I knew that hospitals were worlds unto themselves—with their own clocks and calendars and languages—and that any connection they tried to make with the outside world was awkward, even painful.

Little Dora shared a room with a very old woman who, at first glance, seemed to be dead. She was lying motionless in her bed, covered to the neck with a sheet, her eyes shut and her mouth open. Next to her bed was a nightstand with a bunch of rotten bananas sitting on it, and a small purple teddy bear with a distinct expression of suffering on its face.

The room was separated by three sheets hanging from the ceiling, which were supposed to pull together and create a veil of privacy. But there were cracks between the sheets, and the sheets themselves were so thin you could see shapes and shadows behind them.

On the other side of the curtains was Little Dora, who looked nothing like herself. She was wearing a green hospital gown, and there were tubes and wires snaking out from the gown's neck and sleeves. She wasn't wearing her glasses or makeup, and her hair lay flat against her head. Her face was slack on the left side, her mouth downturned in the corner, her left eye unhinged.

My mother had seen this before and was unfazed. "Hello, hello!" she said. "Merry Christmas! Look who I brought! It's Frankie! Frankie's here to see you!" She was speaking very slowly and loudly, as though in addition to Dora's other problems, she was now deaf and retarded.

Little Dora made a sound of greeting. Her voice was hoarse and she had to push everything out the side of her mouth, like a ventriloquist.

"It's really snowing out there," my mother said. "Look at the hat Frankie made me. Isn't it cute? Look, there's mittens, too. Look what else." She raised up the paper shopping bag she had brought with her. It was full of unexciting items from the drugstore that she had bought and wrapped up as if they were actual presents. "I got you some little presents here. There's lots of nice things in here."

She set the bag at the foot of the bed and started unpacking it, unwrapping each present and holding it up for Dora's approval, then placing the presents all around Little Dora's feet. One by one she unwrapped a box of tissues, bottles of hand lotion and nail polish, tubes of lip balm, a makeup compact, a hairbrush, an issue of *People* magazine. She kept chatting the whole time, saying things like, "I know how you love *People*. There's a piece in here about Tom Cruise, your favorite. He's such a hunk! Look, there's a picture of him without his *shirt*! Can you see that? Here, let me hold it up close so you can see it."

I didn't know how my mother could keep on talking like that, on and on, with no replies or encouragement of any kind. This seemed to be a quality common to all mothers. Often I saw women and their babies in the grocery store, and the women were always talking away, saying things like, "After we finish here we'll go home and have a nice lunch, then change your diaper and have a nice nap. Doesn't that sound good? A nice lunch and then a new diaper and then a nice nap? Doesn't that sound nice?" All the while the babies were just sitting in their carts chewing on plastic keys. I didn't know how they could stand it, either of them.

"And last but not least," my mother said, "the *crossword*!"

Little Dora moaned something, some two-syllable desire.

"I know you want Charlie, honey," my mother said. "I tried every number in your book but I haven't tracked him down. Nobody knows where he is. But I left a note for him taped to your door. I bet you anything he's going to show up for Christmas. Don't you worry."

Little Dora moaned again, the same two syllables.

"Charlie's coming," my mother said. "I can feel it in my bones."

But it didn't seem to me that Dora was asking for Charlie. It seemed to me she was asking for something else.

"Let's do the crossword, shall we?" my mother said. She sat at the foot of Dora's bed and snapped the newspaper open. My mother had been a crossword junkie for as long as I could remember. She'd work them while watching television. Even though our local paper was pathetic and a toddler could solve its puzzles, my mother was often stumped. She didn't have a mind for synonyms and something about filling in a blank really threw her off. I'd be in my room doing homework and she'd yell to me from the living room, wanting to know something painfully obvious, like a three-letter word for *automobile*. Sometimes this was the only communication between us in a given day. Once, on Valentine's Day, she kept missing the easiest clues. "I need a four-letter word for *amor*," she cried. "A four-letter word for *zero*. A four-letter precedent to *bird*. A four-letter word for *pain*."

"Love," I told her. "Love, love, love."

My mother started in. "One across. Five-letter word for *St. Nick*," she said. "Hmmm. St. Nick."

Little Dora moaned *Santa* but my mother couldn't interpret it. "What?" she said.

"Santa."

"Well, let's just leave it blank," she said. "Let's move on and see what else we can fill in. One down is six letters and the clue is *Santa's coach*. Let's see."

Suddenly Dora's roommate burst out moaning. It was loud and tremulous, like the bleat of a goat. It went on and on, rising and falling.

"God," I said.

"I don't think so, honey," said my mother. "It's six letters."

"Should we do something?" I said, nodding toward the room-mate. "Should we call the nurse?"

"Oh," said my mother. "Don't worry about her. She does that all the time. She's not even awake."

I peeked through the curtains at the old woman, who indeed appeared to be asleep. She was so still that it didn't seem possible such a terrible moaning could be coming from her. It seemed to me she must be dying, that she was dying right there in front of us, dying alone at that very moment, and no one was doing anything about it. There was no one to usher her from this life, just a cheap purple teddy bear that looked like a vending-machine prize won for a quarter.

It was too awful. I turned away and stared out the window at the hospital's other wing, which angled away from us. Like our wing it was six floors of gray concrete, each floor a long stretch of tiny windows. And inside every one of them, I imagined, some-one was lying in bed this Christmas Day, perhaps staring out at me, or at the gray sky above us, or the falling snow, or the traffic going by on Route 9, a line of tiny cars speeding past the hospi-tal without a thought to what was happening inside, the suffer-ing and the loneliness, the cries of pain and boredom, the desperate longing for escape. Still the moaning went on. And I wondered what the point was—going off to college, starting careers and families—if we all ended up like this in the end. If at the end of our lives we'd all be stranded in hospital rooms, moan-ing and murmuring, helpless and inscrutable as the day we were born, what was the fucking point?

My mother was still carrying on with her crossword. "Blank *Cane*," she said. "What ends in *cane*? Four letters."

Little Dora spoke again, the same two-syllable desire she'd

uttered before. She was looking right at me, this time. She knew I'd understood her before.

"Oh, *candy!*" my mother said. "You're right! It's *candy!*"

But Dora wasn't saying candy. Nor was she asking for Charlie. What she wanted, what she was really asking for, was a terrible act of love, a little something in return for the sympathy she'd always shown me.

She spoke again, this time with all the effort she could muster. This time it was so clear that even my mother couldn't deny it. "Kill me," she said.

"Well," my mother said. She set down the crossword and picked up the hairbrush she'd brought from the drugstore, started making little sweeps at Dora's hair. "Let's see what we can do about this do."

In January Little Dora moved to a state-run nursing home forty minutes away, and my mother visited her when she could. "You wouldn't believe," my mother told me, "what a *shithole* she's in." According to my mother it was more of a madhouse than a nursing home. There were people wandering the halls in their pajamas, screaming all kinds of nonsense. On Little Dora's hall there was a woman who sat in her room calling out to anyone who passed by. "Come visit me!" she cried, all day long, in the voice of a crow. "Don't visit them, visit me!"

"God," my mother said once. "It's so awful! I can't wait till she *dies!*" Presumably she meant the crow woman, but I wasn't entirely sure.

# 21

Meanwhile Teddy was locked down in an institution of his own. At the start of the new semester he had been put on academic and disciplinary probation, and threatened with the prospect of having to repeat his freshman year. Faced with this possibility, he started attending classes again, and sitting through them without speaking or even moving. He stopped dressing up and putting on shows in the hallway. It was as if he'd been lobotomized, which seemed to please all his teachers. Deep down, this was what they wanted from us.

My mother had grounded Teddy. It was the first time she'd ever tried to impose discipline on him, and for a few weeks he was stunned into submission. He spent all of his time in his bedroom watching television. Occasionally he'd venture out to the kitchen to make himself something to eat, and we'd hear him rifling through the refrigerator. He'd take everything out and make what he pleased, then go off to his room without putting anything away. Sometimes I'd pound on his door and try to get him to come out to the kitchen and clean up after himself. "We're not your personal servants," I'd say, or words to that effect. And Teddy would say something along the lines of, "Eat shit and die." We'd keep at it until Teddy turned up his record player so loud that nothing else could be heard but the voice of Bob Marley, who was always singing about an absence of women and tears.

O n e   d a y I was sitting in study hall and I heard my name burst forth from the intercom. *Frankie Hawthorne*, said the school secretary, *please report to Miss Clapsaddle immediately*.

I had been expecting this. The application deadlines had come and gone and I hadn't submitted to a single school. I'd have to sit there and listen to Miss Clapsaddle tell me about all the terrible things that would become of me. Then she'd outline a plan in which I would apply to community colleges—which were still taking applications and would let anyone in, even a monkey— and transfer out after my first year.

"So?" Miss Clapsaddle said when I sat down across from her. "Were you going to keep me in the dark forever?"

"Well," I said.

"New York!" she said, and clapped. "They called me for your recs and transcripts. You wrote that they were forthcoming from guidance but they never, you know, forthcame. So I sent them!"

"No I didn't," I said.

"There's no use hiding it. I know you applied to NYU. I'm thrilled! We should start talking about scholarships!"

"I really didn't apply," I said.

Miss Clapsaddle stared at me over the top of her reading glasses. As a person without a sense of humor she was probably always suspecting that people were putting her on in some way she couldn't understand. "Well," she said, demonstrating to me once and for all the true meaning of *furrowed brow*, "*someone* did."

Later that day I learned the awful truth, that my mother had applied to college for me. She'd forged applications to all of our state schools, plus a few schools in New York City. "I sent them some of your cartoons," she said. "I wrote a little essay. I'm sorry."

"You're *sorry*?" I said. I tried to imagine the essays she'd written in my name. They were probably full of words like *expecially* and *irregardless*, and just the thought of them made my heart race.

"You'll thank me later!" she said. "When those letters come and they accept you, your whole life will change! You'll go off to school—maybe even New York!—and you'll take art classes and meet new people. You *will*, honey! You'll be so happy. You'll thank me!"

"Yeah, thanks," I said. "Thanks in advance. Thanks a whole lot for treating me like a fucking baby. Like I can't make my own decisions."

"But you can't!" she said. She was starting to cry now. "You can't make a decision to save your life! To save your life!"

"Oh, *please*," I said.

"You don't want to end up like me. Working in a restaurant

and getting old and ugly. All alone." She was really crying now, barely getting the words out.

"You're not miserable," I said. "You're not ugly."

"Yeah, right," she said, and flung herself across the foldout couch. "Look me in the face and say that."

It was true that my mother was aging badly. While her hair was still long and famously blonde, the rest of her was, as she liked to say, "going to hell in a handbag." Her once-brilliant teeth were now hopelessly stained from her two worst habits: chain-smoking and the almost ceaseless consumption of instant coffee, which she loved and hated with equal passion. "This is *terrible*," she'd say, slurping at a cup so hot that she winced. She liked the punishment of it, the searing of her lower lip, the faint taste of aluminum foil. Occasionally I saw her scooping up coffee flakes with her finger and spreading them on her tongue, where they dissolved slowly and bitterly. "God, that's good," she'd say.

"I'm sorry," she said. "I just wanted you to be happy."

"Great," I said, all teenage sarcasm. "I've never been happier!"

"You'll see," she said. "You'll go off to school and you'll thank me later."

She had said the same thing to my father, and it had pretty much killed him.


During the next several weeks I didn't speak to my mother. And when she spoke to me, it was only indirectly. She kept putting on little skits between herself and one of my childhood teddy bears, whose name was Squiggy, and who had been given to me as a sorry replacement for the fallen Boris. I had never loved Squiggy and so his fur was still soft and fluffy, the red bow around his neck still neatly tied. I'd be eating breakfast and my mother would sit across from me and prop the bear next to her. "It must be nice to be young and have your whole life ahead of you," she'd say to him. "When you're young you have all kinds of opportunities."

"That's absolutely right, Gerry," the bear would say. My mother made him speak in a growl, and she often made him chuckle like Ed McMahon.

"If *I* were young I wouldn't go around complaining all the time and moping," my mother said. "I'd make the most of life. I'd think about all the other people in the world who are starving and living in huts with flies crawling all over their faces, and I'd say to myself, *You know what, self? If my biggest problem is that everyone wants me to go to college but I just don't feel like it, maybe I should stop being such a baby and change my attitude.*"

"I couldn't agree with you more," said Squiggy.

I knew that my mother was waiting for me to grab the bear by the neck and throw him across the room, or perhaps go after him with a knife. I also knew that what my mother hated most in the world—what really drove her crazy—was silence. And so we carried on like this.

The worst of it was that I knew my mother was right. I knew that Miss Clapsaddle was right, and even—God help me—Mr. Jolly. I should go off to school and be happy for the chance. The only problem was that every time I tried to imagine all the details coming together—acceptance and scholarships, stuffing everything I owned into a duffel bag and taking a bus to New

York—things took a bad turn in my mind. As soon as I stepped off the bus I imagined that someone would punch me in the stomach and steal my bag, and I'd be left on a bustling street corner with no money and no idea where to go. Finally I'd gather my wits and decide to cross the street in search of a pay phone, but then I'd be run over by a cab and killed.

On rare occasions when I actually managed to imagine myself in a college class, things were no better. I saw myself sitting at an easel, attempting to draw some naked old man who was shivering in the middle of the room, and I'd be so lost in pity for this man—who could only be modeling naked because he was broke and hungry—that I wouldn't be able to draw anything. When my teacher walked up and demanded I draw something, I'd only be able to draw a silly cartoon, a figure reduced to its most obvious components. Seeing this, the teacher would cast me out of her classroom. "What does this look like, the funny pages?" she'd say. "Do I look funny to you?"

"No," I'd say. And indeed she wouldn't. In my mind my art teacher wore a black dress and a black beret, and her lips were blood red. There was nothing funny about her.

"Get out!" she'd say. She and the other students would stand with their arms crossed as I gathered up my things and fled in shame. These students would have gone to private schools and taken all kinds of art classes, while I'd learned to draw from a pamphlet that had fallen out of a cereal box.

In any scenario I imagined, I always came running back home before I'd even been gone for a week.

———

The winter dragged on and we were all just killing time. The days were bleak and cold, and we didn't so much live them as simply cross them off the calendar. People at school were waiting to hear from the colleges they'd applied to, and they talked of little else. Even the fight for valedictorian had stalled out and died. It looked like Wei Zhu's grades would stand, and there was nothing Patty Connors could do about it.

Our family kept unraveling. No one was speaking to anyone, unless you counted my mother and Squiggy, who had developed a hell of a friendship. "This is the most pleasant relationship I've ever been in," my mother told him one morning at breakfast. "You're not only a good listener, you always say just the right thing to make me feel better."

"You're a lovely person," Squiggy said. "It's about time someone gave you the love and attention you deserve."

"I guess you're right."

"Wait till Frankie goes off to college and Teddy winds up in jail. Then it'll be just the two of us. There won't be anyone around to drag down the mood."

"I can hardly wait."

"Maybe you should think about converting Frankie's bedroom to an exercise room. You could get a stationary bike. Or one of those rowing machines."

"What a wonderful idea! Maybe I will!"

In March, in addition to the usual miracle of spring—blades of grass working themselves up through the cold earth, leaves squeezed from dry twigs—something truly strange happened: my mother fell in love. She

came home from her breakfast shift one afternoon and she was actually humming to herself. "La-da-dee," she said, flipping through the mail, which as usual was nothing but bills. "La-da-dum."

"Hi, honey!" she said when she caught me staring at her. "Isn't it a beautiful day? Have you been outside? It's actually sunny out!" She was acting like nothing had happened between us.

"That's nice," I said.

Later that day I found her standing in front of the bathroom mirror scrutinizing herself. She was wearing a red dress she had bought at Filene's Basement years before but had never actually worn. Tags were still hanging from the sleeves. "Honey," she said, and twirled around. "Do you think I can still get away with this dress? Give me your honest opinion."

The dress had a low V-neck and was cinched at the waist with a black patent-leather belt. It was too tight and there was something wrong with the sleeves, which seemed to have been mis-sewn in some typical Filene's Basement way. But still, my mother looked the best I'd seen her in years.

"Can I get away with this? Am I too old?"

"No," I said. Which could be interpreted in two ways. "Where are you going, anyway?"

"I have a date!" she said. "I was visiting Little Dora in that *shit-hole* and I met the most wonderful man in the hallway. He was visiting his grandmother and we started talking. He said, *Friendly's, I love Friendly's*, because I was wearing my uniform. And I said, *Well you'll have to come in some time for a cup of coffee*. And then he said he'd really like that, but he didn't live in town. And I said, *Neither do I*. And it turned out he lives just a mile away, and practically right on top of Friendly's! So we started chatting and chatting, and we were standing there in the parking lot by my car *forever*." She kept twirling around, making the skirt of her dress flare out. "So it turns out we have all this stuff in common. Then he said, *What are you doing later?* And I said, *Nothing!* I mean, I know all the books tell you you're supposed to play hard to get, but I couldn't help it! I think I'm in love!"

I rolled my eyes and crossed the hall into my room.

"What?" she said. "I'm not allowed to be in love?"

"You just *met* him," I said.

"Sometimes you just know," she said. "I think Jim feels the same way. His name's Jim, by the way."


**From then on** it was nothing but Jim, Jim, Jim. My mother saw him every day, meeting him for breakfast or lunch or dinner, depending on her schedule. On her days off, Jim took her to the movies and to concerts, and once they even went to a play. After she came home from a date my mother would wait a few minutes for Jim to get home, then call him. "I miss you already," she said. They'd talk for hours, and every few minutes my mother would laugh—sometimes giggling, and sometimes bursting out in hysterics. "Stop, stop!" she'd cry, stamping her foot on the kitchen floor, making the whole house shake. "Oh, you're killing me, you're killing me! I'm *dying!*"

My mother had dumped her other boyfriends after just a few weeks. This seemed to be the span of time necessary to find out the awful truth about someone, and I kept waiting for her to discover something hideous about Jim. But she kept coming home with glowing reports, chattering on and on about Jim's greatness. He was smart, he was handsome, he was funny. He worked as a foreman for a construction company, and in his spare time he bought old houses and remodeled them, then sold them at a profit. With lots of hard work and diligence, he had saved enough money to bring his entire family here, and they all lived together in a three-decker Jim had remodeled himself. We call it *Casa Martinez*, my mother told us one morning at breakfast. "It's a *blast* over there. His parents live there, and two of his brothers and their families. There's a bunch of little kids and they're always having birthday parties. I can't wait to take you there and introduce everyone!"

"Martinez?" said Teddy. "What kinda name is that?"

"He's from Puerto Rico," our mother said.

"Oh my *God*," said Teddy. "Oh, *man*." He snorted.

"And what exactly is the problem?" she said, straightening in her chair.

"No problem," said Teddy. "No problem at all."

For years our city had been grappling with something that people called "the Puerto Rican Problem." There were always news stories about the wave of immigration to our city, how it was twenty times higher than the national average, and that the trend was growing into "epidemic proportions." The news stories usually focused on how the Puerto Ricans were taking all the jobs, or how the Puerto Ricans were just loafing around on welfare—stories that couldn't simultaneously be true. Earlier that week Chet Burns had run a story on the Puerto Rican "gangs" that stood on street corners. The shocking truth about these gangs, he said, was that they were not actually standing around waiting to kill white people, as commonly thought. Rather, they were gangs of people who were simply hoping to be employed for the day. "People come by in pickup trucks and load these immigrants into the back. Then they drive them to a warehouse, or some other place of employment, and pay them five dollars for a day's work." While this was illegal, Chet said, it was a nice work pool for some struggling local employers. "And," he added, "ordinary folks can stop by and pick up someone to clean their entire house for five dollars!"

"Jim is the most wonderful man I ever met," my mother said. "Once you meet him, you'll see."

But Teddy and I didn't want to see. Apparently we had a problem with Jim being so charming and flawless. Apparently we had something of a *Puerto Rican Problem*. We refused to meet Jim. It wasn't something we'd planned in advance, and we never acknowledged it to one another, but somehow we always managed to disappear whenever Jim came around. Our mother would try to trap us by having him show up unannounced, but as soon as we saw him pull up to the house in his blue pickup we'd sneak out the back door, hopping the fence into the Weatherbees' backyard (the house was still sitting empty, with Midge Durdle's sign collapsed on the front lawn) and crossing around to the side, then out to the street. We'd walk together down Lincoln, killing time like we'd always done when we were kids. We hung out at the pizzeria and in the parking lots of gas stations. Sometimes we'd see a movie. We'd return home late in the evening and our mother would be stretched out on the sofa bed watching television, eating from a half-gallon carton of ice cream. "I don't know what the hell is wrong with you two," she'd say. "I don't know why you can't take five minutes out of your lives and meet someone."

"Oops," Teddy would say. "I guess I forgot."

"I don't know why you can't be happy for me," she said. "After everything I've been through."

"We're happy for you," I said.

"Like hell you are," she said.

After a few weeks of this our mother gave up trying to introduce us to Jim, gave up on us altogether. She started spending all of her time at Casa Martinez. Some nights she didn't even come home. When my college acceptances came in the mail—two of them with scholarships, one from our state school and one from NYU—she wasn't even around to hear about it.

I had to make a decision and mail an acceptance within a few weeks. I kept going over the options in my head. As planned, I could skip college and continue working at the grocery store, maybe move into an efficiency apartment. I wouldn't have any furniture, and as there would be nothing to do in the apartment I'd spend most of my life walking up and down Lincoln, occasionally stopping to buy food from gas station vending machines. Perhaps I'd invest in a small radio and I'd walk around with it pressed against my ear, listening intently, as if there were something very important being broadcast only to me.

Or I could go to school and lose myself in a crush of humanity. I could be one of thirty-thousand students at a state college, which I imagined to be exactly like high school, only bigger.

Then there was New York, which I had only seen on television and could scarcely imagine. I saw myself lost in a mob in Times Square at New Year's, or lining the streets for the Macy's parade, waving my arms as the floats passed by, waving in a way that would be interpreted as a greeting but was really a cry for help.

I figured it didn't much matter what I decided. I was a social failure, a loner at heart, and it was only a matter of time before I wound up walking the streets like the Hawthornes who had gone before me, like one of the Crazies. My mother would wave to me when she passed me in her car, saying to Jim, "Look! It's Crazy Mia Farrow! Doesn't she look like Mia Farrow, only crazier?"

# 22

One night Jim pulled up to the house in his blue pickup and Teddy and I raced each other out the back door as usual. "I'm going to the movies," he told me as we were cutting across the Weatherbees' backyard. "You can come if you want." This wasn't exactly a warm invitation, but still it was nice to be reunited with Teddy, bound by a mutual distrust of a man we had never even met.

"Okay," I said.

On the way to the movies Teddy veered off the sidewalk and walked across the parking lot of an abandoned gas station. "Where are you going?" I said.

"You'll see."

The gas station was a small brick building with its windows

boarded up. Vandals had made their mark on the boards with spray paint. I WUZ HERE, someone had written. And, on another board: FUCK YOU. It seemed to me they had covered everything, written a history of the world in two sentences. This was pretty much all there was to say.

There was a dumpster sitting out back and Teddy positioned himself behind it, then lit up a joint. He smoked like an expert. "Dude," he said, passing me the joint. "You need to learn how to chill out. You're always walking around with this look on your face."

"No I'm not," I said.

"Dude!" he said. "It's like *this*." And he made a face of astonishment, wide-eyed and frantic, as though he'd just been slapped. Then he started looking all around, like he was trying to figure out who'd hit him.

"I don't make that face," I said, though I was making it at that exact moment.

"Just take a smoke," he said.

I did. I felt a burning in my lungs but I didn't choke the way I'd seen people do on television. My lungs, I figured, were already broken in. Our house had been so full of smoke for so long that the curtains and the wallpaper had taken on a brownish tint.

"Hold it in," he said. "Hold it, hold it."

We passed the joint back and forth. Teddy inhaled as if his life depended on it. The joint shriveled away in less than a minute, and we started off down Lincoln again.

"You feel good yet?" Teddy said.

"I don't know."

"Wait a sec."

The theater was on historic Front Street, by the lake. Long ago someone had had the bright idea of dividing up some of the city's abandoned mills and converting them into business space. Like everything else the idea had taken hold at first, and then fizzled. Many of the shops and restaurants had already gone out of business, their storefront windows circled over with soap. The theater was barely hanging on. It had a single screen which the owner had devoted to revivals of movies no one wanted to see. The owner was a short bald man with beady eyes and horse teeth, and he was the theater's sole employee. He'd sell us our tickets and then serve us our popcorn. Before each movie started he stood before the screen and gave a little speech. "Hello," he'd say. "My name is Herman and I'd like to thank you for choosing Herman's theater this evening. Should you need anything please feel free to ask." Then he'd scurry back to the projection booth.

That night Teddy and I were the only patrons, and the movie was *Mary Poppins*. I'd seen it as a kid and I had a vague idea of what to expect: the story of a mysterious nanny who drops from the sky into the dull, orderly lives of the Banks children, and turns their world of rigid discipline into something magical. There'd be moments when Mary and the kids would suddenly stop what they were doing and look at one another, and they'd start singing in perfect pitch about cleaning up their nursery, and everyone in the audience was supposed to ignore the fact that people didn't normally communicate in this way, that orchestra music didn't usually appear out of nowhere, and that the children couldn't possibly already know all the words to the songs they were singing, not to mention the choreographed dance steps.

But I'd forgotten about Dick Van Dyke's character, Bert the chimney sweep, the Cockney foil to Mary's flawless English. In one scene Bert and Mary took the Banks kids on something called a *jolly holiday*, which involved the four of them jumping into a portrait and inhabiting an animated countryside full of dancing penguins and talking farm animals. It occurred to me that the pot was kicking in. Suddenly I was convinced that the world was full of people like Bert and Mary—people who seemed ordinary, but who in fact led secret lives in which they could defy physics in all kinds of ways, flying and turning invisible, changing the weather with the snap of their fingers. Maybe, I thought, people like Crazy Eddy are actually superheroes, and their lives are far more glamorous and interesting than anyone suspected. Suddenly it didn't seem fair that the rest of us— though we had the advantage of warm homes to live in and plenty of food to eat—had to go through life as regular fools, weighed down by the laws of gravity.

During the movie I kept looking over at Teddy, and realized I hardly recognized him. At some point without my noticing he had developed an underbite, and his jaw stuck out defiantly. His hair had grown long, down to his shoulders, and his eyebrows had filled out into a dramatic arch. I wondered how I had continued to see him as the old Teddy, little old Teddy in the striped shirt.

Toward the end of the movie Teddy turned to me and said, "Quit staring at me, you retard." Then he punched me in the shoulder.

But I couldn't stop looking at him. Everything was changing! It felt like I was seeing things for the first time, seeing them as they actually were.

In the last scene Mary packed her bags while the kids begged her to stay. "Don't you love us?" they said. And Mary said, "What do you think would become of me if I loved all the children I took care of?" in a no-nonsense manner indicating that she did not, in fact, love the Banks children. So the kids went off with their father—who had learned to love them in the course of the plot—and Mary stood on the front steps watching them leave. Then the handle of her umbrella—a talking parrot—piped up and said how obvious it was that she loved those children. But Mary simply smiled and opened her umbrella to the wind, which swept her away, and she rose with a stoic expression, high above the trees and rooftops of London.

"Let's go," Teddy said, pushing past me into the aisle. "That movie was so *gay*."

But I sat there through the very end, until Mary was just a smudge in the corner of the screen, until she had disappeared entirely. Something about this scene was speaking to me. I imagined myself floating away to some unknown place, a place where nobody knew me, or knew about my family. The feeling of it flashed through me, and instead of the terror I usually felt there was a strange sense of freedom. *If I stay here,* I thought, *just what do you think would become of me?* My heart was racing.

I caught up with Teddy in the lobby. Herman had covered the walls in framed posters from old movies, which he was trying to sell for three hundred dollars apiece. Teddy was examining a picture of Groucho

Marx, who was looking up and away from the camera as if the presence of an admirer was a great bore. I stood next to him and we didn't speak for a long moment.

"You okay?" he said.

"Fine," I said, shoving popcorn in my mouth.

"Let's get outta here. God, that movie was so fucking *retarded*."

We walked past Herman, who was sitting behind the popcorn counter, asleep in his chair, his mouth hanging open. Teddy fished a piece of popcorn from my bag and aimed it right at Herman's mouth. But he missed, and the popcorn landed in the pocket of Herman's shirt.

Halfway home we saw Crazy Eddy coming toward us. Just as we were passing him Teddy raised a fist in the air and yelled, "The end is nigh!"

"The end is nigh!" Eddy yelled. His voice was loud and reedy, and he spoke out the side of his mouth, just like Ed Sullivan.

We made it home and I walked straight to my room and collapsed on my bed, too tired even to change out of my clothes. The next morning I woke early, feeling groggy and sad. There was a horrible taste in my mouth and my head was pounding. The smell of pot was everywhere, sweet and rotting, on my clothes and sheets and even on my skin. Everything that had been clear the night before seemed cloudy again, and I wondered how Teddy could stand to wake each morning to a disappointment like this. I wondered how long a person could possibly stand it.

Still, without quite knowing why, I walked to the post office that afternoon and mailed my acceptance to New York.

# 23

Finally it was graduation day. The ceremony was held in our school's auditorium. Instead of being a thoughtful or inspiring evening, it turned out to be just another series of lectures we had to sit through while uncomfortable in our seats and clothes, while hungry and wondering what there was waiting for us in the refrigerator when we got home.

Finally it was time for the last speech, Wei Zhu's valedictory address. She had to stand on a step stool in order to reach the podium's microphone. "Good evening," she said, in the softest voice. These were the first words we had ever heard her speak. All year we had assumed that she didn't know English, but now it appeared she knew the language better than the rest of us.

"In my country," she said, with no trace of an accent, "baby girls are not welcome in some families. So when I was born my parents abandoned me in a field. It was only through the grace of God that someone heard my cries, and I was rescued and brought to an orphanage, and then adopted by a wonderful family, who eventually brought me to live here in the United States. Now I stand here today about to start my studies at Harvard University. When I think of the incredible luck I have been granted by God, I find that there are no words to express my gratitude. I want to thank everyone here at West High for being so kind and welcoming to me. I wish everyone the best of luck. May God shine his face upon you, as he has me. Thank you."

There was a profound silence. It was embarrassing to think how petty we'd been, carrying on about our own little problems when all along, in China, there had been babies crying for mercy in open fields.

After the ceremony everyone threw their caps in the air and milled around for a few minutes, hugging each other and signing yearbooks. Vows were being spoken all around me. "We'll keep in touch!" people were saying. And, "This summer's going to be so awesome!" In my yearbook people wrote less enthusiastic comments. *Good luck in New York*, said one. *Hope you don't get mugged.*

I fought my way out of the auditorium and into the lobby. I was looking for my mother, who was supposed to have come to the ceremony straight from work. I wasn't sure if she'd made it. The lobby was packed with parents and grandparents. Everyone was posing for pictures and flashes were going off everywhere.

It was almost impossible to move. I kept getting pushed and jos-
tled, squashed into people I didn't know. At one point I was
pushed against—of all people!—Midge Durdle. She was wearing the same red suit and forced smile she wore in her FOR SALE
picture. She appeared to be alone, standing there for no good
reason, perhaps looking for someone interested in buying a
fixer-upper.

Finally I caught sight of my mother, who was all the way
across the lobby. She was still in her Friendly's uniform and she
was turning around in circles looking for me. Now and then
she'd stand up on her tiptoes and call my name. I was about to
wave to her when I noticed a man standing beside her. He was
the same height as my mother, but much broader. He had an
honest face, round and handsome, with a straight nose and large
brown eyes. He wore his hair in a crew cut, and he was dressed
in a dark suit with a bright red tie. As I got closer to them I saw
that Jim was holding a bouquet of flowers in one hand. His other
hand was resting gently against my mother's back, in a way that
seemed very protective. For a moment they were still and it
seemed to me that they were like a sculpture, a single figure that
had been destined all along, trapped in a block of marble and just
waiting to be freed.

*After three months of avoiding him, Frankie thought, now she was
going to have to meet Jim. Frankie could tell just by looking at Jim that
her mother was right: that once she met him, she'd see that he was a good
guy, and she'd wonder why she'd put it off for so long. That bitch! thought
Frankie. She considered turning away and leaving them there, driving off
in the Buick and never coming home. But her mother was still looking
around and calling out for her. "Frankie!" she cried. And the sound of it*

*was so hopeful that before she knew it Frankie was standing on her toes
and calling back. "I'm right here," she said, and waved.*

Then it was summer, the last hundred days of my life at
home. We were all busy. My mother was working double shifts
at Friendly's, and she spent most of her free time with Jim. Teddy
spent his mornings in summer school and his afternoons working in the deli of the Big G Grocery. I'd quit the grocery and
started working a job I hoped would be more fulfilling.

I worked in the cafeteria at the VA, and my job was very simple. People came through the line with their trays at lunchtime,
and I rang up their orders. Though the food in the cafeteria was
terrible, the vets always piled up their trays with plates of meat
loaf and mashed potatoes, with legs of fried chicken and squares
of lasagna, with fried fillets of fish, with little dishes of Jell-O,
with paper baskets of french fries and onion rings, with dimpled
plastic glasses full of soda, with Styrofoam cups of coffee and little packets of powdered creamer. They seemed to be under the
impression that the food was good, that it was something special,
and this depressed me.

I could never bring myself to charge them full price. They'd
come through with three entrées and two desserts, and I'd ring
them up for an ice cream cone. Some of the older vets were
regulars, coming in at least once a week, and they seemed to
have caught on to the fact that I undercharged. Sometimes
they looked at me skeptically when I announced their total,
raising an eyebrow, then peering guiltily into the depths of
their wallets.

I kept waiting for my supervisor, Betty, to notice what I was doing and fire me. But she only stood at her register poking away at the keys, counting out change from the drawer, grabbing the nickels and dimes and pennies with her swollen arthritic fingers. She was oblivious.

I'd taken the job at the VA because I'd loved going there as a kid. For years Teddy and I had accompanied our father to his appointments, and afterwards we'd always gone down to the cafeteria for lunch. It had been exciting at the time, getting to go through the line and pick out whatever we wanted, filling our trays with baskets of french fries and dishes of ice cream. My father would sit at a table by the window and read the newspaper, and Teddy and I would sit by ourselves at the next table. Sometimes the vets came and talked with us, pretending to mistake us for soldiers. *What company were you in?* they'd say. *Lemme see your scars. Lemme see your tattoos.* And we'd show them, lifting up the sleeves of our shirts and pointing to the faintest scars, scars we had received by falling from swings or falling on ice. *Wanna smoke?* they said, and offered us drags from their cigarettes, then yanked them away as soon as we reached out.

Of all the places our father had taken us, this had always been my favorite.

In addition to nostalgia I had taken the job for a second reason: Harpo. We'd never heard from him after he left, not even when my father died, and the mystery of his whereabouts had always tortured me. I figured there was a chance he had settled nearby, in some lonely efficiency apartment in the worst part of town, and he'd spent the last ten years at some anonymous job, shelving books in a library or working in the mailroom of an office building. I figured that one day he'd come into the VA for an appointment—a checkup, an eye exam, a psychiatric evaluation—and then he'd come down to the cafeteria for a cup of coffee. He'd come through the line and pay, perhaps recognizing something familiar in my face but not being able to place it. Then he'd go on about his business, sitting at one of the tables working the crossword, or talking to the other vets about their blood counts and surgical scars, and he'd never know what had happened. That he'd helped me in some strange way. That I'd been longing to see him for years. Just to look on his face briefly and know he was still alive, know he was out there, know that there was another Hawthorne like me wandering around in the world. Then I'd be able to move off to New York without any lingering questions.

In June the summer had seemed long and full of possibilities, like summers always did when they were just beginning. Every day there was the promise of seeing Harpo, or of something unexpected happening. But then the days started getting away from me and I began to feel troubled in the evenings. I was usually alone, and I'd lounge on the sofa bed, the television on but its volume turned down, and I'd listen to the sounds the house made—the refrigerator rattling in the kitchen, the hum of the dehumidifier, the occasional slap of the window shades as they shifted in the breeze. And I'd think, *Soon you will be gone. The house will still be here, these sounds carrying on just like this, but you will be gone.* Suddenly I'd regret that I hadn't accomplished anything that day. All around me people were living their lives—my mother and Teddy passing through the room now and then, on their way in and out—and I was just sitting there waiting. How long, I wondered, was I going to sit around? Before I knew it half the summer was gone.

In the mornings I drove Teddy to summer school and we had a few minutes alone together. I'd try to talk to him about his classes and he'd answer me with nothing but shrugs and scoffs, or sometimes not at all. If I kept after him long enough he'd eventually burst out with something cruel. "What's your problem?" he'd say. "Why don't you get a fucking life and leave me alone?"

Something had changed. Though Teddy had had a rough year—flunking three classes and getting in-school suspension several times for smoking—he had always balanced his bad behavior with little bouts of solicitude. At night he'd watch television with us, and entertain us with impressions. Or, when my mother was listening to her favorite radio program—*Total Request Love Songs*—he'd call in passionate dedications to her from men with names like Lorenzo and Brock. But that summer was different. Teddy was out with his friends every night, and we had no idea where he was or what he was doing. As my mother was often gone, too, there wasn't much she could do about it. Her only demand was that Teddy pass his summer school classes. "It's bad enough we have to get through four years of this," she said. "We're not going to make it through five."

When I pulled up to the school Teddy would scramble out of the car and slam the door without saying goodbye. I watched him join his new circle of friends, long-haired kids who had flunked their freshman year twice over, kids who stood around in a circle smoking Marlboro Lights with their backs turned to the world. In that circle Teddy came alive, talking and laughing, making sweeping gestures with his arms. And I wondered what it was about those kids that brought Teddy out of himself, what it was about us that shut him in.

Sometimes I sat and watched him and tried to figure how Teddy, my Teddy, had turned into this complete stranger. Once Teddy used to follow me around the house saying, "Whatcha doing?" wanting nothing more than to stand next to me. Once he went around blowing kisses to strangers in the grocery store. Once he carried with him everywhere a stuffed pig named Sherman. And though Sherman was poorly crafted—handmade of a fuzzy pink felt and stuffed with lentils, with dangling button eyes—Teddy had been convinced that Sherman was real. How he tortured himself about the mystery of Sherman's birth! Teddy had found Sherman at a yard sale, lying on his stomach on a card table and looking up desperately, hoping to be picked up and loved. And so he didn't know how old Sherman was, or what day he'd been born into the world.

"Just say his birthday is the day you bought him," I told Teddy, but this didn't satisfy him. He wanted to know the exact date and time of Sherman's birth. Sometimes for fun I'd tell Teddy that I'd spoken to Sherman and he was sad because his birthday had come and gone and no one had thrown him a party. "No he didn't!" Teddy said. "Shermy doesn't talk to you! He hates you, he hates you!" And he'd burst out crying.

Now he was just another punk who went running out the door each night when his friends pulled up in their rumbling red Camaro, their music blasting so loud you could hear it from inside the house. Now he was a kid who'd come home recently with a row of safety pins pierced through his left ear. "What the hell is this?" I'd said, tugging on my own ear.

"Mark did it," he said, referring to Mark Feeney, seventeen-year-old sophomore and driver of the red Camaro. "Cool, huh?"

"Doesn't Mark have the exact same thing?" I said. "Isn't he the kid with the safety pins?"

"Yeah, so?"

"So you're, like, twins now or something?"

"Fuck you," he said.

"Fuck yourself."

"I don't have to," he said. "As I think you know."

This was a low blow. Teddy was referring to the time I'd come home and was heading to my room and saw Teddy and some half-naked girl rolling around in bed together. I'd stood there for a second, in shock, wondering why the hell Teddy had the door open and whether I should close it. Then Teddy had looked up and caught me standing there, and he'd given me a vicious little smile, like a wolf in a fairy tale who'd just scared the hell out of some stupid little girl.

He wasn't supposed to mention this.

As the moral high ground was all I had left I said, "That Pamela, she's really classy," referring to the fact that Pamela wore white tank tops without bras, that her fingernails were two inches long and each painted a different fluorescent color, that she tended to walk around sucking on popsicles in an obscene manner.

"Fuck you," he said again.

"Fuck yourself." And we were right back where we'd started.

# 24

One Sunday morning our mother asked me and Teddy to sit down with her that afternoon for a family dinner. "A real dinner," she said, "with plates and silverware and napkins." I couldn't remember the last time we'd all sat down together, the last time we'd used silverware. Each of us just made meals for ourselves, out of food we didn't need to cook, and we usually ate them with our hands, in front of the television. "The summer's really flying by," our mother said, "and we're all so busy working we hardly see each other. It's a crying shame, is what it is."

When Teddy and I sat down at the table, we were suspicious. Our mother only cooked when she was planning some kind of scene. She made small talk as she piled food on our plates—

mashed potatoes and ears of corn, legs of chicken, buttered rolls—but we all knew it was a preamble.

"Tell me all about your jobs," she said when she sat down.

"There's this old bag that comes in for mackerel," Teddy said, "and everyone disappears as soon as they see her, because we don't wanna touch the mackerel. She makes you take out the bones and everything. It's gross."

"Oh my," my mother said. "That sounds unpleasant."

We ate for a minute or two. My mother was hoping for me to volunteer something, but I wasn't about to. She should have known that much.

"I've got this new regular at work," she said. "And the other day he asked me if he could have a strand of my hair! Can you believe it? I mean, I know people have always gone crazy for my hair," she said, joking, though we all knew she was serious. As a senior in high school she had achieved a certain degree of fame when she took her first and only job as a TV spokesmodel for Maxwell's, a local fur coat retailer. During the commercial, my mother was standing in front of a fan, and people had liked the way her long blonde hair lashed all around, flapping gloriously in all directions. They had been captivated by her. For this reason they flocked to Maxwell's, which was now the most successful fur retailer in New England. My mother pretended to resent Maxwell's for not sharing their profits with her. But secretly, she knew she had them to thank for the attention she still got from old-timers who recognized her, who remembered the way she had run her hands seductively up and down the collar of the coat, saying, "Oooooooh, Maxwell's."

"I can't believe what turns some men on," she said now. "I told him, I said, 'I have a boyfriend and I don't think he'd like it if I gave you a strand of hair.' That's what I said."

"Do you think you can make it through a single conversation without talking about Jim?" said Teddy.

"Gee," my mother said, "I guess we'll talk about something else then."

"Good," said Teddy.

"Frankie?" my mother said. "How's work?"

"Okay."

"Anything interesting?"

"Well," I said, "there's this homeless guy who sits in the cafeteria all day," I said. "Reading self-help books. Like, *How to Make a Ton of Friends and Money in Six Weeks*. He's always got all these trash bags piled up next to him, with all his stuff in them. His hair's really long, and his beard. You can't even see his face."

"Everybody's homeless nowadays," said my mother. "The economy's really in the shitter."

"It's really depressing," I said.

"How's the Buick holding up?" my mother asked.

"Fine," I said.

"It's a piece of shit," said Teddy.

"Don't talk with your mouth full," said our mother.

Teddy swallowed his food and said, "It's a piece of shit," clearly and precisely, like a person teaching English as a second language.

"I, for one, think it's very responsible that Frankie saved her money and fixed up the car for herself," said my mother. "Unlike some people who seem content to borrow cars without permission."

"Well I, for one, think she should have used the money to buy a life."

"Why don't you shut the fuck up?" I said.

"Who wants seconds?" said our mother. We weren't even done with the food on our plates, but she seemed to want to stuff us until we lost all desire to fight, until we collapsed on the table and slept like babies, like the *tiny, darling babies* we once were, so long ago, before we disappointed her by learning to crawl, walk, think, and finally speak for ourselves.

As she piled our plates with mashed potatoes she finally got up the nerve to make her big announcement. "I have some news," she said. "Jim's going to start fixing up the house. Isn't that great?"

Teddy and I didn't say anything. We bit into legs of chicken, chewed, swallowed, licked our fingers. Took a break to work on the mashed potatoes. Returned to the chicken.

"We need a new roof and obviously new paint everywhere. He's going to take up the carpets and put in a hardwood floor. He's going to do all the cabinets in the kitchen. And the bathroom, that all needs to be redone. This house is forty years old, you know. It really needs some work."

We ate our buttery corn, working our way straight across the cobs with our teeth, like typewriters. "Ding," Teddy said when he finished a row.

"Then," she said, "he's going to move in and we're going to live together. Isn't that wonderful?"

It wasn't clear who she was talking to.

"Frankie?" she said. "What do you think?"

"Don't ask me," I said. "I'm moving next month." I hadn't looked up from my plate.

"You're not moving," said Teddy. "Don't pretend you are. You're gonna chicken out at the last minute."

"Watch me," I said.

"Maybe you'll *move* to New York," he said, "but you'll be back in, like, a week."

"It must be nice to know everything," I said. I was being sarcastic, but there was a part of me that thought Teddy might be right.

"It is," he said.

"Hello?" my mother said. "Does anyone have an opinion about what I just said?"

"It's kind of surprising you don't do better in school," I said. "Given the fact that you're such a genius."

"Seemingly," said Teddy. "But the fact is that public high schools aren't set up for geniuses like me. They don't know what to do with us. We have too much mind power. They don't challenge us enough, so we end up flunking everything."

"Hello?" said our mother.

"That's very interesting," I said. "You should consider writing to the president about it."

"I have," said Teddy.

"This is exactly why I decided to move on with my life," our mother said. "I mean, you two are totally impossible."

"What did the president say?"

"He said to hang in there. Stick it out. He said to be careful because the people around me would be jealous and everything. He said that sometimes the siblings of geniuses get really jealous and they can't cope."

"I just want to say," said our mother, "that I know it's hard for kids to see their mothers move on. Especially considering what happened to your father. But it's been a long time and I wish you'd be happy for me."

"It's always been my dream," I said, "to go to summer school."

"Fuck you," said Teddy.

"Fuck yourself," I said.

"Does every conversation in this household," said our mother, "have to end with people fucking themselves?"

"Just the good ones," said Teddy. He stood up from the table and walked off, all the way out the door, letting it slam behind him.

"Thanks a lot, Frankie," my mother said. "I could have used your help, you know."

"Sorry."

"I've had it," she said. She was holding her head in her hands. "As far as I'm concerned you two can go fuck yourselves."

Later that night, as he often did, Teddy asked me for a ride to the movies. He never came right out and asked me. He'd spend a few minutes chitchatting, even though we both knew that he was only talking to me because Mark Feeney was working and I was Teddy's only hope for a ride. Our conversations were always the same, so predictable they seemed to have been scripted in advance. Teddy would walk into the living room and ask what I was watching.

"*Mary Tyler Moore*," I'd say. Or some other show we used to watch when we were kids.

"What the hell are you watching *that* for?"

"I don't know."

"That show is so *gay*. It *sucks*."

I'd shrug, try to concentrate on what Ted Baxter was saying. He was a character I'd come to appreciate.

"You should go out," Teddy would say.

"I don't really feel like it."

"Well, if *you're* not going anywhere, I mean, if the car's just sitting there, how about I take it?"

"You don't have a license."

"So what?" he said.

"So, you can't drive without a license."

"I can drive," he said. "I drive all the time."

This was true. Late at night he was fond of taking the Buick out for a spin around the neighborhood. He'd been doing it for months. But recently our mother had caught him and threatened to kill him if he ever drove again.

"I'll drive you wherever you want," I'd say.

"Cool," he'd say.

That night, after we'd been through this routine, we walked out into the stifling heat, and Teddy started in on one of his favorite topics: air-conditioning. This was his new desire. And as with all of his past desires—cable television, video games, pocket money—he complained about it all the time, with the knowledge that one day my mother would give in, if only to shut him up.

"I hope that bitch at least puts in an air conditioner."

"She said she might."

"I bet she won't."

"She said she might. Jim might put one in."

"Mr. Wonderful," he said, and rolled his eyes.

"He's not so bad," I'd say. "You should meet him."

"I can't believe you're on Jim's fucking side."

"There's no *sides*," I said, and unlocked his door for him.

"This is why you don't have any friends," he said. "You're not supposed to unlock people's *doors* for them."

"It's my car," I said. "I can do what I want."

"But people don't like it," he said. "It's weird. It's like you think we're on a date or something."

"I don't think we're on a date."

I tried to start the engine a few times but it wouldn't turn. Teddy had theories about what I should do: pump the gas pedal or flick the lights before turning the ignition, release the emergency brake and then try the engine while sailing backwards down the driveway.

"It just needs to sit a minute," I said. "It always does this." I was convinced that no one knew the Buick like I did. The Buick and I had our own secret language, a system of tricks and bribes. I thought of us like a circus act, like some lion and its trainer. I could get the Buick to do things that no one else could. If necessary, I could open its hood and stick my head inside, come out unscathed.

We sat and waited. "You're so lucky," Teddy said. "You're outta here in, like, a month. You're not gonna have to *live* with that asshole."

"It won't be so bad," I said. "You're barely even home anyway."

"If she thinks I'm living with that guy, she's fucking crazy."

"Where else are you going to live?" I said.

"Fuck if I know."

The car finally started and I drove Teddy to Front Street.

When we pulled up to the theater he jumped out of the car before it had come to a full stop.

"Hey," I said. "What time do I pick you up?"

"Don't worry about it," he yelled, without turning back.

Usually I dropped Teddy off and went straight home, but that night I parked the car down the street and walked back toward the theater. I knew perfectly well that Teddy wasn't going to the movies, that he and his friends would be hanging out behind the theater at the lake's edge. This was where kids from all over the city stood around and smoked pot, drank beer, and then crushed the empty cans against their foreheads and threw them into the water. They stood around and watched the traffic on the bridge passing over the lake, and when they were drunk enough they walked over to the bridge and crossed it halfway, then hopped its railing and dangled from it, over the water, to the amazement of all their friends.

In the winter, when the lake froze, they stole shopping carts from the grocery next to the movie theater, wheeled them out onto the ice and piled into them, three or four kids to a cart, and they raced toward the center of the ice to see who would turn back first, scared of falling through. Once every few years a group of kids would go too far and they'd sink down into the freezing water, and some of them would be able to fight themselves out of their soaked winter coats and boots and swim to the surface. But occasionally some would die, and their school pictures would run in the paper. In the pictures these kids had their mouths open slightly, as if they hadn't been quick enough to smile when the cameraman told them to.

And so the police drove their cars behind the movie theater

every few hours, and shined their headlights down toward the lake. Someone would yell, "It's the cops!" and everyone would drop their beers and joints, believing that if you dropped these things, the cops couldn't prove anything, even if the joint was burning right next to your foot, they couldn't say it was yours.

I walked behind the theater and halfway down the bank, then hid behind a tree. I stood there and watched Teddy in his circle of friends. He was wearing white jeans and a white T-shirt and his floppy, unlaced work boots, which he never seemed to take off, even when it was a hundred degrees. Every few seconds everyone burst out in laughter and I knew it was Teddy putting on his show, making fun of some teacher or celebrity. Girls stood on the perimeter of the circle in groups of two and three, their arms folded across their chests. I watched as Teddy came up behind a pair of girls and put his arms around them and steered them down to the water's edge. He stood there with a girl in each arm, watching the slow progress of a small boat that was sailing down the lake, with white Christmas lights strung along its rails.

"Hey, mate!" Teddy yelled out, and all his friends joined in, yelling, "Hey, mate!" raising up their cans of beer toward the boat. Whether there was someone on board waving back it was impossible to tell.

For a moment I felt a warmth spread through me, felt what it must be like to be Teddy, to be careless and free. But then it was gone, and in its place came a kind of dread. I started to think that something bad was going to happen to Teddy. What little had kept him grounded was being taken away from him, and I feared he'd lose control of himself, feared it was happening already. The whole scene by the lake struck me as overdone, like something out of a B movie. In those movies there was always a guy standing around laughing, surrounded by girls, and all of a sudden you'd see something glimmering behind him. For a moment you weren't sure what it was. But then you'd realize that what you were looking at was an enormous eye, the eye of some creature whose pupil alone was bigger than a human being. Meanwhile this character was still laughing and carrying on without a care in the world, oblivious to the fact that he was about to be eaten by a giant lizard.

The longer I stood there the more I felt sure that Teddy had a mark on him. Something was going to happen, I knew it. What I didn't know was that it would happen so soon.

# 25

Two weeks later, my mother was having a yard sale. Jim had started working on the house, making little improvements here and there, and my mother was inspired. Suddenly she wanted to change everything, to rid herself of her life's ballast. She wanted her new life with Jim to start with new furniture—a new couch and bed, a new television, new sets of plates and clothes and appliances. So she'd posted signs all over the neighborhood and placed an ad in the newspaper. Bright one Saturday morning, Jim came over and helped her carry nearly the entire contents of the house out onto the front lawn. Then Jim left for work, and my mother woke me up so I could help with the sale. "I need all the manpower I can get," she told me. "You have no idea what these yard sale people are like. They're animals."

Our first customers arrived fifteen minutes early, driving a wood-paneled station wagon. They were an older couple dressed in matching blue sweat suits, and they carried themselves with a professional air. They walked straight for the good stuff—the things that had once belonged to my dead grandparents, and which had been stored in the basement for the last twenty years. There was her father's accordion, her mother's sewing machine. There was a heavy rotary phone with a fabric cord, a set of wine-glasses and a matching crystal decanter, a gold-framed oil paint-ing of the New York hotel where my grandparents had spent their honeymoon.

The asking price for all of this—the last remaining evidence of my grandparents' existence—was a hundred and ten dollars. The old man had pulled out his wallet from a pouch he had strapped around his waist. He stood in front of my mother, thumbing through bills. "I'll give you fifty dollars," he yelled. He had an aggressive stance. He was expecting a fight.

"Fine," my mother said. "Fine."

The man counted the bills into her open palm. "There's twenty," he said. "Forty. Forty-five. Fifty." My mother closed her hand around the money and the old man and his wife started carrying the things to their car. They moved fast, like bandits, loading everything in the back. Then they sped away, giving us guilty little waves. They hadn't understood that my mother wasn't interested in getting a fair deal. She was interested in clearing out the house.

Before the end of the first hour a young couple had bought up all the furniture. They'd bought my mother's bed and dresser for fifty dollars, the TV and its stand for thirty-five. For twenty dollars they'd bought the dining room table and chairs—the table made of white Formica and chrome, and the chairs made of chrome, with the seats upholstered in red vinyl. The couple hadn't believed their good fortune. They were moving into a house down the street, and they kept making trips with their pickup. "I can't believe this," they said to each other. "This is the best day of our lives!"

There was no sense of discretion at the sale. People were talking in loud voices about the uselessness of certain things, especially in the infant and toddler section my mother had set up. "This bib has a *stain*!" said one woman, holding it up for all the crowd to see. "These stuffed animals are dirty," said another. "And who would buy a *used* pacifier?" Our mother had set our entire childhood on the table—the sailor suit and the pea coat that Teddy and I had both worn, our impossibly small pairs of white ice skates, the rattles we'd rattled, the giant sets of plastic keys we'd gnawed on, the soft blue blankets we'd dragged across all the floors of the world, and even Sherman the pig, Sherman who had been discovered at a different yard sale and loved so hard his eyes were falling off. People kept walking up and surveying all of this like it was an installation in a museum. They stood for a moment with their hands on their hips, their heads cocked. Then they walked away and said, "What a bunch of *crap*."

Things got worse as the day went on. For some reason people kept buying things, even things they didn't like, and as the tables cleared my mother filled in the space with her second-string items, her benchwarmers. "An electric mixer with only one beater!" people said. "A footstool with three legs! This is ridiculous!" Nevertheless they continued to buy. They bought my mother's wobbly telephone stand, her rusted measuring cups. They bought her mismatched sheet sets, her half-burned candles, her stained wooden cutting board and matching rolling pin. My mother was making change for people as fast as she could. She was tucking dirty bills down the neck of her T-shirt, into her bra. She was ecstatic, tossing her hair around, flashing smiles.

Meanwhile I was walking around trying not to feel too depressed. I stood in front of the tables, browsing, hoping to blend in, hoping to see things with the same cold detachment as other shoppers. "What in the hell is this?" one guy asked me, holding up a small appliance my mother had ordered off the television. The guy was middle-aged, and wearing army fatigues. He'd probably fought in Vietnam. If he was anything like my father, he wouldn't want to know that he was living in a world whose luxuries included battery-operated hair-braiders.

"I don't know, man," I said. I wasn't about to break the news to him.

"Looks real useful," he said, tossing it back on the table. I didn't like thinking about the fact that my mother had seen something on television, ordered it, used it a few times, then shoved it in the back of the bathroom closet, where it collected dust for ten years. Everything had turned out to be such a disappointment.

At one point Teddy came trudging across the lawn, heading out for the Big G in his deli whites. He had just woken up and his hair was everywhere. He was shading his eyes, which hadn't yet adjusted to the light of day.

"Hi, sweetheart!" my mother chirped, but Teddy walked right past her, out into the street and off toward Lincoln. This had become their routine. Teddy hadn't spoken to her since she'd announced her plans to move in with Jim.

By noon we'd sold all the furniture but the foldout couch, which was priced at twenty-five dollars. A few men had sat on the couch while waiting for their wives to finish shopping. They sat there and dreamed of converting their unfinished basements into personal sanctuaries, where they could watch football in privacy. "Hey, Lorraine," they said. Or Edith or Deborah. "Howsabout this couch? We could put it in the basement."

"In a million years," said Lorraine. Or Edith or Deborah. "I wouldn't allow that piece of furniture into my home."

I couldn't blame them. The couch was truly ugly, upholstered in an itchy fabric, in a brown and yellow plaid. It wasn't even comfortable. It forced you to sit up perfectly straight. It defeated the purpose of a couch.

Still, I was glad that no one wanted it. It was one of the only things in the house I cared about. That and my father's desk, which was thankfully still sitting in the basement. At least my mother hadn't tried to sell that, I thought. At least she hadn't *completely* turned into Yoko Ono.

Toward the end of the sale, in the high heat of the afternoon, a family showed up and parked their Lincoln Town

Car right in the driveway. The parents were very proper-look-ing—the father in a dress shirt and slacks, the mother wearing a navy blue short-sleeved dress. But their daughter was a different story. Their daughter was barefoot, and she was wearing cutoff denim shorts and a white tank top. Her hair was black and frizzy, and it hung down her back. She had about fifty silver bracelets on her right arm. It was Pamela Henderson, Teddy's girlfriend.

The father did all the talking. He seemed to have been briefed in advance. He knew exactly who my mother was. "Mrs. Hawthorne," he said, approaching my mother with an out-stretched hand, "I'm Bill Henderson. I was wondering if we could talk."

"Why, hello," my mother said. "You've missed most of the good stuff, I'm afraid."

"I'm not here for the sale," he said. "Unfortunately." Mrs. Henderson and Pamela stood behind him, looking down at their feet. I could see from the roots of Pamela's hair that her natural color was the same as her mother's—a pale strawberry blonde. The rest of her hair—which was an intense blue-black—was some kind of statement.

I watched my mother show the Hendersons into the house. She was trying to be gracious, smiling and holding the door open, but I could tell she was terrified. We both knew what was going on. I didn't even need to ask. When the Hendersons walked out of the house again and settled into their car, when they drove away—their engine so strangely quiet—it was per-fectly clear to me what had happened inside. I looked for my mother. She was standing in the doorway, shaded behind the screen door. She was frozen. Her arms crossed, her head bent down. It was the posture of a person who had just witnessed an accident. Yes, I thought, Pamela is pregnant.

When Teddy came home—trudging in the house singing, "But I didn't shoot no deputy, oh no," letting the door slam behind him—my mother was waiting for him, lying on the floor of the empty living room. She had an ice pack on her forehead. She had one of her headaches.

"Theodore," she said, quite softly.

He didn't answer, walked straight into the kitchen, where I was making myself a sandwich. "What's up?" he said to me. He opened the refrigerator and stared inside. I watched him in profile for a moment. He was still in his deli whites—the white T-shirt and apron and white jeans. He'd taken out his safety-pin earrings and he looked quite innocent for once, blond and blue-eyed and young.

"Teddy," I said, "you need to go talk to Mom."

He straightened up and looked at me. "Why?" he said.

"Just talk to Mom," I said.

"Fuck that," he said.

"I'm serious," I told him, touched his arm. "Something happened."

He jerked his arm away in a motion that suggested he understood me, that he'd talk to her—but he didn't have to be happy about it.

I took my sandwich outside and ate it on the couch. I wondered why everyone didn't have couches on their front lawn, right up against the street. It was pleasant sitting there watching the neighborhood kids go by on their bicycles. Midge Durdle had finally sold some houses, and there were all kinds of new kids going around. "Hello," one kid said, a little girl with blonde pigtails. She stopped and straddled her bike. "Whatcha doing?"

"Eating a sandwich," I said.

"Out*side*?"

"You should try it," I said. "It's fun."

She shrugged, took off on her bike. A minute later she came around again and stopped. "Whatcha doing *now*?" she said.

"I'm still working on this sandwich."

"How come there's a couch outside?"

I shrugged just like she'd done, and then she took off on her bike again.

I hadn't even finished my sandwich when Teddy came out the front door and bounded down the lawn and out into the street.

"Hey!" I said. "Wait up." I ran after him. "It's gonna be okay," I said. "Don't worry."

"That bitch," he said, not even looking at me, "said she was on the pill." He was walking a few paces ahead of me.

"Everything will be okay," I said. "You'll see."

"I bet it's not even mine," he said. "I bet she's been sleeping around all over the place."

"Mom will help you," I said. "She loves babies."

He stopped, turned around. "There's not gonna be any *baby*," he said. "Jesus." He walked off. There was deli blood smeared on the back of his white jeans.

I walked back and sat on the couch for a while. The girl kept riding by on her bicycle, and we waved to each other every time. Then she abandoned me. Night was falling and all across the neighborhood mothers were calling to their children, making lovely little songs of their names, calling like birds, calling them home.

The next morning, in the empty living room, I found a box of items that were left over from the sale, and I noticed a pink limb sticking out from under a layer of clothes. It was Sherman. I pulled him out and examined him, tossed him back and forth in my hands. I thought about going into Teddy's room and waking him up, giving Sherman back to him. "Sherman's, like, your *soul*," I'd tell him. "You need him now more than ever." But I knew if I did that Teddy would do something awful. Just to make a point he'd probably take Sherman into the kitchen and spread him on his back on the counter, then slice off his head with a knife. I didn't know what else to do, so I stuffed Sherman under my bed.

It was one of my last days at home. My mother was off at work and Teddy was sleeping in. I had an hour before I left for work and I spent it walking through the empty rooms, picturing the things that were gone. The carpets were dented with the footmarks of all the sold furniture. One patch of wallpaper, which the couch had been pushed against, was lighter than the rest. It looked like a painting, something hung low on the wall to brighten up the place, a memory of better times.

Finally it was time to leave for work. But when I stepped outside into the terrible heat I saw that the driveway was empty. Teddy had taken the Buick! Under cover of darkness he had stolen my car and left. I stood there in the driveway for a while, staring at the fluorescent puddle of antifreeze that the Buick had leaked, wondering if perhaps ghosts really did survive on antifreeze, if this puddle was perhaps a kind of footprint, a mark left by someone who had disappeared into another world.

I called in sick to work and spent the day reading. Sometime in the afternoon, Teddy's boss from the deli called. "This is Leon," he said when I picked up the phone. "Tell Teddy to get his ass into work."

"He's not home," I said.

"Is he on his way?"

"I highly doubt it."

"Fine," said Leon. "When you see him tell him I said he's fired."

"He'll be devastated," I said. I suddenly felt very protective of Teddy. I felt like I might kill anyone who tried to hurt him.

When my mother got home, she was all excited about Jim. He'd shown up at the restaurant with an air conditioner, which was all wrapped up in red and green Christmas paper. "He walked in with this huge present," my mother said, "and gave it to me right in front of everybody. They were so jealous!"

"That's nice."

"He knew Teddy wanted one, and that he could really use something nice. So he went out and did that. Can you believe it? Isn't he unbelievable?"

"I can't believe it."

"Aren't you supposed to be at work?" she said.

"No."

"I thought you were supposed to be at work."

"I traded with someone."

"Where's Teddy?" she said. "He'll be so excited. He could use some good news."

"I don't know," I said. I wasn't about to tell her. Soon enough she'd realize that the Buick was gone, and she'd figure it out for herself about Teddy.

"Well, Jim's coming right over to install it," she said. "It'll be a nice surprise for Teddy when he gets home. Maybe Teddy will even meet Jim!"

"Don't hold your breath," I said.

"Could you do me a favor?" she said. "Can you make a sign for the couch? Just make a big sign that says FREE and set it on the couch, would you? I'm beat."

I had to hunt around for a piece of paper. I kept opening cabinets and drawers, finding them empty. She'd really cleaned the place out. Finally I resorted to ripping the back cover from one of my mother's psychology books. FREE TO GOOD HOME, I wrote. The sign was small and unimpressive. No one in a passing car would be able to read it.

Outside, Jim was standing on the front lawn, beneath my mother's bedroom window. He was measuring the frame.

"Hi, Jim," I said.

He looked up, startled. "Hi there, Frankie," he said, and took off his baseball hat. "Good to see you."

"Hot enough for you?" I said.

"Phew," he said. "This air conditioner will come in handy."

"It's nice of you," I said.

"It's no trouble." He was working the bill of his hat between his hands, nervous.

"It's really nice." I was nervous, too. I suddenly wanted Jim to know I was okay with him, even though I'd been ignoring him all through the five months he'd been dating my mother. But I didn't know what to say.

"The Red Sox are looking good," he said. "I think this is the year. The Sox are gonna go all the way."

"Maybe," I said.

"I'm not a big Rocket fan," he said, referring to Roger "the Rocket" Clemens, who was supposed to be Boston's ace in the hole. "Personally, I think he's a crybaby. But he sure can pitch."

"I guess," I said. "You think they can beat the Yankees?"

"No doubt about it," he said. "This is the year."

"This is the year," I said. It was strange to say it. It hadn't been the year since 1918 and might not ever be the year again. Still, people like Jim went around believing.

"Say it like you mean it," he said.

"This is the year," I said. I made a fist and raised it in the air, but it wasn't very convincing.

"That's an improvement," he said, "but you better keep working on it."

"I don't know. I don't like to get my hopes up."

"Just you wait," said Jim. "One of these days, it'll happen, you'll see."

After Jim finished installing the air conditioner we all went into my mother's bedroom and stood in front of it. My mother was smiling, and her hair was blowing back the way it did in the Maxwell's commercial. She looked better than she had in a long time. "Oooh, this is nice," she said. She and Jim put their arms around each other and he kissed her on the forehead.


W h e n my mother realized that Teddy was gone, she called everyone she could think of. She called the Hendersons. She

called the Brownings. She called Mark Feeney. No one had seen
him, and no one seemed to care that he was missing. My mother
had called the police and they'd come over to the house to
gather information. Teddy's name was on the official list of missing persons. The Buick was on the list.

The last days of summer dragged past. Jim scraped off the
wallpaper and painted the walls. He moved in the new furniture,
which I had to admit was nice. He and my mother had bought
a formal dining room set, a plush leather couch, a giant entertainment center. The house was looking better. If Teddy ever
came home, I thought, he would be pleasantly surprised.

In the evenings Jim and my mother sat on the couch holding
hands, talking, sipping beers. She was worried about Teddy and
she was drinking herself into a stupor. Jim tried to comfort her.
"He's okay," he always said. "That kid's a survivor."

A week after the yard sale Pamela Henderson's mother called
to let us know that there wouldn't be any more inconvenience
to our family. Pamela had had an abortion.

T h i s   w a s  how the last days of summer passed. In my mind,
in the world I was always silently imagining, I had hoped for better. In my mind it happened like this: I woke on that last morning before leaving for New York. It was early, before the sun was
entirely risen, and there was a rumbling engine outside. I looked
out the window and saw Uncle Harpo's black Galaxie 500, with
a handmade wooden trailer attached to it. Uncle Harpo and
Teddy were working together, lifting the couch off the lawn, trying to maneuver it onto the trailer. They worked fast, Harpo walk-

ing backwards toward the trailer, then stepping up into it, pulling up the couch, Teddy pushing from the other end. They settled the couch in, then got back in the car and sped away. In my mind, they had found each other and moved in together, and they were keeping each other company. In my mind they were happy.

But nothing like this happened. There was only the waiting and hoping, the endless waiting, and eventually I had to give in to one of life's truths. It was a sad fact of life that you could wait and wait and wait for someone, but just because you were waiting didn't mean they'd eventually appear. This was life. This wasn't, I realized at last, a Doris Day movie.

And so I didn't see Teddy before leaving for New York. On the morning we were supposed to leave I told my mother I thought I might stay. "Maybe I should just wait until Teddy gets back," I said. "I bet he'll be home soon."

"Over my dead body," she said. She took my face in her hands and held it, stared into my eyes. "You're going to New York if it kills you."

Just before I left I took Sherman out from under my bed and placed him on Teddy's bed. I positioned him on his stomach, so when Teddy decided to come home, when he walked through the door and found Sherman there, it would be just like the time they had first seen each other, when Sherman was lying on that yard-sale table waiting for someone, lying on his stomach and looking up, hopeful.

If hopeless waiting was a fact of life, it was also true that sometimes people you *weren't* expecting appeared out of nowhere, and the sight of them could send you reeling. For me that person was Pamela Henderson. On the way out of town my mother stopped to gas up the car, and I ran inside the convenience store to buy a soda. That's when I saw her. She was standing at the register with some friends. She was wearing the same cutoffs and tank top she always wore. One of her friends was saying, "If I get that faggot for history next year I'm gonna drop out of school for sure." Our eyes met, and it was terrible. We barely nodded to each other, and looked away.

I couldn't tell her how sorry I was that she had gotten mixed up with us, that we had ruined what was left of her childhood. How sorry I was that I couldn't stand to speak to her or even look at her. That she carried with her the idea of another dead Hawthorne, and it was too much to stand. I was sorry that she had to walk around with this secret, that she was standing even then with her friends listening to their problems and thinking— somewhere in the back of her mind she was always thinking— about what had happened. I was sorry that later in her life when she straightened out and went to college and met the love of her life, when they got married and had a baby, even then she'd still be thinking about the possibility of this first child, this small idea of a person. *I know*, I wanted to tell her. *This weight of yours, what you're carrying, I know.*


A week later the police called to tell my mother that Teddy had been in an accident. He'd been speeding on Route 20—

a notorious stretch of truck stops and strip joints—and he'd gone off the road, crashing the Buick into a ditch. He had broken his nose and clavicle, and there was a deep gash over his left eye. "He was living in the car the whole time," my mother told me. "Apparently he was just driving around for days." We had this conversation over the phone. I was standing in the lobby of my dormitory, tucked away in an old-fashioned wooden phone booth, its glass door pulled shut, and I remember thinking that I had found the only quiet corner in the entire city.

"He's in a lot of pain," my mother said, "but he'll live."

"Can I talk to him?" I said.

"I don't know, honey. He doesn't really come out of his room."

"Oh."

"He's gotta go to juvenile court," she said. "For drinking and driving. He could be in deep shit. They might make him join the *military* or something."

"God," I said.

"I just don't know what to do," she said, her voice warbling. I heard her light a cigarette, take a drag, force the smoke through her nose. "I just don't know how this happened. I just don't know how it happened."

For a moment I sensed how it must have been in the house, the awful silence, the awkward mingling of people forced to live together, though they all wished it was otherwise. I didn't know how it had happened, either, how the three of us had arrived here, each living in our own private corners of the world, turned away from each other, when once we had leaned together and made shelter.

A sense of loneliness came over me that was so terrible I

actually sank down and sat on the floor of the phone booth. I seemed to feel myself getting smaller and smaller, disappearing into nothing.

"But anyways," my mother said, her voice brightening, "enough of that. Did you go to Radio City yet? Did you see the Rockettes?"

In a flash I realized that I was truly gone, out of the house and out of her sight, that I could tell her whatever I liked and she wouldn't know the difference. I realized how easy it would be to make her happy.

"Yes," I said. "I saw them."

She squealed with delight. "Wasn't it just amazing?" she said. "Weren't they beautiful? Weren't they spectacular? Wasn't it just the greatest thing you ever saw in your *life*?"

"It was," I told her. "It really was."

part three

# 26

Every year our neighbors, the Weatherbees, bundled up in their matching down jackets and trekked through the woods behind their house in search of the most beautiful, helpless spruce they could find. Then they chopped that spruce down with an ax, stood it in the corner of their living room, and invited the neighborhood for a trimming party. My mother loved these parties. She liked to mill around in the stifling heat of the Weatherbees' living room, sipping eggnog from tiny plastic cups. She liked to toss her long blonde hair as she laughed at terrible jokes. Most of all she liked to position herself beneath sprigs of mistletoe and plant flagrant red kisses on the foreheads of passing schoolboys.

My father hated these parties. He hated the Weatherbees, who offended him on an almost daily basis as they jogged through the neighborhood in their monogrammed L.L. Bean sweat suits. The Weatherbees waved whenever we passed them in our car. Big, sweeping, enthusiastic waves. They broke out into wide smiles, their jaws flapping open like puppets. It was all my father could do to reciprocate by lifting one finger off the steering wheel, because he was using the rest of his inner resources to combat the urge to mow them down.

And so it was difficult, on the first Saturday of every December, for my father to wipe his boots on the Weatherbees' welcome mat and shake hands and trade pleasantries. After a few minutes of mingling my father tended to stand at the edge of these parties, alone, taking short, surreptitious draws from his pocket flask. His only source of amusement was watching the suffering of the neighborhood doctor, who stood all night with his hands in his pockets as people peeled back their socks and rolled up their sleeves, presenting moles and rashes and sores. My father and the doctor often exchanged anguished, knowing glances, rolling their eyes while people listed their injuries. Every year, toward the end of the party, my father pulled up the leg of his trousers and asked the doctor to take a look at his prosthetic. "It's the funniest thing," he told the doctor, "but lately it's like I've lost all feeling in my leg." They laughed, savoring the moment. Though my father and the doctor were not friends, they recognized in each other a mutual dislike of parties, of holidays, of people, of milk-based drinks served from giant punch bowls. They recognized in one another the defiant slouch and scowl typical of Vietnam veterans, the preference for solitude, for sitting in dark rooms thinking seriously about death. Both my father and the doctor knew that it was the season to be jolly, to make the yule-tide gay, to go walking along singing a song in a winter wonder-land, to have themselves a merry little Christmas, now, and they hated every minute of it.

Each year my father did his best to fall from the Weatherbees' favor, but they were impervious to insult. "I'm dying of bore-dom!" he yelled out once, at the top of his lungs, but everyone at the party took it for a joke. Another year he stood at the buf-fet table and ate every cheese puff, cracker, celery stick, crab cake, chicken wing, shish kebob, melon ball, and pig in a blan-ket in sight. He did this in the fashion of Charlie Chaplin's tramp, stuffing food into his mouth in quick, greedy motions, with the frantic-eyed guilt of someone stealing from a grocer. He ate until he was sick, then vomited spectacularly in the salad bowl, hoping the Weatherbees would ask him to leave, but they didn't.

After forty minutes at the annual tree trimming of 1979, my father couldn't take it anymore, and he engineered our escape. We were alone in the kitchen, fetching a fourth eggnog for my mother, when the idea occurred to him. It started with the Weatherbees' cat, Mitzi, who was scratching frantically at the kitchen door, wanting out. As always the cat was dressed for the party in a red sweater and a humiliating set of velveteen antlers, and she looked terribly burdened. She turned her green eyes on us, pleading. "Poor bastard," said my father. He set down the eggnog and opened the door for the cat. He watched it dash out into the snow and stood there for a moment, letting the heat out. Then he wriggled his mustache, as he always did when a bit of mischief occurred to him.

"Are you particularly enjoying this party?" he said, and turned to me.

I shook my head.

"Are you sentimentally attached to it?"

"No."

"Are you religiously opposed to leaving it?"

"No," I said, and laughed. He was on one of his rolls.

"Are you politically aligned with the Weatherbees?"

"No!" I cried, and made my hands into fists.

"Are you especially inclined to keep a secret?"

"Yes!"

"Okay, then," he said. He grabbed my hand and we were off.

Outside, the cold air was thrilling. My father took a deep breath and straightened to his full, startling height. He made a fist, shook it triumphantly. "Never again!" he said, and vowed for the thousandth time to suspend all diplomatic relations with the Weatherbees and their insufferable parties. "I don't know what it is about those Weatherbees," he said as we trudged down their driveway, away from their party. "But they give me a bad case of the *heebie-jeebies*, if you will. The creeps, as it were. The spooks. The pukes."

"Me too," I said. "I hate them!" Just then, a wave of laughter crashed from the Weatherbees' house. Everyone in the whole neighborhood was there, laughing, but I could hear my mother's laugh above all others.

"What do you suppose could be so funny?" my father said.

"I don't know. I guess a joke."

"I bet it was that one about the chicken crossing the road," he said. "You know, to get to the other side."

I started shivering, overdoing it a bit, moaning and chattering. My jacket was still trapped at the party, like a hostage, piled hopelessly on one of the Weatherbees' beds. "There's a lesson to be learned here," my father said. "In moments of *extreme duress*," he explained, "there's never time to stop for jackets."

"Okay."

"I'd give you my jacket," he said, "but then you wouldn't learn anything."

"Okay."

"You may have noticed that I never take mine off," he said, tugging fondly at the hem of his army jacket. "That's the first rule I learned in the service."

"Never take off your jacket," I said.

"Right. Even indoors."

"Never take off your jacket, even indoors."

"I think you've got it, now," he said. He stopped and unzipped his coat, took it off, draped it over my shoulders. It was the first time I could remember that I'd seen him without it.

"You just took off your jacket," I said. "You just broke the first rule."

"That's true," he said. "But there are exceptions. *Amendments*, they're called. You've got to be willing to revise things a little as you go along. That's the first rule."

"Amendments are the first rule," I said.

"Unless you amend *that*, of course," he said. He knelt down and zipped up the coat. My arms weren't through the sleeves, and they dangled at my sides. The coat's hem reached my shins. This pleased my father. He started laughing, really laughing, like he did when the Three Stooges clobbered one another over the head.

"What's so funny?" I said.

"You look very terrifying," he said.

"I do?"

"You do. If there was a war, and I crossed paths with you, I'd run for my life."

"Really?"

"Absolutely," he said. "Come on." He started jogging down the street.

"Where are we going?" I asked. We weren't headed toward our house.

"Nowhere in particular."

"I thought we were going home."

"Not yet," he said. "We're on a secret mission."

This secret mission, I soon learned, involved the slight vandalism of outdoor Christmas displays, including the unplugging of lights from their extension cords, the strategic rearrangement of lawn statues so that plastic reindeer appeared to be trampling plastic Santas, so that plastic wise men gathered in circles to adore plastic sheep, leaving plastic newborns untended in plastic mangers. My father did all of this hurriedly, looking constantly over his shoulder, dashing behind bushes when he heard an oncoming car. We ran down the street like this, committing small, hasty crimes. Whenever my father was pleased with his work—when he wrapped a string of Christmas lights around the neck of a plastic snowman and hung him from a tree, like an executed traitor—he put his arm around me and we buckled over, laughing, tears in our eyes, our breath clouding out before us, mingling, then evaporating into the night. I could smell the bourbon on him, his yuletide cologne. He always drank himself through the holidays.

We were almost back to the Weatherbees' when we heard the faint jingling of the cat's collar. We stopped and turned around, and found the cat staring up at us with a cocked head, an incriminating glare. "If you tell anyone about this," my father said to the cat, shaking his fist at it, "I'll kill you."

No one at the party had noticed our absence. For a few minutes my father and I walked around smiling, rosy-cheeked. We mingled gleefully with the neighbors, knowing that they'd eventually return home to the horror of their ruined lawn displays. My father was in great spirits. He even made his way through a conversation with Les Weatherbee. "The dollar is king," Les kept saying. "You can't lose when you bet on the dollar."

"The dollar is king?" my father said. "Really?" He stroked his beard and stared meaningfully out the window.

"You betcha," said Les.

"I wish I'd known that," said my father. "I just converted all of our money to rubles."

"Ha!" Les said, swirling his drink. "You're a card, Randy."

He allowed someone to call him Randy.

Soon enough, of course, the party took a bad turn. Somehow my mother coerced my little brother into performing a Shirley Temple tap dance number, which she had taught him behind our father's back. This drew the attention of the entire party. All of the neighbors gathered around Teddy in a circle, and my mother stood with her hands clasped over her heart. It was the crowning moment of her life. The women who had judged her so harshly when she first married our father and brought him to live in the house, which she had inherited after her parents' death—all of these women were now clapping, admiring her son. And their husbands, the neighborhood's men, they were pulling bright quarters from their pockets and tossing them at Teddy's feet. Finally the neighborhood was accepting my mother! Even though she was a waitress, though she had a husband who grumbled through parties and wore nothing but army fatigues and was living off disability, even with this kind of husband, and with an *ill-gotten* piece of real estate, my mother was raising a *darling child*, everyone had to admit. She had taught her young son to tap-dance, had dressed him in a red corduroy suit for the party, a ruffled white shirt, a green bow tie, and a new pair of saddle shoes, and *wasn't he just the cutest thing*, they were saying, about her son, her Teddy.

When Teddy finished his number the neighborhood women closed around my mother. "Gerry!" they said. "We had no idea you were so talented!" There were church pageants to be choreographed, and my mother was just the sort of person they'd been looking for all their lives.

When I looked for my father, he was gone. He had spent the greater part of his life hating Shirley Temple, and the sight of his son performing a dance number for quarters was probably too much for him to stand. I imagined him walking home, limping slightly, slow and sad and suffering, the way Mr. Bojangles must have walked after a long day on a Hollywood set. I imagined him shivering. I was still wearing his coat.

A f t e r the Weatherbees' party, my mother started chatting on the telephone in the evenings with her new friends. They filled her in on the affairs of the neighborhood: who was unhappily married, who was going to Barbados on vacation, who was in grave danger of having to take in a deranged mother-in-law, who was fired, who was promoted, who was getting a new dish-washer, a new car, a new wife. By far the most popular topic of discussion was the rash of vandalism that had spread through the neighborhood during the Weatherbees' party. No one knew what to make of it. Would the prankster strike again? Would he go so far as to break into homes? People were terrified. Each morning they rushed to their windows to make sure that something obscene hadn't been done to their children's snowmen.

"Mabel Fletcher even called the police!" my mother said one night, at dinner. "And the police said they couldn't help! Can you believe that?"

"It's very appalling," my father said.

"People are even talking about pitching in to hire an off-duty cop. You know, to patrol the neighborhood."

"Thank God," my father said. "Finally a sensible idea. I haven't been able to sleep for fear of my life." He said this, from behind the shield of his newspaper, with the utmost sincerity. But we all could tell, without needing to see, that he was rolling his eyes.

"Well, we have to do something!" my mother said. "Before the neighborhood starts going downhill."

Later in the week our family sat on the couch and watched the Grinch steal Christmas. He mused in his cave, drumming his furry fingers together, plotting to stuff all the season's glorious trappings into his sleigh. "That's exactly what's happening to our neighborhood!" my mother said.

"Yes, Gerry," said my father. "We're all being stalked by a vicious monster. It's very frightening."

"Don't be a smart-ass," my mother said. "That's exactly what's happening. Exactly!"

My father winked at me. We smiled at each other now and then as the Grinch did his dastardly work, cleaning out refrigerators and stuffing Christmas trees up chimneys. But at the end, when the Grinch's puny heart swelled three sizes and he restored everything to its original splendor, my father seemed genuinely confused. "What the hell kind of a story is this?" he said.

# 27

Like most kids, Teddy and I looked forward to Christmas for all the obvious reasons. We spent long hours wondering what presents we'd find under the tree that year, and we counted the days until vacation, impatient for the school break, which we were eager to fill with exorbitant snacking and cartoon-watching.

We also looked forward to Christmas break because it was the only time of year that our father told war stories. Something about the season always put him in a talkative mood, and for a two-week span we'd hear all about his adventures in Vietnam. We never stopped to wonder why the holidays brought this out in him. We simply looked forward to the stories the way we looked forward to the giant ham and the chocolate cake that our mother prepared each Christmas. Every year these stories were better than the last, more outrageous, more spectacular. We spent long afternoons listening to our father. The three of us huddled together in our indoor fort, which we fashioned by draping bedsheets over the kitchen table.

In my father's war stories, he saved lives while sauntering down dirt roads, casually bending to scoop small children out of the puddles in which they were drowning. He revived them—sometimes dozens at a time!—and carried them home in his arms, on his back and hips. They clung to his neck and legs. He walked to the villages and knocked politely on the doors of thatch-roofed huts and delivered these children to their grateful parents. Though he was offered food, clothing, money, cigarettes, and eternal devotion, he refused to accept payment for his services.

Because he was a genius, my father mastered the Vietnamese language in just a few short weeks. He began writing poems, which were discovered by villagers and distributed in pamphlets across the entire country. Soon he was famous. Every mouth spoke his name. People crowded him in the street and begged for locks of his hair, scraps of his clothing. "Our beloved poet!" they cried. He wasn't allowed a moment's peace. Even dogs followed him, wagging their tails, wanting nothing more than his touch.

When he wasn't saving lives or writing poetry, my father was engaged in brutal warfare. He won several bouts of hand-to-hand combat by butting his forehead into the tender noses of his enemies. Because he believed in being polite, he apologized as they held their bloody faces and screamed in pain. At least once a day my father ran into the line of fire to drag his wounded friends to safety. With his left hand, using nothing more than his mess kit, he excised bullets from his friends' shoulders. Simultaneously, with his right hand, he fired his machine gun into dark forests, killing all of his enemies in one clean sweep.

My mother liked to interrupt these stories whenever she got the chance. "When your father returned home from the war," she'd tell us, "he invented electricity. Then he built this house and our car with his bare hands."

"Don't exaggerate, Gerry," our father would say. "You'll confuse the children." We never understood why our mother insisted on lying. Everyone knew that Benjamin Franklin had discovered electricity while flying a kite in a lightning storm.

Usually, in these stories, my father was an army of one. He crushed enemy camps with his own personal tank, then escaped by paddling away down treacherous rivers in his sleek, one-seater canoe, which he had crafted himself from a felled tree, using only his pocketknife. But every now and then these stories included a hapless sidekick named Leonard Holmes. Leonard was a short, skinny kid with downy blond hair and a bulbous red nose. He had baby blue eyes with long, girlish lashes. His two front teeth—one of which was chipped—stuck out awkwardly. "He got those teeth from eating too much corn on the cob," our father told us. "He was a real farm boy, a real hayseed. He'd never seen a flushing toilet until the army."

Leonard Holmes tended to trot at my father's heels, begging to be taken along on important missions. Now and then my father would consent, out of pity. He was the only soldier in the entire army willing to take on the burden of Leonard's friendship, because it was such a terrible liability. Leonard was incapable of completing the simplest tasks. When trying to escape the enemy, he'd accidentally throw the car in reverse and speed toward danger. When trusted with a package, he'd leave it on the floor of a taxicab. He tended to get his fingers stuck in the spokes of umbrellas. He fell with some frequency into toilets. He was always being captured, sometimes even by children, and our father had to take time out of his busy schedule to save Leonard's life, a process which usually involved his swinging across leech-infested swamps on dangerously thin vines. Worst of all, Leonard suffered from unpredictable bouts of stuttering, like Porky Pig. Our father would be trying to extract crucial, time-sensitive information out of Leonard, and suddenly Leonard could say nothing but *abba-dabba* and *badeeb-badeeb*.

But Leonard Holmes wasn't totally useless. Under rare and spectacular circumstances, he'd manage to save our father's life. Now and then he'd unintentionally foil the enemy, like the time he blinded an approaching assassin while applying a finishing coat of aerosol hairspray. Or the time he tripped and landed on his gun and accidentally fired a bullet that pierced the gas tank of an enemy helicopter.

We couldn't get enough of this Leonard Holmes. "Where was Leonard?" we sometimes asked our father when he was trying to narrate the story of one of his daring solo escapes. There he was, dangling by a single thread over a vat of boiling toxins, and we wanted to know about Leonard. Our father would roll his eyes. "Leonard was at Buckingham Palace having high tea with the Queen of England," he'd say. Or, "I believe Leonard was in his tent, enjoying a nice cold Shirley Temple." Sometimes it bothered our father to see us so taken with Leonard. "You're missing the point," he'd say. "It doesn't matter what Leonard was doing.

When you're reading about Batman, do you sit around wondering about Robin?"

"No," we said.

"Of course you don't," he said. "Nobody does. Not even Robin himself."


We heard more about Leonard Holmes during the Christmas break of 1979 than ever before. This was during a strange season, when Teddy and I both suffered from unfortunate ailments. Teddy kept wetting the bed. And I'd had, for ten days running, what my mother called a *nervous stomach*, which caused me to throw up almost every time I ate. Whenever my father had to wash a set of sheets or mop up after one of my vomiting spells, he was reminded of Leonard Holmes, who was often so scared during combat that he lost control of his faculties.

"If you could possibly make it to the bathroom," my father said to me one morning, as he sponged vomit off the living room carpet. Our mother had charged him with the responsibility of getting the house cleaned up for Christmas, and Teddy and I kept spoiling his efforts, staining the sheets and vomiting on rugs and furniture. "Or if you could at least make it to the kitchen floor. That would be progress."

"I'm sorry," I said, sniffling. I always cried after I threw up.

"It's okay, champ," he said.

"I never know when it's coming."

"I know, buddy."

"It just comes out of nowhere."

"I know it does, chief." I hated to see him on his hands and knees, wearing yellow dish gloves. I was crying about this more than anything.

"Cheer up," he said. "At least your mother's not home."

He was right. If my mother were home, I'd be cleaning it up myself while she stood over me, lecturing. She had *had it up to here* with cleaning up after me and Teddy. When she was around, we needed to *grow the hell up*. Many times she had yanked our arms with fury after we had performed our lamentable tricks. Earlier that week she had grabbed Teddy's wrist and ripped his elbow out of joint. My father had to force it back in place. He did this tenderly, lovingly, benevolently, while staring at our mother with abject hatred. They hadn't really spoken since.

"I don't know why I keep doing it," I said. "It's not on purpose."

"Hey, no one thinks that," he said. "Did I ever tell you about the time Leonard saved our lives by throwing up?"

"No."

"I didn't?"

"No."

"Well, we were deep inside enemy territory, and Leonard was really scared. These guys were coming after us, and I pretty much had them all fought off except for one, who was coming at me from behind."

"Oh, no!" I said.

"Well, Leonard's trying to warn me, but he's so scared that when he opens his mouth he *projectile vomits* right into this guy's face, and the guy falls down and dies right on the spot."

"Wow," I said.

"Wow is right."

"Hooray for Leonard!" said Teddy. "Leonard's a hero!"

This seemed to trouble our father. He called us into a huddle and told us that there was something important we needed to know. Leonard Holmes was a nice kid, he said, the kind of guy who shared his gum, and wrote long letters to his mother, and lent money to his friends. But it wasn't enough to be a nice kid. Sure, occasionally Leonard got lucky, and happened to save the day in spite of himself. But more often than not, my father explained, life tended to take a nice kid and *kick him right in the ass*. Nice kids were weak, sickly, sucker-punched, and they were always the first ones killed. We didn't want to be like Leonard Holmes. We didn't want to be throwing up and wetting the bed for the rest of our lives, did we?

We did not.

"You know, I'm not sure if I ever told you two this, but I eventually trained Leonard to be a competent soldier," my father said. "And after that, he never again lost control of himself."

"How come he stopped?" I asked. "How'd he do it?"

"*Mind power*," my father said, and pointed to his temple.

"What's mind power?"

"The ability to control yourself through concentration."

"I'm trying," I said. "I can't."

"You *can*," he said. "I helped Leonard Holmes, and I'm going to do the same for you two."

My father had devised, on the spot, a brilliant plan. "How old are you?" he asked Teddy.

"Six."

"Really?" he said, and frowned. He looked genuinely surprised.

"And how old are you?" he asked me.

"Nine."

"Six and nine," he said, and stroked his beard. "I thought you kids were in your early twenties." We laughed. "Well, you're a little young, but I think we can give it a try."

"Give what a try?" I said.

"Basic training."

"What's basic training?" said Teddy.

"It's when you get your snowsuits on. Hurry up, on the double." He straightened to his full height. He usually walked around in a hunchbacked slouch, but now everything was different. We were about to be trained. Disciplined. He meant business.

We zipped ourselves into our snowsuits. As we walked to the car we saw that our father had tied together the laces of our white ice skates and slung them over his shoulder. The blades gleamed, reflecting the light of the snow. Though we were bad skaters, he always took us to the lake as soon as it froze. Since he lost his leg there were many things he could no longer enjoy, and he went to great lengths to make sure that Teddy and I took full advantage of our abilities.

"We're going skating?" said Teddy when we settled in the car.

"Among other things," he said, and shot us a mischievous glance in the rearview.

First on our father's list was an elaborate snowball fight staged at the lake's edge, which included the shaping of forts and foxholes out of snowbanks, as well as training in basic war tactics: the packing of ammunition, the aiming of said ammunition toward the projected path of a fleeing enemy but not the enemy himself, and the all-important use of surprise. Next we practiced evasion. We dodged snowballs by flinging ourselves into wholehearted belly flops. Our father illustrated these dives with profound seriousness, leaping again and again into the snow, his arms flung out in front of him, like Superman. He landed so roughly that several times his glasses were knocked from his face. "Did you see how fast I was going?" he said. "It takes a lot of mind power to move that fast."

Unlike me and Teddy, my father was not dressed for the cold, and his bare fingers were a raw, suffering pink. Nevertheless he assembled an arsenal of snowballs and launched them at us, sending us diving in all directions. When we managed to avert one of his attacks, which was rare, he made sure to pummel us as soon as we dragged ourselves to our feet. "Bang," he said as snowballs exploded against our suits. "If this was war, you know what you'd be right now? I'll tell you what you'd be. You'd be dead!" He said this jokingly, as he rushed to our aid and pretended to perform surgery on our stricken body parts. "Fix, fix, fix," he said, wriggling his finger over our imaginary wounds. As we lay on our backs looking up at him, we saw that he was a desperate imitation of happiness. A man who spoke the words and smiled the smile of someone else, someone for whom war was nothing more than a game.

After two hours of fighting we collapsed on our backs and looked up at the white sky. We were surrounded in snow. The world was muffled, quiet. All I could hear was the faint flapping of my father's arms and legs as he made a snow angel. He moved slowly, fluidly—making the most impressive of angels with his long, slender limbs. I wanted to stay there, listening to that sound, forever.

But there was more to come. In the next phase of basic training we tied on our skates and raced one another across the lake while our father monitored our progress with a stopwatch. He instructed us to stop and start on the cue of his shrill tin whistle. As he set us in motion, several people stopped and turned their heads, raising skeptical brows. But my father was oblivious. He hollered at us, threatening at the top of his lungs to send us to bed without supper if we didn't skate faster. "In war," he yelled, "there isn't always enough food to go around. You've got to be the first to the table. It's every man for himself!" We scrambled across the ice. Teddy's snowsuit was so bulky that he had trouble moving, and he kept falling down. I left him behind when he cried for help. It was a race, after all.

"If this was war, would you go back and help your brother?" my father asked as we were untying our skates.

I looked at Teddy. He looked like someone being swallowed by a snowsuit. It had completely overtaken his body, its hood secured so tightly over his head that only the center of his fat pink face was visible. He was breathing from his mouth, looking at me with pleading eyes. It occurred to me that if I stopped to help him once, I'd have to keep helping him for the rest of my life.

"I guess so," I said. But I wasn't sure.

Next our father engaged us in games of trust. He stood behind us and directed us to fall backwards into his arms. We were told to fall straight backwards, with our arms crossed over our chests. If we displayed complete trust, he would catch us. If we faltered, winced, hesitated, or made any move to attempt to catch ourselves, he would let us drop. When it was time to fall, I twitched and buckled at the knees and fell on my side. My father frowned and crossed his arms. "Don't trust me, eh?" he said.

"I do!" I said. But when he gave me a second chance, I did the same thing.

"How about you, Teddy?" he said. "Do you trust me?"

I watched as Teddy fell backwards toward my father with complete surrender, and as my father let him fall.

"Never count on another person to save you," he said to Teddy, who was lying on his back in the snow, stunned. With that my father turned away, headed for the car, assuming once again his familiar slouch.

Our mother was waiting for us when we got home. "Where is it?" she asked my father. "Let's see." She was smiling expectantly.

"Oh," he said, and frowned. "I forgot."

"One thing!" she yelled. "I asked you to do one thing!"

"I promise," he said, "I'll do it tomorrow."

"We only have a few days left, for Christ's sake."

"I know," he said. "I'm sorry."

"You're lucky I'm in such a good mood," she said. She picked up a stack of index cards and fanned them out in her hands, held them before us like a winning hand, like a royal flush. "These are all recipes for cookies!" she said. She had been invited, for the first time, to the neighborhood cookie swap, and now she was in possession of dozens of ancient family secrets. "I stopped by on my way home from work. They were so nice! One of them even said she liked my dress, if you can believe it." She was still in her waitress uniform, a black-and-white-checked dress, a red apron. She had pistachio ice cream smeared on her arms, and her hair was in a loose bun, with stray strands stuck to her neck and forehead. Even looking like this, after an eight-hour day, she was beautiful. She belonged on television, in a sequined dress, advertising diamonds. This was what our father loved best about her, what he couldn't resist.

"I'll get the tree tomorrow," he said. "I promise."

That night, as usual, our whole family sat on the couch and watched television. "Look away! Look away!" my mother said to me whenever a food commercial came on the air. "Don't you dare throw up." She was convinced that televised food was the source of my problem. Weeks before, a fuse had blown deep in the bowels of our giant television, and ever since it had broadcast the world in sickening shades of green. People drank green milk and ate green hamburgers. It was enough to turn anyone's stomach. But our father loved it. "We're the only people on the block with a special green television," he liked to say. "We're unique. Eccentric. Avant-garde."

On screen, Jackie Gleason sat down to his green dinner, his festering feast. "Look away!" my mother said, and covered my eyes.

"Don't worry," said my father. "Frankie won't be throwing up anytime soon. Today I taught her a little something called *mind power*."

"Mind power?"

"*Mind power*."

"That's very impressive," our mother said. "I wish I thought of that before now. I wish I thought of using *mind power* to clean up all that puke instead of doing it myself."

When our father tucked us in bed that night, he congratulated us on a job well done. "The first few days of basic training are always the hardest," he said. He told us that nothing was worse for him than that first haircut with an electric razor, which was run over his scalp in quick, merciless strokes. His heart raced as he watched his dark hair fall to the floor. Later, in the latrine mirror, he saw his pale, misshapen, vulnerable skull, and experienced for the first time the sensation of not recognizing himself, a sensation from which he never recovered.

Now that he thought about it, he told us, the horrors of combat dulled in comparison to those first weeks of training, when allies and enemies were forming all around him, when men showered and changed in open rooms, revealing their bodies to be either scrawny and pale and helpless, or tanned and muscled and brutish. In a matter of days all would be decided—who would break and who would rule. And so, he told us, when his friend Leonard Holmes was attacked by a seven-foot three-hundred-pound guy named Jimbo, who punched Leonard in the arm directly after he had received a series of painful vaccination shots, my father couldn't just stand there. It was the pivotal moment of his life. When the bully laughed and turned away, leaving poor Leonard to choke on his tears, my father backed up, took a running start, and kicked the bully right in the ass. "I was wearing *boots*, mind you," he said. "I don't think anyone had ever seen someone get kicked in the fanny in real life, and it caused quite a scandal." All hell broke loose. Bystanders had to choose sides, right then and there. As it turned out, every kid who'd ever been bullied was on Leonard's side, on my father's side. Thereafter my father was the undisputed hero of the barracks. "It was like Charlie Brown finally getting to kick that football," he said. "Or even better. Getting to kick Lucy right in the petoot."

"How come you didn't just punch him?" I asked.

"Because I'm an artist," he said.

He kissed us good night and tucked our covers under our

chins and snapped off the light. "Good night, soldiers," he said, in his best John Wayne. He stayed in character as he swaggered down the hallway, cock of the walk.

We lay in the dark, imagining our futures as competent children. After our first day of basic training, it was clear to us that all the world's people could be divided into categories—the winners and the losers, the healthy and the sick. Those who survived and those who perished. My father wanted to train us against weakness, against the kindhearted tendencies of Leonard Holmes. And who could blame him? We wanted to be like him. Not because of his purple heart, or because he had been lucky and shrewd enough to make it home from combat, but because he had gone to bed each night of basic training an unbroken man. He had slept peacefully on his narrow cot, and he had dreamed the dreams of winners.

We heard about Leonard Holmes all week. Did Leonard Holmes know how to make his own oatmeal? Not at first, no, but once our father taught him, he made the best oatmeal in the history of oatmeal, and he never again had to bother anyone else to make it for him. Did Leonard Holmes know how to clean the house in such a way that his mother would be pleased? No, he did not. And this was perhaps the greatest shortcoming of his character. My father had always meant to show him how to vacuum, how to mop the kitchen floor with the perfect mixture of ammonia and hot water, how to clean the windows without leaving streaks, how to fold laundry, how to dust the furniture, how to scour the bathtub. Did Leonard Holmes know how to clean all of the fast-food wrappers and half-empty packets of ketchup and shriveled, frozen french fries from the darkest corners of his car? Did he know how to organize a basement full of junk? No! "Show us, show us!" we cried. And so in the second phase of basic training, we mastered the intricacies of house-keeping. At the end of each day our father rewarded us with a trip to the grounds of the state mental hospital—a spooky, Gothic-style building that was perched atop the highest hill in the city. We raced our plastic sled down this hill again and again, screaming all the way down, imagining ourselves pursued by all of the hospital's pale, googly-eyed inmates.

"Whatever happened to Leonard?" I asked one night, as my father tucked us in bed.

"What a silly question!" he said. "Isn't it obvious?"

"No," we said.

"You've never heard of *Leonard Holmes*?"

"No."

"Well it just so happens that Leonard Holmes is one of the richest men in the country these days," my father said. "Some-times he's even on the news. And do you know why?"

We shrugged.

"Because of me," he said, jabbing his finger at his chest. "Because of *mind power*. Leonard Holmes was a scared little kid when he met me, and now he's a captain of industry."

"Wow," said Teddy.

"Wow is right," said my father. "Wow is right."

# 28

On Christmas Eve, when he could no longer avoid it, our father took us shopping at the mall. The only thing he enjoyed about holiday shopping was his ability to park in handicapped spaces while others futilely circled the garage, taking long and bitter drags on their cigarettes. "What a space!" he always said, as though it were a matter of luck. "We're right next to the door!" Sometimes I wondered what my father would do if he were asked to choose between these parking spaces and a miraculously healed leg.

He stood inside the mall's entrance and gathered his strength. He was thick in the enemy's territory, amidst the flashing neon lights of a hundred specialty stores, each selling its own brand of frippery. He winced, seeming to hear the scrape of every distant hanger against its rack, every coin against its drawer.

"For God's sake, let's hit the arcade first," he said.

This was the mall's greatest attraction, a place where my mother liked to abandon us while she fought the crowds at Filene's Basement. It was a dark warehouse of video games, ski ball lanes, Ping-Pong tables, and pinball machines. My father sent Teddy and me away with a five-dollar bill. Between games, we saw him sitting by the concession stand, eating hot dogs. He looked sad as he sat there, staring into his lap, licking mustard from his fingers. But Teddy and I were busy trying our hands at winning undesirable prizes, like stuffed flamingos, and we did our best to ignore him.

We returned to him when we ran out of money. He looked surprised to see us. "Finished already?" he said, though we had been playing for almost an hour. On the way out our father bought chances at a stand called the Quacketeria. Patrons of this stand had the opportunity to shoot a plastic rifle at a procession of yellow plastic ducks, who drifted by on a conveyor belt, before a pathetically drawn backdrop of a pond. They were helpless, those ducks, when my father stepped up. He leaned on the counter and pressed his eye to the scope. "Ping," went the gun, and the ducks quacked grievously and fell back, dead. *Ping, ping, ping.* It was a tinny, insignificant sound, the surprisingly hollow sound of death.

"Did I ever tell you boys about the time I shot targets to qualify a buddy of mine for the war?" he said, not looking up from the scope, still taking shots.

"No sir," we said. That morning, as part of our basic training, our father had instructed us to address him as "sir." Six weeks later he'd come to regret it. "If you ever call me sir again," he said one morning, while driving us to school, looking at us very seriously in the rearview mirror, "I'll kill you."

"Well, it's true," he said now, and shot another duck. "This kid I knew in basic training, Leonard Holmes, he actually *wanted* to go to the war." Ping. "Everyone else was running for their lives, but this kid couldn't wait. He was such a bad shot, though, he couldn't qualify. Couldn't shoot a gun to save his life." He was talking about Leonard as though we'd never heard of him before. "So I took the test instead. Our superiors were off at a distance, and I shot his gun for him so he'd qualify." Ping. Our father was taking down every duck that crossed his path. "And he went with us. Off to war." The final duck of the game drifted across our father's field of vision, and he had it in the crosshairs. He watched it through his scope, steady, steady, and followed it as it cleared the field. He didn't pull the trigger.

"He got killed a few months later," our father said. "I got shot trying to save him." He was speaking plainly, without the usual traces of mischief and joy. This was the shortest, strangest, most disappointing story he had ever told us.

"I thought Leonard was famous," I said. "You said he was a captain of industry." But my father didn't answer, only turned away from us and wandered off. He did this sometimes. We followed him at a distance through the bleeping and blinking lights of the arcade. At times like this it was as though he forgot we existed, as though we were the ones charged to keep an eye on him, instead of the other way around. We stood a few yards away and watched as he put a quarter in a fortune-telling machine.

The machine was a glass box with a spooky plastic head inside. The head was painted green and accessorized with a pink turban and a gold hoop earring. For a quarter, the head came to life, jerking back and forth as it spoke in a loud, eerie voice. You could hear the gears grinding inside. "I am the great genie!" it said. "You have requested from me your true and inescapable fortune. Be careful what you wish for!" The machine glowed with green lights, and the genie threw its head back and laughed, and this laugh echoed as my father's fortune, printed on a small card, dropped from the machine.

He stood for a moment and looked at his fortune. Then, as if a spell had broken, he turned and looked for us. We were right behind him, waiting as always, but he still seemed surprised to see us.

"What'd it say?" we asked, but he wouldn't tell us. He didn't say a word as he wandered back out into the mall, staring at his fortune. He was so distracted that he nearly walked into a mime who was performing in classic attire—the red-and-white-striped shirt, the suspenders, the baggy black pants, the painted face. The mime was struggling to make his way out of a cramped, invisible box. People scowled when they saw him, and hurried past, as though they were afraid of catching something. Our father was the only person who stopped and watched as the mime proceeded to push on something invisible but heavy. The mime exhausted himself with his efforts. His face contorted, and he gasped for breath. Finally my father turned away. The mime, having lost his audience, frowned elaborately. Teddy waved to him but he refused to be consoled. He rubbed his eyes with his fists, in a silent tantrum.

"You can be anything you want when you grow up," our father said as we walked off. "Except a mime."

All through the mall, we begged our father to read us his fortune. We hopped up and down, tugged at the legs of his pants. "Please, please, please, please, please," we said. "Oh, please, *sir*, please!" For fun, he pushed us and laughed as we stumbled into clusters of shoppers.

"No," he kept saying. "Shut the hell up." When he finally consented to read us his fortune, he made a big production of it, sighing and wiping his brow. "Help," he finally read, in the softest, most serious voice. "I'm trapped in a fortune factory and I can't get out."

We toured the mall, window-shopping. My father seemed to be under the impression that he had all the time in the world, though it was Christmas Eve and the mall would be closing within the hour. Sooner or later, we were going to have to set foot inside a store.

"What should we get your beautiful mother?" he asked us.

"Flowers," said Teddy.

"Candy," I said.

"Clichés!" he cried.

We kept walking, suggesting trips to exotic locations, fur coats, diamond necklaces, new cars, and hot tubs. "Very good," our father kept saying, "but not quite right." He was searching for the most unique and distinguished of gifts. He took us to Sears.

He gave us five dollars apiece to buy our mother whatever we wanted. The mall would be closing soon, and there wasn't time to mess around. I chose a rolling pin and Teddy chose a cutting board. We knew she didn't really like to cook, but it was the best we could do with our money. Our father didn't do much better. He decided on a nightgown and bathrobe. The nightgown was pink satin, and the robe was a royal purple velour. While it was true that our mother loved pajamas, and that she always changed into them the moment she got home, it was also true that she already had an exhaustive collection of gowns and robes. Every birthday, every Christmas, this was what our father ultimately decided on. He didn't know what else to get her.

Meanwhile Teddy and I suffered with the secret knowledge that our mother had bought our father the present of presents. All year she had been saving her change from her waitressing job with the intention of buying something called a *power shovel*, which was supposed to work like a handheld snowblower. The salesman claimed that the power shovel could clear a driveway in under five minutes. This was the perfect gift for my father, who hated shoveling with a holy passion. During the ninety minutes it usually took him to clear the drive, he never stopped swearing. "Oh, he's just going to *die* when he sees this," our mother kept saying, beaming. "He'll just die!"

"These are good gifts," my father said as we left the mall. "Much better than a trip, which only lasts a few days. She'll get much more use out of these pajamas and kitchen things." He seemed genuinely pleased with himself, and his mood transformed. He blasted the radio as we drove home, singing along with the lamest versions of holiday favorites. He even sang along with the Carpenters, his sworn enemies. That night, when my mother got home from work, our father was still in an exceptional mood, and he surprised her by suggesting that we go out in search of a Christmas tree.

"What's the point?" she said, pulling her long blonde hair from its bun. "It's too late now."

"It'll be great," our father said. "I promise."

"Oh, Randall," she said, and sighed. She often said his name as if it were a curse.

"How about we get some dinner on the way?" he said.

"I don't like this," our mother said. "You can't just make up for everything at the last minute."

"I can," he said. "I will."

"And you won't ruin everything this time, like last year?"

"Of course not," said our father. "I don't know what you're talking about."

# 29

We had a bad history with trees. Our father usually bought the cheapest ones in the lot. And when we decorated these skimpy, yellowish trees, nearly half of their needles fell to the floor. The previous year our father had brought home a tree with a split stem. In the lot it had seemed the tree of trees—a fat, beautiful spruce that was perfect in every way. And it was cheap! What luck! He couldn't believe that other shoppers had passed it by. At home, however, my father and the tree battled like heavyweight champions, my father trying to force the tree into its corner in a metal stand. He discovered, in the light of the living room, that the tree was deformed. Its trunk was cleaved, and it bulged on one side like a can infested with botulism. No matter how tightly my father set the trunk in its stand, it kept slumping over. Just as he'd filled the base of the stand with water and covered it with a red plastic skirt, the tree would begin its slow descent toward us, toward the center of the room. "You filthy bastard!" our father told it, in his most solemn whisper. He tried arranging the tree at different angles, so it would slump toward the wall, but it always fell toward him like a smitten dance partner. Finally my father abandoned the metal stand and opted for a sand-filled bucket, which he retrieved from the basement during a series of crashes and obscene rants.

Once settled in the bucket, the tree seemed to have no choice but to stand up straight. My father strangled it with lights and then instructed us to decorate the rest. By this time the fun had gone out of the whole procedure, and Teddy and I lazily hung the tinsel and ornaments—the glass bulbs and felt candy canes and construction-paper snowflakes—all along the bottom rim of the tree, which amused our mother no end. "Oh it's just *adorable*," she said, clasping her hands over her heart. Then my father turned on the tree's lights and snapped off the overhead and we sat for a happy moment looking at the colorful bulbs. We almost fell asleep, all of us sitting on the couch, mesmerized by those bright lights the way we were normally mesmerized by the television. It was snowing outside, and when the wind shifted toward the house snowflakes pressed against the living room window. They clung for the briefest of moments, then melted away. It was peaceful, sitting there for that triumphant half-hour, watching those flakes take on the red and blue and green and yellow glow of the tree's lights.

But then the tree shifted in its bucket. It was barely perceptible at first, just a slight creak. I looked over at my father. His head was flung back against the couch, his eyes were closed, and he was breathing through his mouth. He failed to notice as the ornaments swayed and the tree began its swift, terrible descent. When it crashed to the floor, spraying sand all over the carpet, our father leapt from the couch and started kicking it. "You goddamned son of a bitch!" he yelled. "I'll kill you!" His voice was filled with rage. He kicked the tree mercilessly. Sparks flew as he stomped out several of the tree's lights and crushed the glass ornaments under his boot. We watched him for a moment, frozen in terror. But then we started to laugh.

"You think this is funny?" he yelled, and turned to us, his face red, his eyes flashing violently behind his glasses. "You think this is some kind of goddamn joke?" His hair was filled with static and tinsel, and it stood on end, which made us laugh even harder. "The hell with all of you," he said, and stormed out of the house into the night, into the great Christmas snowstorm that we had been hoping for.

He came back a while later with snowflakes clinging to his hair, with a sweet, smoky smell on his clothes and an utterly transformed personality. He smiled at the sight of the tree collapsed on the floor, its lights still burning against the green shag carpet. "Voilà!" he said, pointing to the tree. "Behold! An avant-garde sculpture by Randall T. Hawthorne." We laughed. We didn't know what avant-garde meant, but we always trusted that his fancy vocabulary, if decoded, would translate into an impressive joke.

Our father disappeared into the kitchen and returned with two bags of cheese puffs. He settled on the couch and joined us as we stared just past the ruined tree at our television, which was still broadcasting a full rainbow of colors. For once my father wasn't particularly bothered by *The Lawrence Welk Show*, which was our mother's favorite. She loved to watch grown men in plaid suits tap-dance across the stage, and she loved to sing along as young women belted out patriotic songs. She always tried to harmonize with the barbershop quartets. But she didn't know the words, and her songs were filled with "doobie-doos" and "fa-la-las" and "something-somethings." Most of all she loved Lawrence Welk, the man himself, the great conductor who clapped girlishly after each set and who directed his orchestra with the lightest touch of his thin, creepy baton.

It was something of a miracle that our father didn't get up and change the channel at the first sight of a tap shoe. Usually he commanded the television, switching off our favorite programs in favor of the black-and-white reruns that played on Channel 38. This was a channel that seemed to have been conceived just for him. It played nothing but *The Honeymooners*, *The Three Stooges*. It played film marathons featuring John Wayne and W. C. Fields. Best of all it played our father's heroes, the Marx Brothers. "Now *this* is television," he always said. But that night he kept his seat on the couch and made entertainment out of poking fun at *The Lawrence Welk Show*. "Oh, a platoon of powder blue pantsuits," he said as a vocal group took the stage. "How lovely." He snickered as the singers tilted their heads and looked with utmost, heartfelt sincerity into the camera. "Another flock of feebs," he said with each new act. "Another batch of boobs. Another pack of pansies." Teddy and I couldn't help laughing. As our father sat there, making fun of costumes and hairdos and dance steps, cramming handfuls of cheese puffs into his mouth and delightedly licking his orange fingertips, we couldn't help laughing. We were on his side again, happy to be rescued from Lawrence Welk's terrible clutches. Only moments ago our father had been the enemy, but now he was back, and we were on his side, and our mother slouched in her distant, private corner of the couch.

# 30

Now it was another year and we were in
search of a new tree. But first our father was taking
us downtown, to a Chinese restaurant he and our
mother had frequented when they were young and happy, before
we were born. "Chum Lee's," he said to her as he pulled into the
parking lot. "Remember?"

She broke into a smile when we walked into the restaurant.
"Nothing's changed," she said, surveying the small dining room,
with its red vinyl booths. The room was dim. We could barely see
by the flickering light of the red paper lanterns that sat in the
center of each table.

"How are you feeling?" my mother said as we settled into our
booth.

"Fine."

"I think you and Teddy better switch places," she said.

"So you're on the outside. Just in case you need to run to the bathroom."

"I'm fine," I said.

She pressed her hand against my forehead and gave me a solemn look. "No fever," she said. "And you *do* look better." She had been watching me closely since the institution of *mind power*, and she was hopeful. The last thing she wanted was to take me to the doctor, especially so close to the holidays. From her six-week tour of nursing school she knew the most valuable medical information there was to know: that ninety percent of ailments tended to clear themselves up in two weeks, and that most visits to the doctor were unnecessary. You didn't really need to worry about something until it had plagued you for fifteen days. I'd been pushing my luck.

The waitress came and my father placed a reckless order. According to him, our family wanted it all. The soup and the egg rolls, the beef-fried rice, the lo mein noodles, the spareribs, the chicken wings *and* the chicken fingers, the scorpion bowl, the crispy duck. He actually ordered a duck!

"Wow," said Teddy after the waitress left.

"Yum," I said. We were both swinging our legs in anticipation, hitting them against the bottom of the booth.

"Don't you dare throw up," my mother said, pointing her finger in my face.

"I *won't*."

"I don't want anyone throwing up on our nice Christmas dinner."

"Jesus, Gerry," my father said. "Give the kid a break." My father was lucky that he said this casually, distractedly, while examining the Chinese calendar printed on his place mat. If he had said anything more critical our mother's head would have exploded. Instead she opted for a distraction.

"I know!" she exclaimed. "Do Five Little Pumpkins!" Slowly I realized that she was talking to me, and that she wanted me to perform a song I had learned in first grade, a song I thought I had outgrown.

"I don't want to," I said. Singing songs was for the Lawrence Welks of the world. The Leonard Holmeses.

"Oh, come on," she said. "Please? Please?"

"I don't feel like it." I looked at my father but he looked away. He wasn't going to stand up for me this time.

"Don't you want to sing me a song?" my mother said. "Don't you want to give me a nice Christmas present?"

It became clear to me that I was going to have to sing "Five Little Pumpkins," which was a song about five pumpkins sitting on a gate having a conversation. I started singing quietly, looking down at my place mat.

"You're not doing the *dance*, honey," my mother said. "The dance is the best part."

This was the dance that required me to shuffle from side to side while singing. I also had to mime the actions of the five pumpkins. When the first pumpkin said, "My, it's getting late," I had to look at an imaginary watch. When the second pumpkin observed that there were witches in the air, I had to look at the ceiling in terror. When I got to the third pumpkin our waitress appeared beside me with her tray. Our soup had arrived in four steaming bowls. I sat down, never so happy to see a waitress in my life.

"No, no," said the waitress, and motioned toward me. "Continue! Please continue!"

The song's finale required the pumpkins to "go rolling out of sight," which was illustrated by a climactic somersault. I knelt down and pressed my head on the purple carpet, in which was trapped the stale scent of soy sauce, of egg drop soup, of shredded meat, of grease, of rice and noodles and mushrooms, of butane, and of thousands of sour fortunes dropped to the floor. There wasn't time to do anything but look up at my father, who was smiling ever so slightly, who seemed to be expecting it, who seemed to have known all along what would happen.

My father insisted on doing the cleaning. Afterwards, my mother was too embarrassed to remain at the restaurant, and so we had our food boxed to go. When we were almost home my father pulled to the side of the road. "Detour," he said.

"What are you doing?" said our mother.

He pointed across the street. A man was standing by the roadside, under the streetlight, wearing a sandwich board. "Trees," it read, in fluorescent orange spray paint. "Twenty dollars." The twenty had been crossed out and replaced with a ten. These were the last, desperate hours of Christmas tree salesmen. What they didn't sell they would leave by the roadside.

"Forget it," my mother said. "Everything's already ruined."

But my father ignored her. We watched as he crossed the street and haggled with the tree salesman. Twice he scratched his beard ruefully and attempted to walk away from the sale. But the tree salesman relented, calling after my father reluctantly at first, and then desperately. Finally my father handed the salesman a bill, shook his hand, and dragged a tall, skimpy tree to our car. He opened the hatchback and settled it in the trunk, then seated himself triumphantly behind the wheel of the car.

"Five bucks!" he said. "A twenty-dollar tree for five bucks!"

"I still don't like this," our mother said.

"It's Christmas!"

"You say that *now*," she told him. "But in an hour when you're kicking this tree around the living room, it'll be another story."

"Not this year," he said. "This year I have a good feeling."

"Fine," she said. "Let's get home and eat."

We pulled out on the road, then merged onto the expressway. My father hadn't tied down the trunk, and it kept knocking up and down, snapping off some of the tree's lower branches. With all of the jostling, the tree seemed to be slipping out of the trunk.

"Dad," I said, "I think the tree's falling out."

"It's fine," he said. "It's too heavy to fall out."

"It's falling, Dad!" said Teddy. We were climbing a small hill, and the tree was tilted toward the road.

"That's impossible," he said. "A little thing called physics."

Just then we hit a pothole, and the tree sailed out of the trunk and onto the road.

"Dad!" we cried. "The tree fell out!"

We watched his eyes in the rearview as he looked back and saw the tree in the middle of the dark lane behind him.

"Just forget it," my mother said when he pulled to the side of the road. "It's too dangerous. Just leave it there."

But this was the kind of situation my father lived for. He was constantly coming up with excuses to flirt with danger, to climb up onto the slanted roof of the house, where he liked to walk around with a bizarre nonchalance, in search of faulty shingles and chimney pests.

Now he hobbled alongside the road, watching as the oncoming traffic swerved to avoid the tree. There was a long line of cars coming toward us, and my father stood, facing them, his hands stuffed in the pockets of his army jacket. I saw the light reflecting off the circular lenses of his glasses. He seemed to be mesmerized.

Finally there was a break in the traffic and he went after the tree. But instead of simply pulling it to the side of the road by the trunk, he lay down on his back, perpendicular to the tree, and rested his head against it, and stretched his arms up behind him, around its trunk. Then he sat up, heaving the tree onto his shoulders.

"What the hell is he *doing*?" our mother said. We watched as he struggled to stand. We saw the approaching lights of a car that was climbing the hill behind him, and they cast him in silhouette. For a brief, terrible moment, he didn't move. He stood, hunchbacked, bent under the weight of the tree. The car was just yards away, sounding its horn, when he ran out of its path.

Instead of returning to the car he knelt down and settled the tree down on the side of the road, and then stretched out next to it on his back. He spent a few minutes there, looking up at the sky, seeming to be concerned with matters of great importance. He fidgeted dreamily with the buttons of his jacket. "What a moron," my mother said. "He looks like Charlie Brown after he misses the football." We snickered. "Oh, brother!" she said, in a fine imitation of our father's gruff voice. "Good grief!" As we looked at him we could almost see the stars and bluebirds circling around his head, as in cartoons. We all burst into laughter—the frantic, nervous kind—the kind we knew best.

Whenever I remember my father now, I always think of him and that Christmas tree—of that moment by the roadside. I see him rescuing the tree in the same manner that soldiers used to lift their wounded from the ground. And I see him kneeling before it, then stretching out on his back, lying next to it, staring up at the sky. And I remember the terrible pain I felt in my chest as I watched him, as I realized—vaguely—that the story our father had told us in the arcade was true.

That night, after my father rescued the tree, he declined to eat while the rest of us stuffed ourselves with lukewarm Chinese food. He took for himself only the small bag of fortune cookies. He cracked them open and pulled out the thin, fateful slips of paper, one after another, and he winced as he read them. Then he stood up and smiled faintly, and wished us good night. He turned away, starting toward his den, still examining his handful of fortunes.

"What's your fortune, Dad?" Teddy asked.

"Nothing," he said.

"Tell me this," called our mother. "Is putting up the tree in your immediate future? Did they predict that for you?" The tree was lying despondently on the living room floor, several of its branches twisted and deformed.

"I don't think so," he said. We heard the door to his den close behind him. Over the next year it would become a familiar sound, the emphatic punctuation of his regular flights from the dinner table.

I often wonder about those fortunes, those small slips of paper that seemed to pain him so. Perhaps because of the baldness, the brazenness, the absurdity of their lies. "You will be rich and happy," they always read. "Your life will be peaceful and full of blessings." But my father was a man who had recently been reminded of the truth. He had just relived the worst moment of his life, and he knew the score. He was tired of pretending otherwise.

"Your life will be a series of disappointments, ending in suicide," the fortunes should have said.

"You will live forever in a painful state of regret, always blaming yourself for the death of a friend."

"You will not be able to bear the ways in which your children remind you of Leonard Holmes."

"Your new power shovel will not work, simply will not work, and you will smash it to pieces in a fit of rage."


After that night, there were long stretches when our father was his regular self. But then there were days he was off, and when he tried to tell us stories he'd stop in the middle, leaving himself in the gravest danger. "Did Leonard save you?" Teddy asked. He hadn't caught on to the fact that Leonard had died, and this pained me, pained my father. "Come to think of it, yes," he'd say, ever so quietly, his voice cracking. "That's exactly what happened."

Now, of course, we know more about depression. We have a language to describe it. Every day, it seems, some psychiatrist is on the television or radio speaking of flashbacks, of post-traumatic stress, of suicidal tendencies. But at the time we didn't know what was happening. We were angry with our father for drifting off into memories. Sometimes he'd even drift off while driving, and we'd feel the car cruise out of his lane and catch the shoulder of the road before he returned from wherever he'd been and steered us back on course. We blamed him for always leaving us just when we were having a good time, for changing so suddenly and trailing his dark mood through our house, our hearts.

In those last weeks the only time we saw our father was when he joined us to watch television. He almost never spoke, just stared ahead, even during commercials. One night without warning he got up from the couch and kicked in the screen of the television. He said he could no longer stand to see the world cast in green—everyone walking around in green suits, in green skin. Even the most beautiful people with the kindest hearts— they looked deathly, murderous.

The next day he bought a twelve-inch black-and-white set at a pawnshop. On that screen everything seemed small and far away, gray and fuzzy as a memory. Even the nightly news on *Action 13*—which prided itself on being *first to the scene and up to the minute!*—had a nostalgic feel to it. When we watched *The Wizard of Oz* that year, we saw Dorothy step into a magical Technicolor world no more impressive than the one she had left behind in Kansas. That land of emerald castles and yellow brick roads—it was nothing but gray.

My father had loved that television. "Now *this* is TV," he always said, sinking back into the sofa, seeming to let go of his troubles. My mother and Teddy thought he was crazy. "You can hardly *see* anything," they always said. "This is the worst TV in the world."

But I knew what my father meant. He and I belonged to a small fraternity of people who felt we were living in the wrong time. We were two wistful souls. Everything that was said to be obsolete—rotary phones and manual typewriters, record players and push lawn mowers and Buick Skylarks—appealed to us. Everything that was called progress seemed to us like a loss. The next year, when my mother came home with a new television— a set that was twice as big, that was sharp and bright and in full living color—I sometimes felt we had made a poor trade.

For years we kept the black-and-white in the basement, on the floor, and we never watched it. But when Jim finished the basement my mother turned it into a second living room, with the old sofa bed and television in the center of the room, and my father's old things settled in corners. Often my mother spent her evenings there. She was married to Jim by then and they were living a typical married life, watching separate televisions in separate rooms. During college breaks I'd join my mother in the basement, and there were moments—lying beside her on the couch—when I felt like nothing at all had changed. The basement was like a Hawthorne family museum. Our past was preserved there much the way it was in memory—jumbled together, going dark and coming to light in flashes, by the light of the television.

One night, during Christmas break from my last year of college, my mother and I turned on Channel 38 and found ourselves confronted with a Marx Brothers marathon. There was an awkward moment when I considered running away, upstairs and out of the house, all the way back to New York—*My, it's getting late*, I'd say, looking at an imaginary watch like the first little pumpkin—but a paralysis seemed to have come over me, and I just sat there staring at the TV. My mother seemed to be suffering from the same condition. She sat motionless through the final scene of *Duck Soup*, in which the Marx Brothers played soldiers embattled in a ridiculous war. Only when the movie ended and cut away to commercials did she speak.

"I wish Teddy was here," she said, in the softest voice. I had been thinking of him, too. That summer he'd joined the army and now he was stationed in Italy. We hardly ever heard from him. Though this wasn't much different from before—when he had been living at home, shut away in his room, speaking to no one—it was still hard. We seemed to have lost him forever. He liked the army and loved Europe, and I had a feeling he'd never come home. In his last letter to me, which he'd sent in September, he had included a photograph of a girl in a yellow bathing suit, who was sitting on the hood of a tiny Italian car. He and this girl, Teddy had written, rented a car on weekends and drove all around the country together. The only evidence of Teddy I had left in my possession was a dark smudge in the upper right corner of that picture, where he'd accidentally held his finger over the lens.

*Duck Soup* ended and next was *Animal Crackers*, my father's favorite. Groucho starred as Captain Jeffrey T. Spaulding, noted explorer and rogue, whose return from the African jungle was being celebrated by a crowd of stuffy aristocrats. Groucho's entrance was absurd. Everyone in the crowd burst into a song of welcome, and he arrived on a throne carried by four shirtless savages. As soon as he stepped down from the throne he broke into his most famous song, the song my father had loved. *Hello, I must be going*, he sang. He kept turning away, trying to break through the crowd and escape, but always he was held back by his admirers.

The hostess kept forcing him to stay, even after Groucho made it perfectly clear how he felt about her, saying: *If I stay here I'll go nuts!*

For a moment my father had come back to life. I remembered how he'd sung and danced for us in the kitchen that morning, how we'd clapped and laughed and begged for more. I wondered how he could have made it through such a performance, knowing what was coming. I wondered how long he'd been wanting to leave, how many weeks or months or years we'd held him with us against his will. I wondered when, exactly, he had decided that he no longer wanted to belong to our club, the club that counted him as its favorite member.

I looked at my mother and saw that she had turned away from the television, wanting escape. But there was evidence of my father in every corner of the room.

"He was always clowning around," she said, and sighed. "He always wanted you kids to love him."

"We loved him," I said.

"I know you did. But he was always worried that you wouldn't."

Never in my life had this occurred to me. "That's stupid," I said.

"He thought when you got older you wouldn't like him so

much. That you'd stop laughing at his jokes. That he'd seem *lame* all of a sudden or something. I think that's why he stopped playing with you kids those last months."

"That's the dumbest thing I ever heard," I said.

I refused to believe that my father could have suffered such fears. How could he have thought, even for an instant, that we wouldn't love him? How could he have possibly thought that? Suddenly I wanted to go back and do it all over again, to make my father understand that we couldn't live without him, that without him holding us together we would drift hopelessly apart. Didn't he know that? Hadn't he known? The alternative was unthinkable.

"Good night, soldiers," he used to say, after he tucked us into bed. Didn't he know that we were sad to see him go, to watch his silhouette swaggering down the hallway? We lay awake, wondering what adventures he had in store for us the next day. We squirmed in our beds, anxious for sleep, for morning. Anxious just to see him again. Didn't he know that these were the greatest nights of our lives? Simply because he would be there in the morning. Our dreams were hopeful and our futures bright and we loved him, we loved him. Oh, how we loved him.